Way of Love: Book 1

I0630697

RISING LOVE

A SPIRITUAL JOURNEY

PHIL KING

Twisted Hair Publications
an On-Target Words Imprint

ISBN(13):978-0-9990489-0-0
ISBN(10):0-9990489-02

Cover image courtesy of Bonnie King

Printed in the United States

For information on bulk purchases, please contact publisher below.

Twisted Hair Publications
an On-Target Words Imprint
On-Target Words, LLC
4625 Cedar Ford Blvd.
Hastings, FL 32145
www.OnTargetWords.com
(01)386-546-5164

DEDICATION

I would like to dedicate this book to my wife, Bonnie, for all her support and help during the lengthy process of writing and production.

Also, to my publisher, Nancy Quatrano for her amazing finishing touches.

Primarily, I would like to thank the heavens for the wisdom that came through my personal near-death experience, helping me to create this series and ultimately share their own light.

Other books by Phil King

SAINT AUGUSTINE CARRIAGE TOUR

ISBN: 978-1935795834

CHAPTER 1

SHIPWRECKED...

Tom hadn't completely cleared the dream-state before his head smashed into a hard-as-hell wall.

What happened? In the moment of awakening, the only thing he could figure was that he had been thrown out of bed. But no, he was in his bunk in the sailboat. Was that the wall his head was leaning against? If so, it wasn't in the right place....

He tried to put the pieces together. He couldn't see a thing, but the sharp pain on the left side of his forehead wasn't a good sign.

He felt around with his fingers, coming away with warm, wet, gooey stuff on them. *Is all that moisture my blood?*

Now the sounds of his predicament interrupted his thoughts. An eerily-loud creaking gave way to a sharp snap above. To confuse his senses, even more, his entire environment began to whirl, twist, and buck in the dark.

The wind howled outside and Tom could discern the distinct sound of water hitting hard against a fiberglass hull. Oddly, it seemed to be overhead. *What the...?*

Finally, a beam of light pierced the darkness through a small porthole. Tom assembled the interior of his thirty-foot boat bit by bit in his mind, using glimpses of intermittent porthole light.

He was on the floor of the boat's salon, next to the narrow berth where he had slept. But, the port side was up, as the craft listed severely to starboard. Before he could finish that thought, hell's fury hurled his world and tossed his forming picture like a puzzle dumped on the floor by an angry child.

Tom felt himself sliding ahead toward the forward v-berth. The small boat seemingly stood on its nose, while its body revolved around itself. Tom could see a strong stream of water enter through the cabin companionway aft hatch, which was slightly ajar. But, that stingy, illuminating ray was lost halfway through the roll.

Tom realized his left leg ended up under the ladder during that last involuntary maneuver, while his right leg was caught by what was probably the first step. It was too dark to tell and didn't make much difference anyway. All he knew for sure was that his knee now hurt more than his head.

The wind howled, and the boat bobbed until its aft popped above the water line. It still listed dramatically to starboard. The light from wherever flashed sporadically through the starboard porthole as he pieced together a few facts.

He remembered that he'd left Jacksonville yesterday. NOAA had predicted rough seas, so he came down the Ditch, slang for the Intracoastal Waterway to perpetual sailors, by whom Tom had recently been adopted.

His mind flashed briefly on yesterday's arrival in St. Augustine. The beacon at the airport, just a couple of miles north of town, sent out a welcoming search signal above that portion of the Intracoastal. The sun was about to set, and it seemed to him that the town was looking for his safe arrival.

As he passed under the Vilano Bridge, the two-hundred-eight-foot Grand Cross relayed an ancient promise to him that someone or something was looking after him.

Then there was a huge, old fort, a significant structure Tom knew nothing about. Its solid rock construction seemed to lend an aura of stability to his life, which had disintegrated into dramatic bedlam in the past year.

It took less time for those thoughts to form than it did for Tom to review them. Before he could find solace in them though, the reality of his situation demanded his attention. Was water still coming in? Was he still bleeding?

What the hell happened?

The intermittent light from the porthole was barely enough to tell him that the influx of water was also intermittent. There were a few inches of water in a tilted puddle, corresponding to the floor line and the starboard list. Of course, that meant that the bilge, and possibly the engine, were also flooded.

He didn't know if it was salt water or rainwater, and he quickly realized that survival was more important than whether his engine was shot.

He needed better light, but he'd have to stand up to get the flashlight. He remembered leaving a cabin light on when he went to bed and it wasn't on, so he assumed the cabin lights were out of commission, though he'd try to find the switch anyway.

Tom visualized the cabin configuration and began to lift himself to a standing position. His right knee was painful, but he didn't need to go far. He gingerly maneuvered to the flashlight drawer and was surprised, when it was right where it belonged.

Placing his palm on his throbbing head, he pulled it away and checked for blood in the bright LED light. There was a lot more than he wanted to see.

He felt his knees wobble and didn't know if it was the sight or the amount of the blood, or if he finally grasped he might not survive.

He pulled himself together enough to make a rational decision and tied a dish towel tightly around his head. Finally, getting a positive step under his belt, Tom relaxed enough to chuckle a bit as he pictured himself a bloody pirate.

As if it were on cue in a movie, the whistle of wind turned back to a howl. The waves stopped lapping and started to beat on the top of the listing ship. Lines lashed, and unknown instruments joined the percussion outside. The beat became almost as predictive and steady as a march until the crescendo gave way to a horrendous crash into the side of the boat.

Once that began, it didn't stop, although its rhythm changed, and the intensity varied. Tom soon realized that the crashing must be the dinghy trying to get the attention of the mothership.

He had no idea what he needed to do, but the fear clawing at his throat assured him he'd better do something. He worked his way to the window. With the angle of the ship, he found himself looking almost straight up. He finally determined that he was somehow stuck under a bridge.

It had to be the Bridge of Lions that he'd seen on his chart. It wasn't really high like the sixty-five-foot ones that didn't open–it was the old bascule type that opened in the middle.

Okay, now I know my location.

How he got there, why he was sitting at such an angle, and more importantly, how he was to get out, remained to be determined.

It was time to see if there was some way to open the hatch over the companionway without letting in too much water. He flashed the light on the ladder. The boat and the ladder were sitting at such an angle, his knee began to hurt just thinking about that short climb.

If there was water coming in, and that was the only way out, he had to know if it was possible for him to get out.

He realized he hadn't heard the bilge pump yet. Was the listing of the boat causing the pump not to work, or was the wiring or battery shorted out?

Tom's mind raced with questions, many without answers. He grabbed a life vest from the rack over the bunk. "What next?" he asked himself aloud, fighting to keep his thoughts straight.

"Check the hatch!" he answered himself and immediately launched himself through the pain to limp up the lopsided ladder. He yanked at the sliding hatch. It opened a couple of inches then stopped. The quick breath of outside air was delicious.

Unfortunately, it was followed a moment later by the top of a wave. After a few seconds, another wave found its way through the hatch. Tom slammed it shut and then tried to yank it open again, with the same result. It stuck after opening only a few inches. Once more, he tried and then quit. The water coming in wasn't helping matters any.

He thought for a second, then yelled, "Blue Lights!", and yanked it open again only to get another face full of December water.

Tom reached inside his hoodie pocket for the flashlight, set it on its 30 LED BRIGHT setting, and shined it at what he thought had to be the cops. "They're in the street!" he reported to himself somewhat disappointedly.

He shined his light erratically, trying to get their attention. Finally, he tried the old Boy Scout Morse Code, "Dit dit dit, dah dah dah, dit dit dit. Or was it the other way?" he questioned himself.

To be on the safe side, he continued to flash one batch into the next, as he talked himself through it. "Dah dah dah, dit dit dit, dah dah dah, dit dit dit, ..."

Finally, he got a response back from a bright searchlight. More dits and dahs! After a few seconds, the loudspeaker from the squad car hailer belched a more intelligible response. "We are sending for rescue. Are you all right?"

Tom didn't know the appropriate response in Morse Code, so he just flashed his light two long times, hoping that would suffice. It must have worked because they continued hailing.

"It's going to take a while because we have to get a boat out to you. Can you just sit tight?"

Again, Tom flashed two long times which must have satisfied them, because they shut up and started surveying the situation with their searchlight.

Thrilled that help was underway, he breathed a sigh of relief. Only then did the temperature of the water register with his mind and send torrents of shivers throughout his nervous system.

Tom slid the hatch shut, limped down the short ladder, and flopped his back against the tilted berth's pad. So much had happened in very few minutes, that his head still spun with remnants of thoughts and questions. The cops had somebody coming, but it would be a while.

"I need a cigarette," he sighed, remembering he had quit about a week ago. The packs of smokes had been replaced by a box of patches, one of which was on his shoulder, but the stress triggered the urge to light up. Ah well. That wasn't going to happen....

* * *

Was there anything he needed to take care of while he waited? Anything he was forgetting or hadn't thought of yet?

Gaining control of the situation in his mind, he felt a little better and found himself scanning the disheveled cabin with the flashlight beam, for his phone and radios.

A white microphone dangled on a stretched coil wire from an ICOM VHF marine radio. There weren't any lights lit, even after Tom played with the controls.

"Just as I thought. No power!"

As if to make him a liar, suddenly, the subtle sound of a bilge pump came on. Tom figured that had to be the backup bilge pump which was mounted a little higher than the primary system.

That rhythmic gurgle was a comforting sound for a second until Tom remembered that he'd used the old primary pump for a backup, while he put a new high-capacity one in for the primary. It was just temporary and seemed like a clever idea at the time.

"I guess we'll find out how smart an idea that was."

He sighed. Seemed he'd made a long list of bad decisions of late. He sighed and shook his head gently. What did it matter, really?

Help was on the way. Tom shook with the cold, then resumed the search for his handheld radio and phone. He looked through a pile of books that had fallen off the desk and landed beneath the ladder.

As he followed a trickle of water up toward the hatch, he saw it was steadily coming from around the base of the companionway door. Tom's mathematical mind analyzed the path of the water and the depth which made that into a right triangle with equal sides. The boat was listing forty-five degrees.

That isn't good. It wasn't coming in there a few minutes before. Maybe the boat had shifted. With the storm and waves still raging, what he had been noticing was the stillness of the boat, yet the waterline was moving...

"Oh, no! The tide is coming in!"

Tom flashed the light over the desk to the tide clock. He had set it to the local tidal charts when he got into St. Augustine Harbor last night.

The single-hand was halfway up the left side of the clock face, moving toward high tide. The clock usually provoked a peaceful feeling in him to know how he stood with Mother Nature. And, he usually envisioned the face of Claudia, who had given it to him, before they parted months ago. But, there was no peaceful feeling now.

Tom wiped a tear off his face. "We, or rather I, am obviously stuck under the Bridge of Lions with my keel in the mud, steadying my bottom. The tide could pop that up, but something is holding us down. Got to be the mast is too long to fit under the bridge since we're close to the road. I'm wedged in. The higher the tide gets the tighter it will be!

"But, that doesn't explain the stuck slide on the hatch. It doesn't slide back far enough to allow the door to the cockpit to be lifted out. I guess if I really have to get out, I could bust it out with something heavy. Dang it, where are those rescue people? Where is my phone or handheld?!"

Tom began to panic. He was again pawing through the books and papers on the floor. His head pounded like mad, and he had to set his right leg stiff-legged to the side while kneeling on the floor. The papers were soggy, and many of his charts were ruined. At the bottom of the stack, he found his radio, just as the water began to cover it. He found his phone next to it, but under the water.

The waterproof, handheld radio chirped joyfully when Tom turned it on. After tuning it to the maritime emergency channel 16, he spoke loudly and clearly, "Mayday, Mayday, Mayday!"

"This is Sea Tow. What is your emergency?"

"I am stuck under a bridge, and I am taking on water."

"Are you under the Bridge of Lions in St Augustine Harbor?" Sea Tow asked.

"Yes. I think the cops saw me here quite a while ago. Is anyone coming?" Tom asked impatiently.

"Yes, Sir. The St. Augustine Police reported you to us six minutes ago. A boat just left from here about one minute ago. It should reach you in about fifteen or twenty minutes. How many people are on board?"

Tom replied, "Just me."

"Was anyone else involved in the incident?"

"I don't think so. I just woke up on the floor of the boat. I don't know what happened."

"Do you have a life vest on?"

"Yes, Sir," Tom quickly replied.

"Are you injured?"

Tom told them about his head and knee.

Sea Tow talked to Tom on the radio, while their inflatable tow boat approached him. The tide was moving in at the fastest part of its cycle, causing the pressure to increase against the companionway door. That door was made of individual boards that lifted out when the hatch cover slid forward. Unfortunately, the hatch cover was jammed, and the door was stuck in place.

The water was rising fast, and Tom was in over his waist, even while he stood as high as he could on the ladder. When he stepped down a rung to look out the porthole and watch the red and yellow lights bounce toward him, the water was up to his chest.

"Hell, I might just make it out of here after all," he said aloud.

* * *

Two large men in yellow rain gear and orange vests surveyed the situation quickly and tied up loosely to Tom's boat when they determined it was almost stable.

The biggest of the two climbed onto the lopsided sailboat with a smile and a loud joke. "Well, at least you were able to get out of the rain! Are you all right?"

"Yeah, I'm right here," exclaimed Tom while flashing his light near the intersection of the hatch cover and the door. "Get me outta here!"

"Stand back while I destroy this jammed hatch," he yelled before demolishing the door.

Tom watched as a large hand reached down.

"Give me your arm and grab my wrist," commanded the man who was rescuing him from his death capsule.

"My name is George. And, if you listen to what I say, I'm going to get you into that inflatable boat and back to safety."

Flashing red and yellow lights distorted George's features, while a white searchlight silhouetted his large frame. Although his long hair whipped fiercely in the wind, the halo of his yellow rescue hood lent credence to Tom's deliverance from disaster.

"Now, hold on! You are coming up out of there," George said as Tom was pulled out through the water-filled hatch.

"Hold onto that stay cable for your life, while I get you turned around so that you can slide down into that tow boat there."

A few skillful maneuvers from George and Tom felt himself slip into the bottom of the rescue craft.

"You just lie there for a minute, and we'll have you over to the City Marina, where Rescue is waiting for you," George said.

He unleashed the lines, and the Captain gently shifted the two 250-horsepower Yamahas into gear. As the boat began to move, it rocked and rolled with the wind and waves.

Tom closed his eyes to relax in his cold body and began to drift away. He awakened a few seconds later with George shaking his shoulder.

"Hey, you, wake up! We don't want you dying in our boat! Your body's freezing and wants to shut down. Now open your damn eyes, listen to what these guys say, and do as you're told! You gotta give them some information, so they can help you!"

George scared Tom awake with his gruff admonition, as they pulled into the dock next to a waiting, plastic covered gurney.

They continued to ask him things he had no interest in answering. His clothes had been taken, and he shivered uncontrollably until they placed a warm water bottle on his groin and one under each armpit. That's when they placed a really comfy, warm blanket over him. *Ah, much better.*

They kept asking him questions, as he began to enjoy his new warm surroundings. They got personal with questions about his family and wife. He really didn't feel like talking about any of that.

He wanted to enjoy the warm blanket and the heating bottle. Tom closed his eyes and pretended he was falling asleep until he did.

CHAPTER 2

HENRY'S HOSPITAL…

Flagler Hospital was named after Henry Flagler, John D. Rockefeller's partner, and the brains behind Standard Oil's success. He built the railroad down the east coast of Florida to bring patrons to his world-class hotels.

He opened Flagler Hospital in 1890 to care for his wealthy patrons and to treat the indigent population. Tom belonged to the latter.

Before being seen by a doctor these days, billing information is of primary concern for all except the most urgent of cases. Tom was listed as homeless and indigent since he no longer had a home, job, or health insurance. He was told to speak with a social worker during regular business hours about his medical bills and his living situation.

* * *

St. Augustine, America's Oldest City, is a modest size town, and Flagler is a modest size hospital. It is seldom overcrowded or overwhelmed. Being the middle of the night, Tom was treated promptly and courteously in the Emergency Room. His injuries were not severe, and they were quite obvious.

They bandaged his head and admitted him to the hospital for the hypothermia. After x-raying his right knee and finding nothing, they told him they would have Orthopedics see him for his knee later.

His condition was not serious. They just had to bring Tom's core temperature up a few more degrees. Under normal circumstances, a patient might have been able to go home after a few hours under the warming blanket. Since Tom had no home to go to, it was best for him to stay there for the night. If he could convince the day staff, maybe he could rest up until the following day, before being put out on the street.

After that short Emergency Room visit, he lay in the exam room waiting for medical orders to be written. The midnight shift never seems to be much in a hurry anywhere, and this was no exception. Tom just lay on his gurney, waiting to be wheeled at a moment's notice, down some hall. He closed his eyes to shield them from the bright, fluorescent lights and methodically recalled his harrowing experience.

Memories turned into dreams. Dreams evolved into nightmares. Soon he had left his water-filled boat to search through an unending basement in the dark. Light filtered in through cracks in the walls or around heavily shaded windows. He continued to search for a way out, only to be met by another room of darkness, sometimes walking through ankle to knee deep puddles and squishy deep mud. Another room, dim and dank, led to only another room in his mind.

Finally, a voice called out from a distance. "Tom! Tom! Tom! Time to go for a ride" rang out the somewhat melodic voice. At first, Tom thought it was his wife's voice. Then he realized it was just outside the fog of his mind, and he pulled himself out of the trancelike stupor.

He looked up into the face of a sweet, smiling, Latino woman probably in her late twenties. "Thomas? Thomas Porter?", she said twice. Tom noticed an exotic, foreign accent when she spoke.

He reopened his eyes enough to see her. A pleasantly charming look matched the voice he replied with. "Yes, I'm Tom. Whom do I have the pleasure of meeting?" There was enough sugar and honey in his tone to sweeten a lemon.

It must have worked, because she came back bubbling, "I'm Maria, and I'll be taking you to your room on the fifth floor. I guess they are going to keep you for a while. But first, what is your date of birth?" Maria finished her identification check.

"By the way, before you ask, I am from Brazil and my accent is Portuguese. People don't usually know that is the language down there," Maria continued her introduction.

"Are you going to be my nurse, Maria?" Tom asked with a little more than a normal ration of interest. He had already assessed her as demure, petite, and voluptuous. Her long, black, loosely braided hair couldn't cover the sensuous curves that her unisex scrubs failed to hide from Tom's probing eyes. He certainly wasn't too ill to become aroused by a sensuous, Brazilian woman.

"No, but I work on the fifth floor mostly. So, I'll be seeing you around some, I'm sure."

Maria seemed to be toying with the obvious bait.

As they entered the elevator, Tom continued, "So, what do you do here, Maria?"

"Whatever they tell me to. I'm just a medical assistant. I handle all the things the nurses don't have time to do," she replied.

Tom came back quickly, "I'm sure you are more than just an aid. I'm sure what you do is very important. You are probably the one who really cares for the patients."

By the time the fifth-floor elevator light came on with a 'bong', Tom's charm was beginning to work its way. "Are you going to take care of me?", he said with a wink, as he caught her eye.

Hospital women were accustomed to being hit upon by guys. They had to be nice to the patients, as long as they were inside appropriate bounds. Tom was a little different. He was immediately charming, and he was good looking. Even the bandage on his head lent an aura of vulnerability. Of course, being good looking stretched the 'appropriate bounds' category a little, too. Tom knew that and used it to make his wink acceptable.

"I work on the fifth floor usually, so there's a good chance I'll be seeing you soon. Honestly, I don't think you'll be staying too long. You look in pretty good condition to me," she tried to return his wink, but it was easy to see she hadn't had much practice.

"You'll visit me, at least, won't you?" Tom continued his playful pursuit.

"If I have too, I will, but only if I have a reason to visit," Maria said coyly. "I'm all business around here. Here's your room, Mr. Porter, 522. Your nurse will be in to see you in a moment."

Before Tom had a chance to reply to her cute accent with one of his preprogrammed hints of intimacy, in walked a pin and capped, standard issue RN right out of the '60's. Before women demanded their own identity, she commanded hers. "Can you stand up and get into your own bed, Mr. Porter?" She knew what was going on, and she needed no introduction.

Tom responded like he was talking to his mother. "Yes, Ma'am!" Then he backtracked a bit, "I think I can." He stood up gingerly and gave a wince. "Ooh!" He moaned like it hurt a lot.

"I'm glad that didn't hurt much, Mr. Porter. You should be good to go in no time. I was a trainer for the Jaguars, so I know what real pain looks like. You'll be ready to walk out of here by tomorrow," Nurse Pritchard said. "Just for the record, give me your full name."

"Thomas David Porter," he replied.

"Date of birth?"

"January 12, 1988."

"And what day is it, Mr. Porter?"

"I guess it must be Monday, by now."

"One more. Do you know where you are, Mr. Porter?"

"St Augustine. In the Hospital. St. Augustine Hospital."

"Flagler Hospital, Mr. Porter," the RN got the last point, as she finished her exam. "Good enough. You better get some sleep after I'm finished with your vitals. It's almost three now and we start waking patients up about five."

"What about my pill?", Tom asked quickly.

"What pill is that?" Nurse Pritchard asked, with an attitude.

"The pain pill, for my knee," Tom responded.

He watched her eyes roll, as she stated, "The medicine cart starts its rounds at five. You will just have to wait your turn."

Tom heard a little disdain. He knew not to push and uttered a surrendering, "Thank you."

"Go to sleep, Mr. Porter," was her compassionate reply.

Tom laid his head on the pillow. He was tired but edgy. It would have been nice to have that pain pill now. Nurse Pritchard was right. He didn't really need it. He could feel his right knee hurting just a little by the lower left edge of the patella, as he laid there. It hurt more when he walked, but nothing he couldn't bear. Nurse Pritchard was a bitch, but she knew what she was doing. The doctors were a little easier. Mention a pain and they prescribed a pill. That's how they showed that they were doing something. That made the hospital money, too.

There was a big profit margin there, even in a not-for-profit hospital. "They have to pay those six-figure salaries somehow," Tom mumbled as he let his thoughts ramble on in his head while enjoying the starched white sheets and his fluffy pillow. Much more comfortable now than his wet boat, and a lot safer too.

Tom worried that the wrong people might find out where he was since he had to give his real identity. Hopefully, the discovery would take a while. By that time, things would change. Tom dealt rationally with his fears from his own perspective. The comfort of the sheets and pillow overrode his edginess. He gave his thoughts freedom to roam through more pleasing possibilities.

His thoughts drifted to Maria. She was a pretty girl. It seemed like they had made a connection. Maria appeared a little lonely too. No ring on her finger. She was probably fending for herself. They could use each other for a while. He'd check out her family situation the next time he saw her.

Tom gave thanks for his good fortune. He was alive and in a comfortable bed. His near future had decent possibilities. He didn't pretend to himself that he was perfect. That wasn't part of the bargain that he'd been offered when he'd gone to church. He just had to surrender himself, and his prayers would be answered. God or the Holy Spirit would change him if they wanted to.

Tom surrendered again and he saw the face in his imagination of the one who controlled his fate. Tom was rather true in his beliefs, even though they didn't jive with the rest of the world's. He paid his weekly homage and received his rewards. It wasn't his job to judge what was due.

A few moments later, the face in his mind morphed into the face of Maria. Again, he gave thanks. It wasn't thanks just for gifts of the past, present, or future. It was an all-encompassing "thank you" that included all three plus eternity.

Judging by the results, Tom knew how to pray. He knew that only things in the universal plan would be granted, and he was grateful for being part of that plan. He didn't know his role, just that he had a part. It was a heck of a ride, and he was glad to be on board. In a roller coaster with so many seats, Tom knew he couldn't drive. That job was taken, and the platform was crowded with people waiting for that seat.

Tom's imagination whirled through the ride, sitting next to Maria. Tom didn't know whether he was dreaming about or living the up and down excitement of the banked turns that he was experiencing. He felt safe in his crazy, exhilarated enjoyment. What a ride!

He saw Maria had a wide-eyed smile that emitted enough energy to warm both their hearts. A feeling of sharing that exuberant contentment filled his soul, and it made no difference if it were dream or imagination.

* * *

Tom left the company of his dream date, Maria. He wasn't ready, but he didn't have a choice. The subconscious orchestrates the music there. It is the producer, director, stagehand, and the rest of the cast. The dreamer even speaks scripted lines but gets to add the emotion to them. In this act, Tom felt like he spoke his own words, whether they were or not.

A pleasant but loud voice interrupted Tom's sleep, "Good morning, Mr. Celebrity!"

When Tom opened his sleepy eyes, he saw a nurse in light blue scrubs. He was tired and didn't want to deal with anything right now. It seemed that he had just gone to bed. What time was it? Where was he? What happened? Those were the questions he slowly answered for himself. Now, Tom wondered what that celebrity status was all about.

"Good morning, Mr. Celebrity!" repeated the cheery, voice. "Did you see your picture on the front page of the paper? I've got the St. Augustine Record right here if you'd like to see it," she said proudly. I always pick it up off my driveway and bring it here. I caught the headline in the locker room and one of the other nurses told me you were here. I thought I'd bring it to you. You want to read it?"

"Sure, sounds interesting," Tom replied, still groggy.

"Okay, you can look at the front page, while I take your vitals. Just give me your left arm," she prompted, wrapping the cuff around his bicep.

Tom saw a great picture of red and yellow lights framing a brightly lit area under the end of the bridge. The newsprint picture was a little too grainy to discern, but he could make out the Sea Tow inflatable boat next to his. Tom's boat was at a very awkward angle with its slanted mast wedged under the I-beam roadbed of the bridge. He could even see the small newspaper pixels showing George yanking him out of the hatch. Tom was glad that his face was unrecognizable.

Although the article was short and hastily written, it was not exactly what he wanted to see. It was Tom's first time on the front page. It did make him a celebrity for the day, but that's not what he wanted. Fortunately, the incident happened late enough in the night that the reporter couldn't gather and print his personal information. He was still hoping to slip out of town quietly and start a new life for himself. With luck, his identity would not be front page news by the next day. That info could spread too easily and be dangerous.

* * *

There was family money that he'd left town with, that was supposedly under the control of his wife. More dangerously, there was a gambling debt owed to someone who took debts very seriously. Tom had gotten swept up in all of that and no longer dealt with it rationally. He always had a plan, but this one now had a wrinkle.

Everything was going to be all right as soon as he could get everyone to see things his way. He thought he knew everything. That was probably a result of the coke he'd snorted for a while. Luckily, he couldn't afford the good stuff and gave it up. Thankfully, he considered himself above doing crack.

He didn't want his wife to know where he was. Life had gotten very uncomfortable. Tom had developed some seriously bad habits.

The habits had overtaken him. He'd always liked to drink, but that had led to doing drugs, gambling, and running around with women. All of that fed upon itself.

Tom had nearly become an alcoholic. He had been a hard worker for quite a few years and ran several trendy businesses, from antique shops to art galleries. He didn't own them, but he did well riding each coming wave with the smooth talk of a salesman.

Happy Hours were the happiest times, boasting with buddies and flirting with women. Money ran plentifully along the Carolina beaches. Tom acted the part with boasts and toasts with the pretty but petty people partying with the good times.

Tom married a beautiful young lady, who enjoyed his steady cash flow. His new bride had a twelve-year-old daughter with whom he got along well–for a while. He was a proud husband and cool step-dad for a couple of years until things went south.

Tom's drinking buddies were making a bundle in the fast-paced building boom. Deciding to jump aboard, Tom bought a new Kubota tractor on credit and began digging ditches for drainage and plumbing. He loved that little orange machine and soon bought a larger size with a dump truck to match.

He hired operators to handle those and the next set he bought. Tom always enjoyed operating one whenever he had the chance, letting the operator be the gopher or shovel man for a while. Tom and the banks had a booming business with the payments to show for it.

The construction bonanza had taken him along with it to prosperity. He was working ten-hour days, with two-hour business meetings at Happy Hour, with bands, karaoke DJ's, and other party people. Tom did the best he could, but it was a struggle to manage work, play, and family life.

Tom liked to call his after-hours, networking meetings. There he kept up on a lot of business news and opportunities. He got more leads and made more deals there than anywhere else.

He also enjoyed more sweet smiles and fluttering eyelashes at those after-hour meetings, than he probably should have. However, Tom handled himself and his bolstered ego quite well for a married man who loved the ladies. Although he charmed and flirted with as many as he could, he drew the line at what he considered harmless welcoming and departing hugs, with a few pecks on the cheeks thrown in.

Of course, his bride got an earful from her divorced, diva friends. When they were done selling real estate or shopping at the mall, they'd bring their bling to Ocean Annie's, just north of Myrtle Beach.

Starting at two in the afternoon, Ocean Annie's Beach Bar, amidst the seven 'Dunes' hotels, drew golfers from all over the country. Its live, beach music invited bikini-clad girls up three steps from the beach and onto the dance floor. It was the perfect atmosphere for selling condos to prospective customers or just enjoying a little fun in the sun.

Jimmy Buffet music played as deals were being made. It never hurt a contractor to know other contractors and the real estate people. Tom knew his share of both. People knew Tom, too. And their opinions were not always positive. Some saw him as a player, while others saw him as an opportunist. Others didn't care and just saw him as part of the party.

Soon Claudia, his sweet, arm-candy wife, asserted herself as head of household, and Tom had to change his tune to suit her taste in music. Not only that, but his cute, twelve-year-old stepdaughter turned into a troublesome fifteen-year-old. Daddy had to take care of a family in revolt.

He admitted that he had been a neglectful parent and repented in flamboyant fashion. Tom used his new-found fortune for an opulent cruise. That way he could show his wife and daughter what a wonderful provider he was. Off they went to explore the islands of the Caribbean in style.

Unfortunately, his daughter was bored to death by shuffleboard, old folk's musicals, and corny comedy shows. She needed other fifteen-year-old girls and drama queens to hang with her. Rap, rock, cell phones, cars, and computers were what they enjoyed. And boys, lots of boys! If you can't talk, text, get online or ride around in the back seat, it's like living in solitary. For a teenager, a cruise is like a floating prison, where you stop in a port to leave whomever you met, forever.

Of course, that was all his fault. Tom's cruise with Mama wasn't much better, although it started out well. When they went to the pool and drank ten-dollar margaritas, Tom's eyes naturally followed a few of the shapely bikini bottoms longer than he should have. That's when the fireworks started.

"What's the matter? I'm not enough to keep you satisfied anymore? Put your tongue back in your mouth and your eyes back in your head," hissed Claudia.

"I knew that I should have had my sunglasses on," Tom joked.

Claudia retorted, "You don't think I know what you are doing when I can't see your eyes. I do and I'm tired of it!"

Once upon a time, she'd thought Tom was funny, but that had obviously worn thin. Tom was a flirt, but he had been surprisingly well-behaved in his after-hour partying. It must have been all the 'friends' his wife met, whenever they went out together, that made her jealous.

He tried to be silent and let Claudia and her daughter, Lisa, get past their anger. He hoped they would relax and come around soon because he wasn't too good about keeping his feelings from reflecting their moods.

Claudia and Tom spent a lot of time drinking the rest of that cruise. Nothing was really resolved, but at least Tom knew to wear sandals, as he walked on eggshells. It flared up again when they were dining onboard, and Claudia saw Tom roll his eyes when she came back to the table with a second helping of lasagna.

"I know I eat a lot more than I ever did before. I had to do something waiting for you to come home from whatever bar you were closing."

What could Tom say? He'd admittedly been selfish, flirtatious, and negligent. He was just drinking with the boys. After all, Claudia wasn't the same centerfold girl he'd married. He had a big ego, and the larger-sized Claudia no longer satisfied his pride when they went out together.

That was just the beginning of the downturn, that ended with his sailing away in the middle of the night. Many families lived with and adjusted to much worse circumstances. His might have also if the economy hadn't collapsed.

That ten-day cruise cost well over twenty-thousand dollars, a heavy price to pay for a week and a half in hell. The bar tab was more than three thousand, while the casino losses were over four thousand. The surprisingly largest expenses though, were the Internet and cell phone charges that Lisa somehow activated. Claudia did more than her share of shopping for art and larger sized clothing too.

When they got home with their cash spent, the news came out that the largest recession since the Great Depression was about to descend on America and the world. Building immediately stopped and so did Tom's income. Suddenly the trucks and backhoes he was so proud of owning were no longer assets. Work for them no longer existed. The payments on nearly three hundred thousand dollars were still due in monthly installments.

Tom tried to get more work, but just couldn't. He let one piece of equipment at a time be repossessed, in hopes that the economy would turn around. Meanwhile, Tom did what he had always done. He networked with his construction friends at the bars. He also tried to sell his services to every legitimate business in town during the day, but no one was hiring.

Happy hours began sooner every weekday, but fewer of his old friends showed up. Many of the contractors, that Tom had shared bar stools and stories with, had taken any job they could find. Tom saw more of them working at McDonald's and Wal-Mart than he did at Happy Hour.

Some of the more established contractors worked small construction jobs themselves, often doing grunt work of banging nails and digging ditches. Others, who were more solvent, threw in the towel and retired. Their equipment sat in a barn waiting to be sold someday as another leg of their pension.

Unfortunately, Tom hoped against hope that he would find something to bail him out of an impending bankruptcy. He put on the same cocky smile every morning, hoping his good old boy charm would win him a chance in the backhoe seat. He missed those buckets full of pay dirt. He held out just long enough in the musical chair game to be the last man standing, without a seat. Finally, his winning smile no longer fit, and he went home without it.

His winning ways had worn out long ago with his wife. Claudia was no longer impressed. Their marriage had turned into little more than a business relationship. While Tom was out trying to save the business in his way, Claudia was home at her desk trying to save the money. She had a much more realistic outlook on the business world than he did. She knew to separate their money from the corporation she set up for him. He told himself right then, that he needed to keep some money hidden.

Tom's income paid the business expenses. What was left went for the house payment and into a bank account. To protect against bankruptcy the house and the bank accounts were in her name. There was one, five-thousand-dollar account that Tom's business had for expenses. Everything else was hers. He took that out in cash before she could get her hands on it.

Unfortunately, they didn't have the desire to work together. Tom liked to drink, brag, and flirt. Claudia was insecure in herself because of Tom's ways and her weight gain, so she went into protective mode and spent her time hoarding assets. Lisa no longer got as much attention or as many things as she wanted, and began rejecting her replacement dad. Love, the glue they needed to hold the family together, just wasn't strong enough to do its job.

CHAPTER 3

BETWEEN THE THOUGHTS...

Tom lay in bed thinking of all that when he felt the dressing on his forehead being peeled off. It hurt for him to open his eyes, but he saw two caring eyes close to his own.

He followed them as they examined his wound. Only the finest of lines hinted of her maturity. The warmth of her tanned skin set her sparkling green eyes off like gems.

Deftly, her left hand went to his wound and he noticed an empty ring finger.

"That's certainly raw. Does it hurt much?" she asked. "You already have pain meds prescribed. The med-cart nurse didn't give them to you because you were still sleeping at five. We can start those now if you need them."

Tom thought fast and came back with a great reply. "I better take them now, so the pain doesn't cause me to put my hand on it in my sleep and make it worse."

"I've got it right here. It will definitely help you sleep through some of the commotions today. You were up really late last night. Here's the water to take your pill. I'll be back later to check on you."

As Tom handed back his water glass, he let his gaze drift lower to her name tag just in time to say with a slight wink, "Thank you, Madelyn, you've been very kind."

"Take care of yourself, Tom, and get some sleep."

It wasn't exactly a wink, but Tom caught a warm glance and perhaps a self-conscious glow from her, as she turned to go.

"I'll see you later," Tom replied almost questioningly, as he enjoyed watching her go through the open doorway.

* * *

When Madelyn returned an hour later, Tom was breathing deep and sleeping hard. The medicine evidently had done its job, but not before a fitful time of it. Madelyn readjusted his disheveled bedding, while he slept.

As she gently pulled down his sheet, his muscular physique impressed her. Tom's arms were well developed, not like a bodybuilder's, but more like a hardworking man. His biceps and triceps bulged slightly but smoothly, even in his relaxed position. She knew that he was nearly ten years younger than she, but Madelyn found herself thinking, it was still a reasonable age difference.

As she continued to pull down his wrinkled white sheet, Madelyn was surprised to find the bottom hem of his hospital gown raised above his taut abs. It surprised her, even more, when she found herself staring at more than she should have, and much more than she would have expected. Madelyn felt her face flush and heart flutter before she thought to adjust the gown and pull the sheet back up. Tom smiled in his sleep.

She found herself returning an hour later, hoping to talk with him before her shift ended. It was unlike her to be drawn to a man that quickly, and she even questioned herself. She stopped questioning when she saw him sitting up in bed smiling.

Madelyn immediately went into full nurse mode to cover her embarrassment. "Hello, Mr. Porter. I just stopped by to see if you were able to get some good sleep after your meds."

"Yes, I did, Madelyn. Thanks to you! Call me Tom, okay? I even had some great dreams," he answered.

Still embarrassed and feeling herself blush, Madelyn made her visit short. "Very good, Tom. You have a great day!"

Again, Tom gladly watched her softly sway out of his room.

* * *

A moment later, Maria stopped in. "How are you doing, Tom? I stopped by in the middle of the night, but you were sound asleep. I hope you're feeling better today."

Still thinking about Madelyn when Maria appeared, Tom switched his thoughts quickly. "Thanks for stopping. Is this official business?" Tom asked jokingly.

Maria blushed. "I wasn't certain that you would still be here by tonight. I wanted to give you my number before I go home. I know you're new in town, so just in case you need something after you are out." Maria slipped him a small piece of paper.

"Thanks! That means a lot to me. You are my first friend in town. I'll call you! Thanks again."

"See you later. You have a much better day, and welcome to St Augustine!"

* * *

Leaving in a rush, Maria almost ran into Madelyn in the hallway. Tom watched Madelyn's face. She looked surprised, but not too happy, as she continued past her.

Tom tried to relax. Soon he received his ration of breakfast. "Pears, scrambled eggs, bacon, English muffin, and coffee. All the standards, and not bad for hospital food," he thought.

With a full stomach and a pain pill, Tom began to drift back to sleep again. His mind was at ease for now. His name hadn't hit the papers yet. He had a couple of days before anyone would be looking for him.

In his semi-conscious state, he reached out in gratitude to what he referred to as his Absolute of The Universe. In his own way, he quietly gave thanks that he had been spared, at least for another day or two, from an unpleasant encounter with the underground collection agent.

* * *

"Mr. Porter, Mr. Porter, time to wake up! Your doctor will be here in a minute. Just sit up and let me update your vitals."

A nursing student stuck a thermometer in his mouth and watched the gauge on the blood pressure cuff, while she listened through her stethoscope. "Thanks. He'll be in here shortly now."

It wasn't long after she left the room when a white-coated, white-shirt-and-tie-guy came in and started asking questions. "Hello, Mr. Porter. I'm Dr. Barganer. May I call you, Tom?"

"Sure, everyone else does."

"Tell me what happened to you."

Tom reiterated his story, even as he realized that his tale wasn't important to the doctor except as a diagnostic tool to judge how alert and coherent he was.

He sized up Tom mentally, physically, and socially, by what he said, and how he said it. In the same manner, the doctor looked at his body, in his eyes, ears, and mouth for telltale signs of economic and personal social status. Of course, he listened to his heart and lungs, and then he palpated various parts of his body for any signs of ill health or discomfort.

Combining his exam with labs and observations, he concluded that Tom was in relatively good shape and health. His body temperature was restored to normal, and his head wound was superficial. With the probability of proper care and cleanliness, he could be released. The hospital frowned upon supporting an indigent longer than necessary.

"How's that knee today?" Dr. Barganer asked.

"I can walk on it a little, but it still hurts."

"Orthopedics is supposed to be here soon. Probably just a light sprain, but we'll see what they have to say about it," the doctor replied.

The physical examination showed that Tom had adequate hygiene and health habits and could be trusted to take proper care of himself if he were in the right setting.

"Where will you be staying, Tom, when you are released? Do you have the means of supporting yourself?" The doctor asked.

"I don't have a place to stay, and I don't have any money. What little I did have was on my boat, when it got wrecked." Tom neglected to tell the doctor about the cash in his money belt. "By the way, where are my clothes? That's all I have left!" He wanted no one to know that there was nearly three thousand dollars in that belt. That was what Tom planned to have for rebuilding his life.

The doctor was not going to get involved with that. "Ask your nurse about your personal effects. I'm sure she will be able to help you. The thing I'm concerned with is where you'll stay when you get discharged from here. I'm going to schedule you an appointment today with our social worker. You need to get that done so you can get out of here. You may be able to leave here today."

Tom agreed to consult with the hospital social worker.

"Is there anything else I can do for you, Tom?"

"Before you release me, could you prescribe me something for the pain here," Tom pointed to his forehead wound.

"That seems rather superficial. The abrasion should heal quickly. Does your head hurt inside?"

"Yes, it does. I took a pretty hard fall last night. It might take a while to clear up." Tom did his best sales job yet.

"Your X-ray didn't show any concussion, and I believe any narcotic I would prescribe for you would cause you more harm than good in your situation. They are nothing to fool with. I will see that you get some Tylenol and a stack of bandages to keep your wound clean."

Dr. Barganer politely let Tom know he wasn't going to play that game. "If the pain gets a lot worse, come back, and we'll do more testing. When I hear from orthopedics and the social worker later today, I'll set up your discharge. Good luck, Tom, and try to keep it between the lines."

* * *

That afternoon the hospital social worker, Suzanne, requested Tom in her office. She wanted to arrange a bunk for him at St. Francis House. Suzanne warned that the local homeless shelter wouldn't be anything fancy. It would be a clean bed in a room with about fifteen other men. Clothes, toiletries, and other necessary items would be available. Food was plentiful, and it was generally a decent shelter. Of course, the price was right, free for the first week, and then only five dollars a day, if he was able to work.

Tom questioned Suzanne about the hospital's privacy policy. He confided to her only that it could be a life-threatening problem if certain people were to know his whereabouts.

Suzanne agreed to keep details out of the records and put in only that he would make his own arrangements to stay with friends. When the time came for his discharge, he was to call her to push his wheelchair to the waiting car. Tom respected her offer to stretch the limits of her job's reporting requirements to accommodate his needs. He picked up her business card from the desk, as he thanked her for her understanding.

* * *

In her job as a social worker, Suzanne had heard wild stories, but she was somehow enthralled with the intrigue of Tom's urgent request. It was common for indigents and homeless to present a pretend persona, but Tom drew her into his drama in a way that made her want to participate. It must have been the collusion in his smile or the intimate twinkle in his eye.

Suzanne had warned Tom about Roberta, the director at St. Francis House. She was a former correctional officer, and she could smell a snake from a hundred yards away. She demanded complete adherence to the rules. There were plenty of rules, but Roberta could impose, dispose, or make rules up as she went along. She made no bones about chewing anyone out on the spot if she felt the need.

But, at least the place was clean and safe. A far cry from what it was before Roberta had taken over, when the toughest client ruled, and drugs were the currency. There would always be complaints, but most clients would tell you that it was the best homeless shelter they had ever stayed in, as long as you did as told.

The case manager from St. Francis House would pick Tom up when Dr. Barganer was ready to discharge him. He would even bring some used street clothes over for Tom since his clothes had been cut off by the paramedics.

Tom had finished his social worker visit with a serious discussion about his privacy rights. He made sure all the staff would be instructed not to give out any information about him. No family, no newspapers, no supposed best friends were to be given any information about him, not even that he was no longer there. And of course, if he were to go to St. Francis House, he didn't even want that in the hospital records.

"Get back into your wheelchair, and I'll give you a push back to your room," Suzanne said, letting Tom know that the interview was over. As he gingerly rose from the more comfortable office chair, she extended her hand to shake, but it turned into a polite, but warm embrace, ending with a shared awareness in their eyes.

They talked casually on the way back to his room. There certainly seemed to be chemistry in the air. Suzanne smiled and quickly left him at his doorway, while she still had her professional dignity intact.

* * *

Back in his room, basking in his success with Suzanne, Tom thought about his money belt with three thousand dollars in it. The hospital staff had put it in a safe. He was ready to strap it back on and plan how he would use the money to change his life and his juxtaposition in the universe. He walked out to the nursing station to put in his request.

While Tom was at the counter, a short, curly-haired guy came up and abruptly started a conversation.

"Hi, I'm Larry. I'm the one who called 911 when I saw your boat going under the bridge. I've been sailing here a long time, and I knew there was no reason for anyone to be going under that part of the bridge." Larry was a talkative, friendly sort of guy. "I saw your mast hit the girder and I knew something was wrong when you didn't come out the other side."

Tom was a little surprised to meet Larry, and he was put on guard by meeting him just as the nurse handed him his belt. Tom didn't want anyone knowing that he had money, but he responded appropriately, thanking the nurse and then turning to Larry.

"Thanks! Another few minutes and my cabin would have been full of water."

"It was pure luck," Larry said. "I just happened to be coming out of A1A Ale Works and going back to my car, when I saw your mast go under the bridge. I had to come to the hospital today to visit a friend anyway, so I thought I'd stop and see how you were doing."

"I'm glad you did, Larry. I really appreciate all you did, and I'll have to look you up and buy you a drink when I get out of here. What was the name of that bar where you were?"

Larry reached into his wallet and pulled out a card, "Here's my info. Give me a call. I'm always glad to get a free drink! That was the A1A Ale Works, right across from the Bridge of Lions."

Tom extracted himself from the conversation, "I'm waiting for my doctor to show up, so I better get back to my room. But, thanks for checking on me. I'll give you a call or see you at that bar sometime."

Larry looked harmless, but Tom didn't want any information about him getting out just yet. He was deathly afraid of what could happen if the wrong people found out where he was. Maybe it wasn't paranoia. Maybe his intuition and fears were real.

CHAPTER 4

TAKE CREDIT OR GIVE CREDIT...

Tom was concerned about the money in his belt. Three thousand dollars wasn't much, but it was far more than nothing. It was his legally, but he owed that and more to a bookie. Thirty-seven thousand, three hundred and seventy-two dollars to be exact. That was a lot of thousands when you only had three—and the interest rate was high.

Tom liked to drink. When he drank, he liked to act important. Maybe he'd fool the people around him, or maybe not. He'd even fool himself, but never the bookie. Sometimes he'd win, buy a round, and be a hero. More often, he'd wake up the next day feeling like the ass that he was.

He didn't always like the way he acted when he drank, but anything past three drinks he attributed to that *other* self. He was trying to cut down. Some days he would only drink beer. Some days, just wine. He was even trying to cut back to five days a week, but that wasn't working so well. Without a good income, liquor quickly went through any walking around money he had in his pocket.

Tom had even started going to church. He finally realized he couldn't change on his own, so having gone to a couple of AA meetings, he thought he'd put his problem in the hands of a higher power. At first, he was just testing the waters, but there were lots of pretty girls in church, and they were friendly, too.

If he didn't get too wasted on a Saturday night, it was fun to get up and go on Sunday mornings. Some of the teachings began to sink in, but he was definitely more enthralled by the friendly, female faces. The music wasn't bad at the contemporary service. He found himself singing along, although mostly under his breath. He felt a bit guilty going for what he got out of it, but then he rationalized, that could just be God's plan. He liked that analysis.

What really amazed him was after he followed a funny feeling to put a fresh, ten-dollar bill in the plate one Sunday morning, he won a one-thousand-dollar bet that afternoon. Then he remembered it was a fifty-fifty chance anyway, but he *did* win.

Tom found himself having fond memories of those times in church. The healthy girls with honest smiles stood out in his mind most of all. Was that so bad? He even went to a couple of Wednesday evening services when he needed a fix and hadn't had too much to drink. What the heck, Tom imagined that even Jesus drank–although he probably didn't condone drunks.

That's when Tom's house of cards started to fall in. The bookie had confronted him with the initial, veiled threats. Tom's wife and her lawyer were beginning to put the squeeze on with real threats. Credit card companies were sending overdue notices. People that Tom had regarded as friends were asking aloud at the bars for their loans back. A few young women that Tom had been dating were starting to talk down about him. The large husband of another was looking for him.

It was time to move on. Even the landlord of his cheap apartment harassed him. He found his one stroke of luck at a bait shop bar, where he'd started going when the other watering holes got too uncomfortable.

The second time he went to Bait & Beer, he met Todd, whose sailboat was ready to have a lien put on it for six months of late dock rent. A few beers later, and a deal was dealt. A thousand dollars cash would take the title of the thirty-footer, sails, engine, and all.

They went to Todd's boat right then for an introduction and inspection. The eight horsepower, two-cycle Mercury outboard started right up after three pulls of the cranking cord. The inside was almost empty, as Todd was moving his things out. It needed a little TLC, but it was presentable enough. Dig a little dirt out of the corners and put a gallon of fresh paint on the walls, and a guy could live on it quite happily.

If it wasn't for the recession it would easily have sold for five or ten thousand. During the recession though, it was only worth six months delinquent rent.

It had a galley with a two-burner propane cook stove and a two-person table by the port side bunk. There was a starboard side bunk with bookcases, car stereo, and a twelve-inch TV/DVD player above it.

There was a head with a shower, just large enough to turn around in, and a mirror above a downsized vanity with a round stainless sink. In the bow, there was a nice size V berth, more than ample for two.

They sat down on the side bunks with a couple of cold beers to figure out the details. Tom admitted that he really didn't know much about sailing, but he said he picked up things quickly. He'd been on sailboats before, but he needed some finer points drilled in. Todd said he would be glad to teach him, but they needed to get out of town tomorrow.

If Tom could have the money first thing in the morning, before the marina owners were there, they could load Tom's things on the boat. Then they would go to the County and transfer the deed. After that, they could get on the boat and slip quietly out of town. Todd could teach him how to sail on the Intracoastal Waterway. They could even go for a while in the open sea.

Todd wanted to go as far south as Beaufort, Georgia, and he felt that Tom should have the idea by then.

"You just have to solo to learn the rest on your own. Talk a lot to boaters about everything you want to learn, and they'll be happy to share their knowledge for rum or beer. Stay out of the bad weather and pay attention to what you are doing. Just don't go out in the ocean, unless you have someone experienced with you."

They gave each other high fives, hippy handshakes, fist bumps, and finished bonding with cheers and beers.

Tom went home to pack. In the morning, he left the pickup he was driving at the all-night Wal-Mart lot to be discovered later and returned to Claudia, whose name was on the title. He took a cab from there to the boat.

Todd had stayed the night on the boat to get things ready for sailing.

* * *

Tom lay on his hospital bed remembering the beginning to this leg of his life's adventure. It was hard to believe he had gotten to town just a day ago. Things were moving too fast. Everything was changing again. Thoughts of slowly meandering down the lazy water of the Intracoastal, tiller in one hand, beer in the other, led to thoughts of flirtatious faces of friendly women singing hymns in harmony. Those thoughts blended with others until they yielded a dream that Tom would carry with him forever.

As he closed his eyes, he found himself sitting on his old back porch, in the springtime, looking past the fresh, green grass into the woods. The forest was sprinkled with newly opening buds, just beginning to show their pastel colors and impart a tinge of green throughout. Pinkish white blooms covered the dogwood trees, giving a gala appearance to the onset of Spring, but the early May blossoms did not yet block the view into the dense woods.

A darting movement suddenly contrasted against the near-evening stillness and drew his attention and curiosity. As it came closer, Tom could see that it was a young, white lamb. The little fur ball explored the forest with youthful spunk and agility, while it made its way down the hill towards him, and frolicked in his yard.

About a minute later, Tom heard someone in the distance calling, "LIFO, LIFO, where are you?"

The crunching of last year's leaves and crackling of twigs led Tom's gaze to a stumbling figure, obviously stalking the lamb. The runaway juvenile hid behind a small evergreen bush and watched its pursuer, as he tripped and tumbled the last few yards onto Tom's lawn.

It was the Good Shepherd himself, who shook his head and acknowledged Tom with a chuckle, as the little lamb neared him to see if he was all right. The shepherd gathered himself to his feet and brushed himself off. Then the impish, curly-haired creature darted away again in renewed play.

"Help me catch him if you would," he pleaded to Tom with a laugh.

"What's his name?" Tom asked.

"I call him LIFO. He's the Last In, First Out of the pen every day. He loves to explore and experience everything on Earth and in life, every chance he gets. He just doesn't stay in line like the others or do as he is told. But, you know, I just can't help but hold a special place in my heart for him."

Tom got at one end of the yard and helped corral little LIFO toward the shepherd. After he zigzagged between them for a while, LIFO jumped gingerly into the outstretched arms of his master, who hugged him tightly. and then hollered back to Tom, "Thanks a lot. I better get him home."

As they walked away together, heading up the hill, little LIFO looked back with his head on the shepherd's shoulder and gave Tom a contented smile.

Tom knew how LIFO felt being snuggled in caring arms. Seems like Tom had played the same game more than once himself.

* * *

Tom opened one of his eyes gingerly, not wanting to return to the real world too soon. *What just happened, and where did it go?*

Already it was blurring in his memory. Only the looks on the faces of the lamb and its master remained in his mind. It was the look of unabashed love. Tom drifted off with those images in his mind, while the feelings they stirred comfortably feathered his thoughts.

* * *

The orthopedic specialist walked briskly into Tom's room.

"Mr. Porter, I'm Dr. Sickles. Sorry I'm a little late in getting here. What is going on with your knee? It says you were in a boating accident. Tell me what happened."

Tom told him the story about wrecking his boat and hurting his knee when he slid into and under the companionway ladder. It got bent in some painfully strange way, but he couldn't see, as it was dark. "I wish I could be of more help, but that's about all I know."

"That's all right. Let me take a look at it. We didn't see any fractures in the X-rays."

The doctor poked and prodded like they do, feeling the tendons and muscles and listening for telltale screams at certain appropriate moments. Then he did the customary extending and rotating, testing for tenderness and for Tom's tolerance of pain. He asked Tom to stand and walk, noticing the grimace on his face from the slightly feigned, but mostly-real limp.

"Well, it seems you have a sprain. It should heal itself in time if you take care of it. I'll get you an elastic brace to help stabilize and heal. For the next few days put ice on it for about fifteen minutes every hour and stay off it as much as possible. Come see me in a week, or go to the walk-in clinic on the first floor of this building. I don't know why they call it a walk-in clinic, when you may need crutches!" He laughed as though he'd told the funniest joke in the world.

"They have a sliding scale for payment. I'll give you some muscle relaxers to let it heal. Anyway, it should be better soon. A couple of weeks if you take good care of it. Good luck."

Then, realizing that the file said "indigent/homeless" on the paperwork, he continued, "Do you have a place to go?"

"No, not really. Maybe into the woods," Tom replied, not wanting to have St. Francis House put in the records. *Everywhere has woods, right?*

"I'm going to recommend that you stay tonight, to give your knee more time to rest. You might want to check into a shelter like St. Francis House tomorrow," the doctor suggested. "Or, someplace else. I understand they only have an upstairs dorm for men. That could be tough on your knee, but I think you could do it, if necessary. In any case, you will probably have to leave tomorrow, but that's up to your primary doctor. Take it easy on your knee, and I wish you the best."

When the doctor left, Tom began to fret. "Since I can't pay for this, or won't, how does that work? I wonder if they have my address. They probably have my old address on my license. That means the bills will go there. That means my wife will know that I was here. At least that should take a while. Maybe I could have the bills sent somewhere else. But if I send them to anyone I know, they will either forward them, give them to my wife, or send them back. That would buy a little time, but I need more. If I give them an address in care of the guy I bought the boat from, the marina would either hold onto it in hopes that he comes back, or if they would send it back, in which case the post office would probably forward it to him, if he puts in a change of address. Since he doesn't know where I'm at, it would buy more time. Who knows where I'll be by then?" He couldn't part with the money in the belt until he was ready, but would they let him walk out without paying something?

"Well, at least I'll have another day here," he thought. "This damn shipwreck could really mess up my desire to slip away quietly into the sunset, though. Something will come along, but I could sure use a drink right now!" Tom ruminated in frustration, "God, there's got to be a damn answer to this! What the hell is it?"

Having verbalized his exasperation, Tom let it go. He laid on his hospital bed, turned on his TV, and let his mind wander.

* * *

As he began to doze, Madelyn, the pleasant nurse from the morning, came in with a non-narcotic Naproxen for his pain and a Flexeril to relax his muscles.

"Hello, Tom! I'm glad to see you're still here. I did stop in to see you earlier, but they said you were out for an appointment. Hope you're making progress in your recovery."

He smiled. "Good to see you too, Madelyn! Things are going well. I'm feeling better, and it looks like I'll be getting out of here tomorrow. I'm hopeful that I'll see your smiling face again in the morning. You make me feel better by just walking into my room."

With a flirting look, Tom told the truth and joked at the same time. He figured that he might as well be straight-forward since she seemed to be sending out inviting signals, although subdued. He was running out of time if there was something cooking here.

He could tell that Madelyn came from a socio-economic background slightly above him. She had excellent posture, and her teeth were straight, probably from braces. Her scrubs were like new and her speech was perfect.

She was beautiful to watch, but Tom knew he should tread lightly with a gentleman's confidence. He needed his personality to prevail over his nervousness, and his humor and good nature to keep her smiling. Fortunately, her gracious ways made that easy for both. Their gentle banter left each of them looking forward to their next meeting.

"Dr. Barganer prescribed you something a little lighter for pain, but Dr. Sickles gave you Flexeril which should help your knee heal. So, go ahead and take them, and I'll see you in the morning."

Tom took his medicine from Madelyn's right hand and a fresh glass of water from her left, sensing an urgency in her voice. Before he finished washing the pills down with water, he heard her say, "Goodbye!" He read her body language, as she walked out the door. He put down the glass with barely enough time to get out a hurried, "Goodbye".

The Flexeril did more than take care of his knee muscles. It blocked the pain from reaching the grey matter in his head. Soon he didn't care about anything and slipped into a mellow, relaxed state. He laughed with Ellen on TV and even felt like dancing with her, too. He didn't care that Ellen was gay because what difference did it make to him what she did in her bedroom? She was fun and he always cracked up with her.

Tom fell back to sleep. The Flexeril really was "just what the doctor ordered." It made his dreams better. The colors seemed brighter, and the images, more intense. Yet his enjoyment was calmer, like a warm, swaying breeze, carrying his mind to where it needed to go.

Questions seemed followed by obvious answers as if everything in life was easy. The drug probably had little to do with it. Tom was now well rested, and his mind had surrendered control of everything, allowing simple solutions for difficult problems to flow through.

* * *

He drifted past the surface thoughts that morphed from sense to nonsense. As sleep caught up to him again, one thought replaced another, each seeming to be reasonable in the realm of dream fantasy. A pinpoint light grew in the darkness, becoming the shape of a keyhole. Eventually, it became large enough and close enough for Tom to peep through it. The brilliance of the light forced him to shut his squinted eye. Still, he could faintly hear a sound from the other side, as it echoed through the passage made for a key.

The heavy vibration was indiscernible but powerful enough to cause Tom to maneuver himself into a position to listen through the hole to its emanation. "Take credit or give credit, it is up to you!"

Tom was dumbfounded. What was that all about? Credit for what?

Give credit? For who, where? What a crazy dream, he thought as his ethereal body floated away from the keyhole, but the message floated into his mind.

In the darkness, Tom spent his restless slumber searching for something, but he didn't know what. Something eluded him. Tom slept deeply through the evening, but not well. He tossed and turned restlessly in his dream, and finally realized he had lost his peace when he missed the clue. Revisiting dream after dream, the search became its own nightmare.

Finally, the keyhole appeared again, and as he drifted slowly by, he heard the clue again, riding out on the white light.

"Take credit or give credit, it is up to you," was what he had been searching for all evening. He remembered it in his dream. But as dreams are, he probably would have lost it again, if he were not brought to consciousness with it on his mind.

* * *

"Tom, are you awake?" she asked, hoping that she didn't sound too excited to find him still in his room when she'd come on duty.

"Take credit or give credit, it is up to you," he mumbled as he came to.

"What are you talking about, Tom? Are you awake?" Maria asked softly again.

"Take credit or give credit, it is up to you," Tom repeated. "I'm sorry. It's too complicated to explain. Just something I was dreaming. What are you doing here, Maria?"

"It's ten-thirty at night. I'm ready to start work at eleven. Just thought I'd stop by and see if you were still here. I'm glad to find you." She had no idea why she was acting such a fool over someone she didn't even know, but she didn't really care.

"Oh, sorry. I'm still groggy. Crazy dream. It's good to see your smiling face," he said, making her happy. "I'll be leaving tomorrow."

"Where will you go?" she asked as she straightened his blanket and smoothed it out.

"I'm not sure, yet. I'm going to try to find an old friend that moved here." He looked away.

Maria wanted to tell him that he could stay with her, but she decided that would be putting way too many cards on the table. She had just met him yesterday and really didn't know him. Mostly she thought it was better if she weren't too forward. She didn't want to scare him away or be so easy that he wouldn't respect her, and perhaps take advantage of her generosity.

After taking another second to think, she replied, "Well, if you need something let me know." Maria made a minor offer without a major commitment. "You've been through a lot. God bless you!"

Maria held his gaze as long as Tom would allow, and then followed it with a knowing chuckle and darting look as if she really knew his thoughts. But what she'd seen only confused her more. She cleared her throat.

"Well, I better clock in. It's getting close to eleven. I'll look in on you during the night. Let me know if you need anything."

Maria extricated herself from what might have been an uncomfortable situation. She had sensed an interest in regard to her openness and the blessing she extended to him but she knew it was too early in their friendship to expect anything.

It was time to let go of her feelings, and let nature take its course. The rest was up to him and the ways of the universe.

She went to the break room and poured herself a cup of coffee, but Tom stayed firmly fixed in her mind.

She'd noticed the half-formed tear in his eye when she'd blessed him and could only surmise that she had awakened a sore spot. Maybe it was a hurt, a longing, or just a tender heart expressing itself.

Maria had closed her eyelids to focus on the Third Eye area of his brow and allowed his aura to engulf her. She'd had that gift since she was young but usually avoided viewing auras, not wanting to invade the privacy of others.

She could not ignore Tom's though, as his colors surrounded her and drew her in. His aura was lightly visible with her eyes open but intensified when she absorbed them blindly. She saw blue and green and felt his calm, comfort, and loving heart.

She visualized the controversial, vivid reds of his base chakra. Maria found the abundance of the powerful red color to be sexually attractive, but there were muddy red pockets that she knew to be repressed anger, too.

Maria could feel all of Tom's myriad of qualities by just being in his presence. He was passionate about his desire to improve himself in almost every aspect of his life, though he had a long way to go in most areas. He was one who believed that love could heal.

"There I go again," Maria muttered to herself, "wanting to fix a mess that's not mine." She could see Tom's confusion and conflicts plainly in his auras and feel them intensely when near him. She could sense similarities between them. Would she have the time to find out if there was something special for them?

The time clock clicked without Maria noticing. Several people punched in before she became aware that the midnight shift was beginning. "Stay on task and forget about that stranger in there," she silently reminded herself and smiled.

Tom had his own thoughts. He could sense Maria's subliminal invitation to join in her life. There was the distinct possibility of becoming more than just friends and his body reacted to that thought.

But he had a lot to do. He had to get rid of his past before he could start a new life, and there were things he had to do privately. Maria was nice, but he didn't have that "forever" feeling about her.

Tom was attracted to Madelyn, too. She'd been a little short with him at the end of her shift, though. Tom didn't know any reason for that, but it made him wonder. She was a classy woman with many refined traits. Maybe she was married or involved. Some women didn't wear rings in a job like hers. Maybe he just wasn't in her league?

Hell, he fell in love almost daily, anyway. Something–or someone– would come up when he had time to fit that into his schedule.

Meanwhile, he had a plan, or one might say a dream, about elevating his life in a spiritual direction. He didn't belong to any religion or sect. He drew upon all the established beliefs and on some of the unestablished New Age philosophies. He wasn't religious, partly because that required following too many rules and codes of conduct. What was more important though, was that he had never found a religion he could agree with completely.

Tom drew much of his belief system from Christianity, although he personally considered much of the Bible to be metaphorical. He liked Jesus' message and ideas about loving all others. Unfortunately, he hadn't found very many role models in Christianity.

It seemed to him, that if someone didn't live as prescribed by their certain sect, then rejection, disdain, excommunication, or even death, although mostly in years gone by, might be the response. Even though most sects weren't that dramatic, many well-meaning Christians got carried away by their fervor and totally misinterpreted Christ's understanding, forgiveness, and loving words.

Tom drew many of his beliefs from the ethereal pictures and words of internet gurus of various persuasions. There were plenty of old hippies who had paid their dues to corporate America and were old enough to let their "freak flag fly" again, like in their glory days. Many were retired with surplus time on their hands to fill Facebook pages with tie-dyed pictures from Photoshop and their new digital cameras.

Twenty-megapixel Canon shots led the peaceful protests on social media. That's where Tom saw his niche. He had wanted to post recycled pictures from other sites along with quotations from various authorities, including himself.

It was a dream he'd had for a long time, but finally, he would do it full time. He could add a couple of posts each day and build a base of Facebook followers by recruiting new friends upon old friends. He could foresee the thousands he would rake in through the media for marketing his wisdom-filled books, music, and art.

If televangelists could raise millions, internet pastors could do the same. The time and price were ripe for an enterprising and passionate pastor, of sorts, to lay the groundwork for a spiritual source of innovative ideas.

Tom chuckled. He'd be the "Pay Pal Pastor."

"Take credit or give credit, it is up to you," rolled through his mind.

A lightning bolt epiphany shook his being. Suddenly he knew. Suddenly he understood. Although he had heard that in his dream, it now became an overwhelming revelation!

If he wanted to take credit for everything he did on his Facebook page, then he had to do it alone. There would be no more lucky coincidences.

His work and his words would not flow as effortlessly, as they could. Instead, if he were humble and gave all credit to the Spirit that facilitated his work, then he would be assured of Divine guidance.

Tom was elated. He immediately felt proud—and sure—of his new adventure. Then he realized, that's exactly the wrong attitude to take.

He couldn't take the credit. He only had to give it.

CHAPTER 5

DANCING BLACK CURTAIN...

Tom felt blissful. All his tensions were released. He felt as if his project had received a stamp of approval from Above.

He was happy, but he was too relaxed to celebrate. After lying on his hospital bed in that state for a few minutes, he found the remote and clicked off the television. The eleven o'clock news had ended, and he wasn't on it. That was a good thing. Hopefully, his location was still a mystery to the outside world.

He relaxed into the pillow with a profound feeling of satisfaction. The future, although it looked rosy, was still uncertain, but it always was. Now he felt like he had just finished Thanksgiving dinner, and the tryptophan was kicking in. With a fixed smile on his face, he drifted off for the night.

Although Tom was cozy and relaxed, he could have been ready to wake up and face the day. In his dream state, Tom suddenly saw road signs reading, "Construction Ahead" beneath flashing lights. Orange pylons narrowed the highway to secure a safe place for hard-hatted workers to dig and make dust.

Through the brown haze, he could barely make out the form of a flagman with a SLOW sign, pointing to a freshly cut, rough ramp stretching beyond a sign, TO ELSEWHERE.

Since he found himself in a place where he didn't want to be, Tom took the turn. Only when he approached the flagman closely, did he recognize his old spirit guide and guru.

"Just keep to the right, and you'll find it," he hollered as Tom inched by him with a knowing wave.

Finally, Tom was alone. He left his jumbled thoughts behind and continued on the path as directed. The guide drew him forward into an emptiness in his mind. Its vastness amazed him.

In the darkness, the hem of a large stage curtain danced lightly on the floor. Barely a single line of light escaped beneath, with one ray falling directly upon Tom. He had the feeling of being bathed in the purest of light, love, and creativity. He was without desire, yet totally filled with complete satisfaction.

It was the understanding of all the knowledge of the universe, all the beauty of existence, and love eternal, not only all at once but all as one. His mind did not try to comprehend it. He just accepted it. Without expending an ounce of energy to grasp or reject it, he only allowed it to happen. Tom sat effortlessly on the path, he had been shown by the flagman, the path between the thoughts. He sat without all the ideas that usually saturate the mind, preventing Divine visitation and suggestion.

The black curtain stood between him and the Other Side, the spiritual side. It was real. It was there. He got a glimpse of it. It was powerful. It was beautiful. Yet, how could he see it, and how could he feel it again. How could he get there? How could he communicate with it? He desperately wanted to engage himself, but he didn't believe he could handle it all at once.

The slim line of light beneath the hem of the curtain was radiantly gold, while the ray that shone upon him was overwhelmingly white. It was filled with so much knowledge and wisdom that his thought process shut down to protect itself. He had to resort to his senses and feelings to experience the astonishing deluge of this all-encompassing wealth. It was the non-material pot of gold, everything good that he could ever have hoped to imagine.

His eyes opened almost immediately after his imaginary encounter. It was still vividly playing in the foreground of his mind. Its meaning was obvious. Still, Tom had to focus and rethink immediately, before it faded and joined the pile of outdated dreams, too soon forgotten.

Tom wondered what he had done to deserve that gift. He hadn't done anything superior or magnanimous. He knew that he wasn't perfect, or even good, for that matter.

He realized that he had so much to correct in his life. He whispered to himself, "I don't know how all this ties in, but it fits into the puzzle somehow. It's got to have something to do with that phrase, 'Take credit or give credit, it's up to you,' from my dream just last night."

It was getting late, and Tom wanted to get up early in the morning. He was expecting to be discharged, and there were certain things, he needed to do. He was becoming too comfortable in the easy life at the hospital. It seemed like it was his home, even though he had been there less than forty-eight hours. It was almost a new life, not much to do and no real responsibilities. He was getting lots of sleep with lots of dreams. He really did enjoy the dreams.

He was under the care of everyone else, and he didn't have any obligations. It seemed that he could surrender his worries to whoever was in charge. It was quite nice to be able to do that. He wanted to carry the idea further.

"Wow, I think that I've got something here! The key to the universe is humbly surrendering the ego. Why didn't I see that before?"

Tom continued to quietly rave to himself. He proudly envisioned himself like a preacher or a teacher presenting his discovery of humble surrender as the key to life and the universe.

Then it hit him hard. He had become so proud of this discovery, that he took credit instead of giving credit. "What was the old saying?

'Pride goes before the fall?' So, if I take credit for a great discovery, then I lose everything. If I give credit, what do I gain?" Tom tried to reason it all in his thoughts. "That's right! The key to the Universe! What more could I want?"

Excitedly, he felt like it was the first time he'd heard this message. He recalled how most preachers were humble. He also remembered several religious people saying, "Praise God!", giving credit whenever something good had happened.

He'd always assumed that they were just showing off their religiosity. Maybe they were just giving credit–or maybe they were doing both. Wasn't that like offsetting penalties in a football game, where you win and lose something at the same time?

He decided he just needed to leave it there. He had received a wonderful gift tonight. He needed to be thankful for it and give credit, where credit was due. He would, but right now he needed to get some rest. This incredible message was a lot to receive at once and he needed to mull it over.

He whispered, "Thank you, God."

* * *

"You are welcome, I'm sure," Maria said as she walked into his room. "I'm sorry. I didn't mean to interrupt your prayer. I just wanted to see if there was anything I could get for you, but it seems that you have someone else taking care of you."

It seemed that Maria always knew where Tom's head was. "Oh, thank you, Maria. Yeah, I just had quite a dream! It's given me a new insight into how things work. I don't have everything figured out yet, but I do have this new insight."

Looking at Tom with an intense look, Maria said, "Your aura is amazing. It's prominently blue-green as usual, but it has brilliant, white flecks sparkling through it. I've never seen anything like it before!"

How powerful had his dream been? She could sense a warm, nurturing spirit encompassing him and his aura. She didn't want to say more because few people can see auras and fewer still can comprehend them. She didn't want to scare Tom, but he had a spiritual gift like she had never encountered. She probably understood much more than he did, but she didn't have his gift.

Tom rested on his propped-up bed pillow thinking about what she had said. He chuckled. "I don't know what you're talking about Maria. I did have an enlightening dream, I think. You have this knowing look in your eyes. Your lips are turned up at the corners too. It's like you want to laugh at me."

He laughed back at her. "What's going on with this aura thing?"

Maria leaned in and spoke quietly, "I have some ideas, but you would have to tell me more about it because it's happening inside you. Maybe you should contemplate it tonight. I've got to get back to work now. Call me in the morning after my shift. You've got my number. We could talk more then, but I'll probably see you in the morning before I leave. Are you still being discharged tomorrow? Do you know where you're going?" she asked softly.

"Yeah, I've got that figured out. I'll be all right. Don't worry about me." Tom replied, deliberately not answering her questions.

She wanted to know exactly where he would be staying. What she really wanted to hear, was that he was at least going to spend some time with her. Although it might be premature, Maria wanted a relationship with Tom. She did, however, have enough self-respect not to push herself on him. She wished him well and offered her own silent prayer that just maybe, Tom would be part of her future.

* * *

Tom woke early the next morning, before the sun. He had plenty to do and he was excited. He needed to get out of the hospital and start his new life. He didn't have anything to pack. He couldn't even get dressed until the guy from St. Francis House brought him some clothes, but Tom didn't know what time that would happen. While it was still dark outside, he began to make a list of how he wanted to start his new life and what he needed.

A cheap smartphone with lots of features was the first thing on his list. He was becoming Mr. Penny Pincher, no more Mr. Big Shot. It wouldn't cost him much to pursue his plan of starting a new Facebook page with spiritual advice. He felt compelled to give advice to others, as to how they could live their lives better. Maybe it was what one might consider a calling. It was always on his mind. Not that his life was a model of perfection, but he had an overwhelming desire to help others find what would be best for them.

He wanted his Facebook page filled with beautiful photos and inspiring quotes that would help people find their spiritual path through Eternity. He'd build himself up as a spiritual guru. Religion was a product that would sell big time.

People who liked a certain brand would gladly give ten percent of their income to be a part of it. He was confident that he could build a ministry, and people would turn to him for guidance. He would make more than a modest living in the process, too. It did sound a little cold when put that way, but it was the truth, and there was nothing wrong with that.

The clergy was well respected throughout the world, but they had to market their own brands in a way that people would desire to participate. There were plenty of standard brands of religion. They required a certain amount of certification, degrees, and ordinations, that he didn't possess.

But, there were also nonsectarian churches that were not affiliated with any governing body, and although nonprofit, the preacher's salary was set by the preacher-owner. That would work for Tom.

The ability to make a large profit depended on the faith of the followers and the salesmanship of the preacher. Tom was confident he was a good enough salesman to do it well.

He'd begin a radically nonsectarian church, Internet-based and able to reach the disenfranchised New Age seekers. They were of the personality type who might mistrust traditional religions, as they'd been ostracized or stigmatized by them in the past. Or, like Tom, just disillusioned.

Tom considered himself as a follower of Christ's teachings of love, humility, sowing and reaping (karma), and a rewarding afterlife. Most importantly, he did not feel the Grace of God was exclusive to a limited number of sects whose rules God supposedly liked. To Tom, God was God, is God, and will be God to all who accept Him, regardless of their religion.

There is one God that cannot be limited by manmade rules and regulations. He does not need our help in judging others' beliefs and actions. It is His job, His creation, His laws of nature, and His love that pervades His universe. Our job is to learn and accept or adapt to His Way.

Tom thought the masculine "He", only because it was an English convention. He believed the seldom-used pronoun of "One," capitalized to differentiate it from the common use of the word, was probably much more accurate.

Although Jesus most likely had a penis, the faceless forms of the Father and the Spirit had no need for one. And although that point might have been a good one, he decided it wasn't worth a fight or even a heated discussion.

In Tom's heart, a person's true being is his Spirit, not his Soul which is the essence of mind, will, and emotions. The Spirit is the part of us that connects the soul with God. To Tom, Jesus Christ's real being was His Spirit, not the body that died on the cross.

Therefore, when Christ said, *"No one comes to the Father but through me."(John 14:6)*, Tom was confident that man came to God through the Spirit of Christ, not the physical body. That Spirit could have dwelled in many bodies all over the world and in ways that different peoples could understand. The Great Spirit of the American Indians came to Tom's mind.

Yet, the misunderstood, divisive quote, *"No one comes to the Father but through me,"* is possibly the unintended cause of the greatest slaughters ever. Hate and war mongers, on all sides, used that quote throughout the world and history to alienate religions and perpetuate their own profitable purposes.

* * *

He continued with his Wal-Mart list. He would need a small tube of toothpaste and a toothbrush. He also needed soap, disposable razors, deodorant, pen, paper, a Bible, and of course, a good, but a cheap cell phone.

If he bought himself a phone for a few hundred, he could get a decent service plan there for $40 a month. Not a bad price to be in touch with the world, and he could hold his church in the "palm of his hand"!

Tom suddenly realized he was whistling a happy tune when he was interrupted by Maria.

"Hello, Sleepy Head," she said affectionately. "I came in to visit during the night, but you were deep asleep. You certainly sound happy now! Glad to get out of here?"

"Oh, yes! Time to move on. I want to thank you for all the hospitality, while I was here. You made my stay really enjoyable. I'll give you a call. You have been genuinely nice to me, and I'd like to get to know you better. Maybe we could go out for a drink or something."

"I don't drink much, but a glass of wine is nice now and then! I'd enjoy that. Just give me a call."

"Sounds like a deal! Give me a chance to get settled and a few things done, and we'll talk. I'm looking forward to it."

"Did you get things worked out with your friends where you are staying?" she asked as she checked his chart.

"Things are working out fine. I'm excited about everything."

Just then his hospital room phone rang. Maria gave a little goodbye wave and a giggle, as she made the telephone sign and mouthed the words on her way out the door, "Call me!"

Answering the phone, it was Larry, the guy that called 911, when he got stuck under the bridge. "Hey, Tom. I've got good news for you. I was talking to a guy that has some dock space available, and he likes to be able to help some people in need when he can. He said he read about you in the newspaper. If you need a place to put your boat while you are getting it back in shape, he might be able to help."

"Yeah, Larry. That sounds great! I need to see if everything works out with Sea Tow. I'll give them a call and see if I can move it. Give me his name and phone number. I'll call him when I find out my boat's status."

Tom was ecstatic about maybe getting the boat back. That would be a bonus he hadn't thought of yet. He'd have to take care of that right away before he accumulated big, storage charges.

Finding the card he had from Sea Tow, he called even though it was only seven in the morning, and the dispatcher answered. Tom found out that although his boat needed lots of other work, it was floatable. If he had it moved within the next four days, the charge would remain at four-hundred dollars, the weekly rate. Hopefully, he could get that done and move it to his new dock.

He was amazed that there were so many nice and generous people in St. Augustine. Larry barely knew him, and the guy with the dock didn't know him at all, yet they seemed to genuinely want to help him. Tom liked it here so far. Everyone seemed friendly and outgoing. He remembered the Grand Cross he'd passed as he floated into town from the north. There seemed to be a lot of love in St. Augustine.

During that thought, Madelyn, the morning RN, came in. She was in a friendlier mood than yesterday. "Howdy, Sailor! Ready to move on with your life? How did you sleep last night?"

"Good morning, Madelyn," he answered. "I'm ready to leave when they'll let me! And as far as the sleep goes, I didn't get much. Too many strange dreams. Good dreams, but really intense."

Madelyn put her nursing face back on, "I saw on your chart that they are giving you the smoker's patch. Those patches can give you some dynamic, colorful dreams. Some people don't like that. Does it bother you?"

"I didn't know that. No, it doesn't bother me! I love those kinds of dreams but they make it harder to sleep. They make my mind wide awake. I'm still wired."

"Well, here's one for today." Madelyn waved five patches, with a little wink. "Be careful about using them though. No smoking, while you're wearing them. I don't want to see you back in here with a heart attack! You keep using them. Smoking cessation is one of the most important things in your life right now.

"I'm putting these in your bag for you. You seem tense. Let me see how I can help. I don't want you leaving here this uptight. Lie down on your stomach right here," she said smoothing out the sheets for him. "You definitely need a massage."

Tom surrendered to Madelyn's skilled hands. She started at the top of his head, massaging his scalp. His mental image of her faded into the gentle sensations of her warm fingers and their deliberate advance from the top of his head to the rigid muscles of his neck. Repeating each stroke three times, she inched steadily downward. That predictable rhythm, coupled with the appropriate pressure for each muscle, relaxed his body in an orderly and steady progression.

From his neck and across his shoulders, her hands separated to knead the left and right muscle groups. Strong fingers pressed firmly and massaged his back, with her thumbs kneading deeply into his muscles. As Tom verbalized his feelings with moans, Madelyn hushed his sounds.

When she reached the small of his back, she increased the pressure, still digging deep into the tense tissue. "This is where the devils lie." Her thumbs smoothed and stretched the tightened sinews, and Tom felt his body relieved of all aggravation.

The skilled RN then changed her technique and began gentle, long strokes, following the muscles upwards from just below his waist to the level of his heart. Madelyn followed one hand behind the other, causing one continuous motion up his back. A set of six motions fell into one flowing pattern, moving from right to left across his now submissive back tissue. When she was done, she said, "Lie there and relax for a while."

Tom found himself in a drifting state, much like floating on a rubber raft in a lightly rippling pool. He was somewhere between euphoric and erotically aroused. Sleep overtook him and blended his thoughts colorfully into dreams. Ambitious plans for his day disappeared in his misty mind, while his last brush with awareness envisioned something being softly slipped into his hand.

CHAPTER 6

TEACHER OF LIGHT SAID...

A bell rang loudly. Tom was startled from his deep, comfortable sleep. About halfway to awareness, he realized it was only his phone.

His mind took its time coming up to the surface, pacing itself to answer by the last ring. It was the social worker, Suzanne, calling about his discharge. A man named Shane would pick him up in about an hour and he'd have clothing for Tom to change into before leaving.

Shane would drop the clothes off to Suzanne and then wait in the St. Francis van for her to push Tom out the main door of the hospital on his free wheelchair ride. She was still willing to protect his right to privacy.

As Tom hung up the hospital room phone, he realized he held a card in his hand which read, "Madelyn Holt, RN, (904)555-7483." Tom was confused. Madelyn ran hot and cold. At first, she was upbeat and friendly. Next time she was cool and remote. Now, it looked like she wanted him to call her, and after that sensuous massage, too! That was an event he'd really like to repeat soon. Unfortunately, he had other things to do right now.

He freshened up a bit, then gathered what few belongings he had and sat down, waiting for Suzanne to show up with clothes and a wheelchair. It hadn't been a bad stay, but he wanted to get on with his life. He sat in a chair in front of the never-ending news on television and drifted off into a disengaged, waiting state.

It wasn't long before Suzanne showed up. She handed Tom a plastic bag from St. Francis House filled with used clothes and another with slightly worn shoes. "Here, put these on. Time for you to bust out of this place."

* * *

Tom gave a smile, a wave, and a polite, "Thank you!" to everyone, as they passed the nurses' station. He felt a lump in his throat, as Suzanne pressed the '1' button in the elevator. He'd made friends during the two days there, and he held expectations of something to develop from that time. He was transitioning into his new life after enjoying two rather surreal days of rest and recuperation.

On the ground floor, everything was different. He had first come in through the back, emergency door. As he left through the front door, he felt a new life beginning. That was confirmed when a plain, white van pulled up in front of them. It was time for him to get up from his complimentary, discharge ride and stand on his own feet.

"Good luck, Tom! If you need anything let me know," Suzanne spoke with sincerity, looking deeply into his eyes.

"Thanks, Suzanne. Thank you for everything." Tears welled up in his eyes.

He turned quickly to climb into the passenger seat of the waiting van before departing became more uncomfortable. Looking back at Suzanne, he saw his feelings reflected in her eyes. She forced a little smile and a slight wave.

"Fasten your seatbelt," he heard as the van began to roll. "I'm Shane, the Case Manager at St. Francis. You must be Tom. Heard you were in a boat wreck or something."

"Yeah, the anchor let go, and I drifted under the bridge," Tom replied.

"You from around here?" Shane put Tom on the spot.

"I'm from the Carolinas, but I'm going to ask that you keep that to yourself. I'm going through a divorce and have some messy situations up there. That's the reason I got in my boat and left. Nothing illegal or anything. I'd just rather not let anyone know where I am now."

"Well, we have to run some background checks. If you don't have a real violent past or sexual offenses, you'll be okay. We do have a privacy policy, and I'll remind the staff not to talk to anyone about you."

* * *

Shane was comfortable with not knowing Tom's details for now. One thing he had learned during three years on the job was not to believe anything that anyone told him. Not that he disbelieved everyone immediately, he just didn't want to judge everyone on everything. His job was to help those who came to him, no matter what. No sense cluttering that up with the truth.

Most people in the homeless shelter spoke what he called a *convenient* truth. There could be lies involved or maybe just an added, decorative gloss to make themselves and others feel better. Shane didn't care. Lies hurt the liars a lot more than they did him. He was there to do his best for them regardless. What they did with that was up to them.

Besides, if he didn't judge them or unnecessarily pry into their business, he was more apt to get their trust and truth. Shane often told them in counseling, that he didn't care if they lied to him, he just didn't want them to lie to themselves.

"So, what happens now?" Tom asked.

"I'm going to take you back to the shelter and get you more clothes and toiletries. I'll let you know what's what and where. You can put your stuff in your bed locker if you want. Lunch will be served at eleven-thirty.

"After that, you can do what you need or want. You'll have to be back at 6 pm. That's when you will check in. You must check in every evening at six, or you lose your bunk. Then supper is served. You'll have some chores and then free time. You'll need to be back for bedtime at nine. Wake up is early at four, and breakfast is served thirty minutes later. Then you are expected to be at Day Labor or looking for work all day.

"Have you been in St. Augustine before?" Shane finished up.

"No. Been here two days, but that was just in the hospital."

"I'll show you around on the way back to the house. We are on US1 North right now, the main artery through town. We are coming up to State Road 312 here. There are lots of restaurants, stores and shopping centers here. It's a good area to look for work. Wal-Mart is just south of here. K-Mart's gone. Target's up ahead on the right, behind those trees. Further on the left is Winn Dixie, the Super Market. The road at the light is State Road 207. It starts here and goes out about seven miles to Interstate 95 which runs up to Jacksonville.

"US1 keeps going forty miles straight up to Jax, too. The county library is about a mile up that way. You can get on the computer there to find work. Another mile north past there is State Route 16, which also goes out to Interstate 95.

"I'm turning right on King Street now. Its name refers to King Philip II, the Spanish King who sent a pirate hunter, Pedro Menendez, to found this town back in 1565. Its primary purpose was to safeguard Spanish ships carrying gold back to the homeland. You'll be staying in the historic district of the oldest town in this country!

"That big building with the towers is Flagler College. It was built by John D. Rockefeller's partner, Henry Flagler, with help from Thomas Edison and Louis Comfort Tiffany. As the Ponce de Leon, it was the finest hotel in the world in its day. The first building with hot and cold running water plus electricity in every suite, thanks to Edison.

"We're going to turn right here onto Granada Street. This fancy building was a Flagler Hotel called the Alcazar, now the Lightner Museum and City Hall. That one over there was another Flagler Hotel, called the Casa Monica Hotel, our finest hotel now.

"We are coming up to St. Francis House on the right. It has three buildings. Martin Luther King used two of them as his headquarters when he launched Civil Rights marches from here. This town was quite the hotbed during those times, although the city would as soon forget that period of its history."

Shane changed the subject. "I'm just trying to help you get familiar with your surroundings. You'll be expected to go out looking for work, so you'll need to have some knowledge of the town. I'm going to suggest that you take a walk all over town today, to learn where everything is located. Tomorrow morning you will have to hit the pavement to find a job."

Pointing to the lime green, Victorian building, he continued, "You'll be staying upstairs in this building. It ain't much, but it's all we got. I'll get you more clothing and toiletries."

Shane pulled the minivan into a driveway with a picnic table under an awning and asked, "What kind of work have you done, or can you do? Do you have any specific skills?"

Tom responded, "I've done a lot of construction work, mainly running a backhoe. I had my own business until the economy failed. Lost everything, even my home, and family. That's why I set sail in this direction. Might as well seek out some new horizons.

"Since the construction business is in the dumps now, I'd like a change of occupation. I'd like to follow a more spiritual calling. I know that I must make some money, too. I've just come to a point in my life, where I need to pursue a new direction."

Shane listened to Tom as he led the way to the clothes closet. When Tom paused, Shane began to lay down the rules.

"Well, let me explain how it works here. The first five days are free. After that, it costs you five dollars a day to stay. If we feel that you are making an honest attempt to get a job and pay your way, we will try to help you. If not, you are out of here. Also, no drinking or drugging while you are staying here, even off the premises. We can give you an alcohol or drug test anytime that we think it's appropriate. As long as you pay your rent and follow the rules, you will be allowed to stay a month. Since the economy has been so bad, if we think you are trying hard and need a little more time to get it together, we might let you stay another month.

"You'll have to sign a list of rules this evening when you officially check-in. That will be your best guideline. However, this isn't a free society, and you don't get a vote. Roberta is my boss, and she runs the place. If she is unhappy, you'll be unhappy. If she says you are out of here, you are gone. I don't argue with her, and I suggest you don't either. This is the only homeless shelter in five counties, and we have only sixteen beds for men and eight for women. If you want to leave, that's up to you. I don't want to sound harsh, but I just thought you should know."

He unlocked the well-stocked clothes closet and pointed to a section of large shirts. "These should be your size. Pick out three more that you want. Another pair of pants and some shorts, too. Here, take these four T-shirts. Do you like boxers or briefs? You get four of those. Grab another pair of shoes or sneakers, too. They're arranged by size. We don't have any boots in your size now, but we'll try to get you a pair if you need them for work."

When they were finished, Shane locked up the closet, while Tom thanked him profusely. "If you need more later, let us know. We've got a washer and dryer to keep them clean. I'll show you the bunks now, and then I have to work. You can leave the extra clothes up there for now, but you'll have to come back at six to sign in."

Tom asked, "How much do those buses cost, and when do they run?"

Shane replied, "I'll give you a schedule and a couple of tokens. You can catch the Blue Line by Flagler Auditorium, across from City Hall. It's a yellow bus but has a sign on it that says, Blue Line. The buses are all yellow, but they have eight different colored routes."

Tom hoped he didn't look as confused as he felt.

Shane continued talking, as they climbed the stairs to the men's dorm, stepping over piles of termite droppings on many of the steps. Pulling out his huge ring of keys, he soon found the green plastic one marked for the dorm and opened it.

There were four sets of two bunks in each of two fourteen by fourteen-foot bedrooms. There were two locked plywood cabinets under each set. They were solid wood and simple but well-crafted out of two by fours. The many coats of thick paint gave their age, not in years, but in use.

Tom certainly wasn't impressed by the accommodations. One shower, two toilets, and two sinks filled the small bathroom. He didn't see how sixteen guys could get ready for work in the morning.

The smell of dirty socks dominated the air. It wasn't dirty if expectations weren't too high. The alternative was no meals and a blanket out in the elements, hot or cold, wet or dry. What the homeless called, "No hots, no cots."

Shane let Tom know that he could have Number Six bunk and set his recycled clothes on the mattress. Thanking Shane, Tom knew that it wouldn't be a long stay, but a few days would be an education.

He followed Shane to the office, where he received his two tokens and a bus map. "I'll give you two tokens, but you'll find walking instead of riding far more educational in learning the town. Besides, we only get a hundred tokens a month, and they are primarily for medical and employment reasons."

Tom's knee was feeling better, and he thought that he could probably walk back from the library if need be.

Shane opened a Sunshine Bus Map of St. Augustine and showed it and the accompanying schedule to Tom. The 9 AM Blue Line had just left Flagler Auditorium and wouldn't come by again for an hour and a half. Tom asked Shane if there were a quiet and pleasant place nearby where he could meditate while waiting. Shane recommended Maria Sanchez Lake about two blocks away.

Shane slipped behind his desk for his daily dose of unending help requests for all kinds of difficulties of the less fortunate. He started each day with a silent prayer, "Lord, help me to help you bless those in need, without undo judgment." He then hit his Easy Button from Staples. "That was easy!" it said, making Tom laugh and setting his mood for the first of many encounters of pending futility.

With map in hand, Tom set off on his first solo venture in St. Augustine. He found Maria Sanchez Lake to be pleasant like Shane implied. It was peculiar that it was as rectangular, as the vacant city blocks it occupied. This was a small, tidal lake with a dam. It retained the high tide water at a specified depth when the tide receded. The dam simply allowed the excess salt water to overflow back through acres of marshland into the Intracoastal Waterway, as the tide went out.

Saltwater foliage provided calm sanctuary with wetland birds in the midst of the historic Lincolnville section of town. Rumors suggested that those waters concealed skeletons of St. Augustine's less-than-perfect past. That day, a lone bench provided the perfect place to meditate on the many nuances of love in St. Augustine.

Sitting comfortably, he silently repeated the sound of his mantra in his mind. The vibrations of its melodic echo lulled him into a deep state of relaxation, which preceded a transcendence of consciousness. As each errant thought tried to occupy his pattern of thinking, Tom set it aside, deliberately choosing to ride the floating drift of his meaningless mantra. Finally, a thought gained the right to carry him along with it, blazing a path into his subconscious. This fully-formed idea came to him, without even seeking it.

It was plain and simple, but important. After mulling it over for a short while, Tom slowly opened his eyes. Coming to, he reached for his pen and wrote it down in his pocket notebook.

The Teacher of Light said...
Relax, completely and totally relax
Open your mind
Open your body
Open your soul
Allow the multi-color bits of light to permeate your being
Allow yourself to be connected to the universal Deity
It is the Deity of the universe
It is the Deity of your ancestors
Allow it to impart its wisdom

Allow it to impart its love
Allow it to impart its health
Allow it to impart its wealth
Allow it to impart its peace
Allow in its goodness
Allow in its creativity
Allow in its understanding
Allow in its humor
Allow it to be one with you
It is your path to eternity
It is your path to others
It is your path to all
All can be part of you
You can be part of all
All you have to do is accept these gifts
All are yours
All are you
You are all
Allow yourself to be connected to the universal network
Allow yourself to share with the universe
Allow the universe to share with you
Love and be loved
Laugh and hear it echoed
Cry and feel all embrace you
Share your feelings
Feel the sharing
You are connected to all
All are connected to you
All is connected to you
You are connected to God
God is connected to you
You are a part of God
God is a part of you

Just relax
Completely and totally relax
You are where you need to be
The kingdom of God is within you

Tom loved it when he became inspired during his meditations. Many times, he would just relax with his mind wandering and sorting itself out. This time, however, he felt he had received a distinct message. The words he had jotted may not have been the same words that were presented to him. In most cases, they were presented to him more as feelings or concepts. When he began to write them down, the words flowed out of his pen without his effort or thought. They obviously belonged on that page and had arranged themselves there much better, than he could ever have created in his own logical mind. He loved it when his actions were on autopilot.

Tom knew when it was time to close the notebook and put it away. That was a gift he began receiving soon after he began meditating. It was a natural part of a two-way communication with the higher power.

It wasn't uncommon, but Tom didn't talk about it much. Many people probably couldn't or wouldn't understand. He didn't understand it all himself. Tom wasn't a religious expert. He just went by the wisdom that he received. He studied and researched the best he could, gaining an understanding similar to what preachers taught, only with a personal relationship to the source.

It was time to catch his bus and get on with his life. Tom tucked his spiritual thoughts away for the moment and hustled towards the bus stop. He arrived at Flagler College Auditorium, just as the bright, yellow bus with the 'Blue Line' sign arrived.

He boarded leisurely and chilled in the front row, while the driver took a cigarette break before starting his next lap right on schedule. A couple of guys whom Tom figured to be homeless boarded and gave him a knowing nod. A girl about thirty also got on and gave him a pleasant, toothless smile. Everyone in St. Augustine seemed to be friendly, so far. Although Tom was out of his element and former character, he felt at home.

The Sunshine Bus passed by many places that Shane had pointed out only a few hours ago. That quick review gave Tom a strong déjà vu feeling. Although he had been in town only a few days, he had already made some friends and was learning his way.

That same realization immediately included feelings of missing Maria. There was comfort in her presence. An overwhelming acceptance enveloped his being when she was near.

Although she knew very little about him, he sensed that she recognized his inner spirit. Thoughts of her now eased his worries, as if he was sinking into a feather pillow. He relaxed with her on his mind.

Those warm thoughts urged him to make a mental note to give her a call. In some ways, he really didn't want to do that. He had just gotten into town and wanted to see what was available before he got into a relationship, but he felt so comfortable with her. "Okay," he answered himself. He would call her when he got his phone.

Tom's attention went back to the scenery, spotting a Burger King and KFC just before the bus went south beyond Flagler Hospital. An almost deserted mall, followed by a Chevy dealer passed his window before they turned into the tree-lined parking lot of Wal-Mart. Tom disembarked almost directly into the next chapter of his life.

He planned to buy a smart cell phone that would facilitate the vision of his next career. A half hour later, he emerged with the scientific wonder that would put the power of a worldwide stage, screen, and magazine in the palm of his hand.

If the media is the pillar of power for governments and corporations, this two-hundred-dollar toy could propel his rise to fame and fortune in the near future. For less than two dollars a day, thanks to Wal-Mart, he could reach more people than NBC, Time Magazine, and The New York Times, combined.

Tom just had to have faith. He knew that. If faith could move mountains, then faith could support his vision as high as his sincerest belief. He knew that. He also knew that a pinpoint prick of doubt could pierce his balloon, let out his hot air, and drop him flat with a splat.

CHAPTER 7

A NEW TOY IS THE KEY...

Tom excitedly boarded the bus holding his new toy. After consulting the bus schedule, he chose the White Line, a connector that ran straight up US 1 to the Main County Library. There he would get on Wi-Fi and learn all that his new phone could do. He deliberately placed it in the box while on the bus. Watching the view to learn all he could about the layout of St. Augustine was far more important.

After the bus crossed King Street and passed its two liquor stores, he had a new view to absorb. A sparkling body of water, that his map designated as San Sebastian River, was on his left. There was nothing else on the left but railroad tracks and then the scenic headwaters of the river.

Oyster bed islands dotted the middle during its low tide, but the river's other side was void of any development.

On his right side, there were numerous businesses including a bank, Village Inn, McDonald's, and a few other spots not worth remembering. Tom debarked at the Main Library which was rather new and was adjacent to a small family park with an active carousel. Several homeless guys and girls sat outside the library on the steps in the warm sun and cool breezes of December. 'Just hanging out.

Tom felt more akin to the homeless, now that he was one of them. He could feel the covert stares and overt glares of the library patrons. Maybe he was imagining it, but it seemed that the wheels were turning in their minds, as they tried to guess why he and others didn't have full-time jobs like them. Were they druggies or alcoholics, or were they just crazy or lazy?

There were a few looks of compassion, but many of masked derision. Tom might have related to this perception, remembering his own suspicions when he was a member of the working class. With his new insight, he viewed them differently and began to understand how Jesus felt when He began his mission as a homeless vagabond. Tom now realized why He came to Earth with a low station, so He could understand walking a mile in the shoes of one who has none.

Once inside the library, Tom found the clerks pleasant and helpful. He was told, if he just wanted to use the Wi-Fi on his phone, he could sit anywhere. If he needed electricity to charge his phone, he should choose an out of the way outlet on the wall. To use a computer, a library card was required, for which you had to show a St. Johns County address on your license or ID card. For those who needed a license and didn't have thirty dollars, St. Francis House could help. Tom was ready to begin!

He took a seat by the wall and read the instructions, while his phone charged more fully. When he felt comfortable enough to learn by doing, Tom made his first call to the marina to ask about getting his boat back. He made a tentative date to retrieve it in four days. Surely, he could make any necessary arrangements by that time. His head and knee were healing well, and he wanted to get on with his life.

Following the same train of thought, Tom called Larry to see if that Saturday morning would work with the dock owner. "The dock is ready when you are. It is the first one you will see when coming up the river. It's in the little cluster of seven docks, right next to the boat with the Jolly Roger flying. I'll give you a hand if you need it. Just call me Friday, and we'll make plans. I've got a skiff if it needs to be towed."

Tom was happy to hear that the plan was going so well. "People around here are incredibly friendly and helpful," he repeatedly muttered to himself. He was confident that he'd be back on his boat within the week.

There wasn't anyone else he wanted to call except Maria, and since she had worked the night shift, she was probably asleep. Besides he didn't want to seem overly anxious. That might give her the wrong impression.

Tom refocused on his self-training with his new Galaxy phone and he learned how to use its camera, Wi-Fi, and Internet browser. He set up a new email address which allowed him to start a blog and open accounts on Facebook, Twitter, and LinkedIn. Then he added HootSuite to link and manage them all at once. In short time, he was ready to rock. Free was such a good price for him, too. As interest grew, he might have to upgrade to the pro versions with more analytics and education. For now, though, he was golden!

Next, he went to sites that he respected, to garnish information. He envisioned his own web presence to have spiritually insightful quotes and whenever possible, inspirational music and imaginative graphics. There was so much free content out there in the public domain! He could place an array of it on his site to capture the attention of people that he needed to build his Internet "friendships".

Perhaps "followers" was a better word to use. He couldn't build a church because he didn't have the credentials. But, that's basically what he was doing. He just didn't feel he should reveal that yet. Not that he was trying to be deceptive. It was just way too early to see what direction things would go. The followers he was attempting to attract, were the people who, for whatever reason, did not want to get involved with an organized church or religion.

On the other hand, those same people were ripe for the picking. Those he wanted to begin drawing were those who had a leaning toward 'spiritual' existence. They were basically good people who felt there was something beyond physical existence that interacted with humans and the universe on an unseen and unexplained plane. This might include free thinkers, New Age, New Thought, Law of

Attraction, Law of Intention and Desire, and so many others, often so lightly defined there was little distinction.

Tom believed that there were few true atheists but many who had yet to define their beliefs. His weren't all defined either.

He knew that goodness and love were primary tenants of any belief system that he could embrace. Truthfully, Tom's roots were in Christianity, but he'd familiarized himself with other philosophies that he encountered. He could understand the thought patterns of other sects, but personally, he was attracted to the universal love, faith, and forgiveness values of Christ's teachings. Ironically, he hadn't found a true following of Christ's values in any Christian religion.

Tom knew many good spiritual people, that didn't want anything to do with organized religion. Sadly, a large number of them had bad experiences in their past, just as he did.

Although overall church attendance had dwindled over recent years, the numbers of believers might even have gone up. It's just that many didn't know what they believed, or whom they could trust. This is what Tom wanted to provide. He wanted to provide an intellectual and spiritual product that many craved without even realizing it.

He didn't like the term, "product", but that is what it was. His plan was to produce a loose amalgam of philosophy, psychology, rhetoric, belief, music, visual and aural effects, and even tactile, taste, and olfactory perceptions. The combinations would be subtle but powerful, to the point of addiction. Tom felt we are all seeking this, and his goal was to provide it through the talents of his followers. Today he would begin with beautifully spiritual, pictorial presentations online.

Tom's main concern was not to slander any religion. He did not want his product to be considered blasphemy by any open or close-minded follower of any religion. It should be supportive of the tenets of most beliefs. Loving God and loving others were the two pillars of his philosophy. Tom reasoned that Jesus believed that all else depended on those two premises.

With that in mind, Tom began scanning Facebook for something he could 'share' to his page on his first day of his service to humanity.

He had to laugh a little when he realized that he was starting from a very humble beginning.

It took only a minute to find a beautiful picture on Spiritual Networks of an exquisite sunset over the ocean with the quote, "Love is the secret password for every soul."

Wow, this was his philosophy! That was easy. Tom thought his plan might work out easier than expected. Then he got worried. If his philosophy was that prevalent on the web, he might be further behind than he thought. Maybe someone is already doing what he wanted to do. Then he conceded, "If God really wants me to do it, then it still needs to be done."

Steadily he found more on the same spiritual site that he needed. There were also many links to other like-minded sites. A wealth of information was there for his picking. But, what about copyrights? He answered himself quickly, that if everyone put it out there to share, that's exactly what he intended to do. Besides, if they wanted to sue him, he was broke.

Suddenly an overwhelming feeling of fear overtook him. He was embarking on a change in his life that he had wanted to do for a long time, but had no real idea of how to do it. There was just so much to consider, and he had so little experience doing it. Alone and very scared, he had no one in whom to confide.

"Sometimes," Tom thought, "it seems that when I have a good thought, a bad one jumps in there to counter it. Maybe that's the devil trying to stop me. But I don't even think of the devil that way. Well maybe, but I think of him more like the opposition rather than some red horned monster with a pitchfork. He might not have horns or a pitchfork, but there is a part of my mind that has to argue with every good thought that I have."

Tom could feel his blood pressure rising, his face flushing, and his ears tingling. "I've got to calm myself. I'm starting to rant inside my mind like a lunatic. I would prefer to talk this out aloud and rationally, but I don't have anyone that I trust. I need a cigarette or a drink, or both. Maybe just one cigarette and a drink, and I'd be okay. Damn it!

There I go again arguing with myself, or with the devil! Who knows! Damn! It's all the same thing!

"I've gotta talk to someone. Maria seems to understand me. But then, the one who gave me that massage is really hot. Here I go again. I've got to talk to Maria!"

Tom fought with himself and won this time. That was not always the outcome. And, it was never over. Negativity in its various forms always waited around for the next weakness.

Tom pawed through his old leather wallet until he found the crinkled piece of paper with Maria's phone number on it.

Tom neither paid attention to the time nor gave any thought to whether Maria would be asleep. His frustration forced him to charge into a solution for his problem. It might not have been the calmest approach, but it got him to an almost rational decision. Before he had the chance to think again, his fingers had "dialed" his new smartphone. Tom felt himself breathing hard as he listened to Maria's phone ring.

Expecting the ringing to yield to a voicemail message, he was completely caught off guard, when a groggy voice answered softly, "Hello?"

He tried to conceal his inner turmoil, as he began to speak. "Uh, Maria, this is Tom, your favorite patient from the hospital. I'm sorry. I forgot to check the time, but I don't know what time you sleep until, anyway. I hope that I didn't wake you. I just wanted to talk with you."

"Is everything all right, Tom?" She asked.

He was embarrassed, yet relieved that she understood him. "I got out of the hospital this morning, but I've far too many things on my mind to keep it all straight. Just felt like I needed your sympathetic ear to help me sort out what's right and wrong."

"Well, I don't know if I can help, but I'm a good listener. What's going on?"

Tom was a little taken back when she put him on the spot. "I'm a bit confused about all I've got to do. Do you think you could meet me in a little while, and we could talk? I'm at the library now, but I hear there's a cozy restaurant on the water, Hurricane Patty's, down by King

Street. I could meet you there in about an hour for a bite to eat, and we could talk."

Tom looked at the screen on his new phone. 1:57, it showed. How convenient. He had also heard that Happy Hour started at three.

Maria hesitated just long enough before responding, "I know where it is, but let's make it about 3:15. That'll give me time to shower and get there. Do you want me to pick you up at the library?"

"No. I need the walk. It's only about a mile from here. Great! I'll see you there soon."

Tom's mind already envisioned a frosty pitcher of beer, two mugs, and a cigarette. Drinking while staying at St. Francis House was not allowed, but he would deal with that later. His subconscious had already decided, while his conscious mind was on the phone. Besides, he wasn't officially checked in yet.

He had a little over an hour to walk there, so maybe he could get there a little early, order his beer, and enjoy a cigarette to even out his frayed nerves. His smoking cessation patch was running past its twenty-four-hour life. His dependent system was calling for more nicotine.

Tom figured that the best thing to do was to remove the patch and wash the skin, while he was still at the library. By the time he walked down US1 to Hurricane Patty's, he would be ready to smoke again. He knew his plan was counterproductive, but the nicotine and the devil had already joined sides, and it was two against one.

The idea of waiting until he met Maria also occurred to him, but his thoughts were already out of his control. Tom immediately put his plan into action in the library bathroom. Ten minutes later, he was walking south on US1.

It was an exhilarating walk. The December air was crisp and clear. He smiled when he saw the large, white egrets along the tidal pools and the low marsh grasses of the San Sebastian River. There were several pink birds with oddly shaped, wide bills. They weren't the famous Florida flamingos. Not quite as deep pink, but very unique. He made a mental note to ask some local about them.

Quickly, Tom's mind returned to the cold beer and cigarettes available only half a mile down the sidewalk bordering the pleasant four-lane road. With each step he took, the draw of his old habits pulled on his heartstrings.

Finally, he saw the two liquor stores at the corner of King Street and US1. There was no way around it, so he crossed the road to Broudy's Liquor Store. The older building appealed more to his addictive tendencies than the upscale appearance of the ABC Liquor Store.

He got a pack of Marlboros to satisfy one addiction and a four-ounce flask of Jack Daniels for the other. He felt guilty buying both, but it was out of his control. He watched himself hand the clerk a crisp twenty-dollar bill and had no power to override his hand from doing it. Only an addictive personality could understand his problem, but he had seen himself do it many, many times.

As soon as Tom stepped outside of Broudy's, he lit and inhaled his first Marlboro. Stepping beside a parked truck, he tipped the flask of Jack up with a quick, nonchalant flick of a practiced hand. A brisk jerk of his head and two ounces disappeared. He resumed walking towards a used car dealership, where he would turn off the main road toward the water.

At the other end of River's Edge Marina, Hurricane Patty's sat with its wrap around deck on the edge of the San Sebastian River. Only a ten-foot-wide, wooden dock separated it from the slips, filled with boats of all kinds. More than half were sailboats, and many of them were live-aboard. It was not only the nautical appearance but the accompanying local color of entrenched sailing life that Tom loved. Some boats were in seasonal North/South transit between the upper East Coast and the Caribbean. Others rarely moved, and their sailors rarely sailed. They just enjoyed the ambiance and lifestyle of living on the water. To accommodate them, it was always Happy Hour at Hurricane Patty's for anyone associated with a boat in the marina.

Tom walked up to the restaurant's deck to ask a passing waitress in shorts and a bright tank top if it was Happy Hour yet. She pulled her cell phone from her black apron, glanced at its clock, and replied that he had twenty minutes to wait. Her tables on the deck seemed slow, so it afforded an opportunity. Tom confidently looked into the bright sparkle of her blue eyes and gave his best shot to initiate a conversation with her.

"How much do you save on a pitcher of beer during Happy Hour?" he asked.

"Almost three dollars," she responded without much judgment.

"I'll wait a bit and take a walk around first if that's okay. It's my first time here. Looks like a lovely place. Seems really down-home, and I love being on the water. You might have read about me. I'm the one who got my boat stuck under the bridge a couple of days ago."

"Oh, yeah. I saw your story online. Are you all right?"

"Just got out of the hospital this morning, but I'm doing okay. Just waiting to get my boat back now. By the way, my name is Tom."

"Jan!" she replied with that same twinkle of blue. "I'll be your waitress if you sit out here."

"Great! I'll be back in a few minutes. Just want to check out the docks. They won't mind, will they?"

"Nobody will care, as long as you don't touch the boats. Are you going to dock here?"

Tom replied, "No, but I'll be somewhere on this river. Just don't know the name of the marina yet. Well, I'll see you in a few minutes, Jan." Tom gazed into those gorgeous, blue eyes again and punctuated his glance with the fast flicker of his trademark wink, almost too quick to consciously register.

"Good meeting you, Tom. Have fun," Jan smiled, blushing instantly.

When Tom got around the corner and out of sight, he pulled out the Jack and swigged the remaining two ounces of courage. He wasn't sure if he was nervous about meeting Maria or just in need of a fix. Either way, that swig would soothe him.

Tom wandered the docks, while the serenity of the scenery mixed with the Kentucky bourbon. The gentle sway of the wooden docks added to his meditative mood of the moment. He felt that there was just something unexplainable about the undulating motion of being surrounded by water. His only thought was, "Life is good."

Tom sat patiently on the restaurant deck, as Maria pulled into the parking lot. It was a slow Tuesday, and there were plenty of spaces available. She worked her way across the gravel to the broken pavement in front of the restaurant. She could see down the boat ramp into the water and view the haphazard assortment of boats in their slips. It was obvious this ramp was not used to launch many boats. The foot-thick muck would suck the boots off any fisherman. It was low tide now. At high tide, the water would be about four feet higher, and launching a dingy would be easier. It was only for locals with local knowledge anyway. The tourists could go to the Lighthouse.

Tom went over to the steps to greet her. He walked down to the bottom and waited for Maria to ascend to the first stair, so they were even. It was perfect for their first hug and peck on the cheek. They were still in that casual friend stage. Tom's gaze pierced her eyes for an extra second, letting her know that he was interested in her inner being.

"I've got a table up here on the deck by the rail," he said, directing her with a magnanimous sweep of his arm.

Maria led the way, looking back a little questioningly.

"That one, right there." Tom pointed to the two-top table. He popped a couple more breath mints into his mouth while she was looking at the pitcher on the table.

"I see you've already started," Maria said as she took her place opposite the half-full mug in front of a wicker chair.

"I'll just have a sweet tea," she said to Jan, the waitress, who had curiously followed them, as they walked over to sit down.

Tom wasn't sure if he detected a hint of sarcasm about his alcohol consumption, remembering that Maria had mentioned that she didn't drink much.

"I hope you don't mind if I have a couple of beers. It's been a crazy week. Although everything seems to be working itself out, I am really overwhelmed this afternoon. I need to relax and I need to talk to you!"

"To me? What for?"

"To be totally honest, I was feeling overwhelmed earlier. I got out of the hospital first thing this morning. So far, I have an arrangement to get my boat back in a few days. I've gotten some 'almost new' clothes, a place to stay, and a new smartphone with a big screen and good camera. I've gotten onto all the social media to begin promoting my new vocation, too. Things are happening so fast, I'm just a little nervous. I'm not used to making so many decisions with so much depending on them. I'm feeling scared and alone. I know it sounds silly, but I need someone to talk to about everything, and you seem to be the perfect person."

Maria's dark complexion blushed noticeably, "Why me? I mean, I'm glad you thought of me, but this is an unexpected, though pleasant surprise."

"Well, first of all, we talk easily. I mean, somehow I get the feeling that we both have a similar spiritual outlook, and this is the direction my life is leading me," Tom began to explain.

"I feel I have a calling to start a social media ministry that's nondenominational. I don't really know where I am going with it, or how I'm going to get there. Yet, I feel I'm being led to start on this path, and I'm to follow it, wherever it takes me. Everything I am doing is totally new. I need someone I can relate to, and someone to be totally up front with me."

Tears were beginning to well up in Maria's eyes, and she tried to hide them from Tom.

Before she could speak, Tom responded to her feelings. "That's okay. We need to be honest with each other, feelings and all. What I'm saying is, well, I don't know what roles we might take in this or in our lives, but I don't want to play any games. We could be dealing with things on a universal plane, where hiding anything could not only be impossible but also dangerous. I know, all this seems a little far out, and I shouldn't get so deep so quickly, but that's where I feel we may be heading."

"Wow, I knew something like this was in the air when I first met you! I couldn't help being amazed by your auras. They are prominent, and they change with your moods and passions. Hopefully, you don't think I'm weird, but I really do see auras. Not everyone's, and I've never seen one as intense as yours. They're so clear and obvious, like none I've ever seen."

Tom looked keenly at Maria with an expression of excitement. "I don't know much about auras and chakras, but I understand they are related to spiritual energy within our bodies and with the Divine. You've got to tell me more!"

"Okay! What I see very clearly around you is a radiant turquoise aura. The way I understand it is this. The chakras are energy centers within your body. These energy centers are quite constant but can change over time. You might look at life differently and your chakras could change, maybe because of a brush with death, or a career change. Your aura is more temporary, coming from how you relate to things at the moment.

"Your turquoise aura is blended from colors of your dominant chakra's, your green heart chakra and blue throat chakra. The tone and intensity of colors are modified by your present perception of life right now, creating your aura. The way I perceive you probably affects how I even see your aura.

"The green tells me you have a good evolving heart and with a desire to express your love. The royal blue says that you are spiritual or intuitive and want to communicate with others and the Divine."

"Wow!" Tom responded again. You can see all that by just looking at me?"

"Well, it's not really looking. My eyes have little to do with it. It's more like a feeling of color. You have an unusually clear, turquoise aura. To me, that means it is not muddied by holding onto hurts or grudges from the past. You have some fears of intimacy as most people do, and I see some cloudiness wafting by now and then. At least with me, it disappears after a few moments, and that makes it easy for us to talk and understand each other."

He broke in, "I don't see auras, but you have probably described me very well. Now, how would you describe yourself?"

Maria blushed a little, "Well, I don't see myself, of course, but I have always seen the auras of others. I remember in third grade, when I was supposed to draw pictures of family members, I would always put colors around their bodies. The teacher would ask why I scribbled around them. I just told her that was the way I saw them."

Maria continued, "I'm not weird or strange. I go to a Christian church. I really like how Jesus changed the way we need to look at everything with the New Covenant. 'Forgive and love instead of kill and hate.' No more eye for an eye, etcetera. The Old Testament was all about war, while the New Testament doesn't have any war in it.

"Unfortunately, many of the so-called Christians seem to still be following the Pharisees and their old laws. They like to judge others as being wrong about everything. I'm sorry. Don't let me get started. I don't have a lot in common with many Christians, but I enjoy learning about Jesus. I don't consider myself a Christian, really. I consider myself a follower of The Way. That's what His followers were first known as. He was The Way, and everyone considered themselves followers of The Way. Now, Christians are just followers of a religion. Strange, huh?"

"Wow! You know, I feel much the same," Tom replied. "Churches complain that people don't attend as they did, but they've driven many of Christ's followers away. There are probably more people like us than we realize. Hopefully, they haven't just given up and hung their faith upon a nail somewhere. These are the ones, that I need to reach."

"There used to be a church in town for people who didn't like religion. It was great until the pastors found religion. Now a pastor comes out shaking his finger and yelling that everyone is going to Hell unless they do as they're told. Their service is like a show. It's a hit and apparently profitable. I guess people like that stuff, and God Bless them if that's what they want to hear. Many were brought up to respond to fear, rather than love. I chose the love. That's why I moved on."

Tom agreed with her. "Yeah. Too many religious people spend their lives steering from fear. They are always afraid they are going to do something wrong. I'd rather be led forward by love."

Then Tom changed the subject, "Hey, want to take a walk out on the docks? This place is really nice. Maybe I could move my boat here when the time is right. I'll pay the check, then let's walk around." He flagged Jan and gave her fifteen bucks which included over a fifty percent tip.

Jan responded with a grateful smile and her expressive twinkle, as she thanked him. With Maria behind him, Tom quickly looked into Jan's blue eyes and gave her his signature wink, which made her blush again. "Thanks, Jan. I'll see you soon."

Placing his hand gently on Maria's elbow, he moved them forward. "Let's go out this way," he said, leading her towards the back deck that overlooked the boats. "This view is incredible. I wandered around a bit before you came. Wouldn't you like to wake up here every morning?"

She was quiet a long time and Tom wondered if she'd heard him, but judging by the look in her eyes, she'd heard him. And she was thinking hard about an answer.

Finally, she came back with, "Yeah, I'd love it."

He couldn't keep a smile off his face. She was definitely interested.

They walked up and down the docks even though the unlocked gates had signs that said, "BOAT OWNERS AND GUESTS ONLY". The boaters weren't that uptight, but they needed a recourse to get rid of troublemakers. Most boaters were proud to have outsiders look over their boats, wishing that they could enjoy such a laid-back lifestyle. It's always five o'clock at a marina.

After passing the second boat dock filled with different boats, some of which might be classified as yachts, Tom's hand touched hers, and they naturally clasped.

A romantic charge united them, as they toured the third dock. By the time they got to the end jutting out into the river, they turned to embrace each other. Saltwater, warm breezes, and solitude mellowed them and their lips met to explore each other. It was a perfect step towards a possible romance. The gentle swaying of the floating docks intensified their lightheadedness from the kiss and caused them to back off while still balanced.

Tom wasn't exactly sure what path he wanted this relationship to take. For the time being though, a sweet dream was unfolding as gently and enjoyably as the breezes that seemed to enwrap them. He thought the dreamy look on Maria's face indicated she wanted more.

Enjoying the stroll back to shore in silence, each was quiet. For a while, no words could duplicate the exchange that had so instinctively occurred. Energy tingled between their entwined fingers. Words could not replace the communication that flowed as they walked in their cloud of sensual serenity.

Finally, their long-shared silence brought an awkwardness to their intimate encounter. Then sighs of wonder broke the silence, as each echoed the other's feelings.

Maria's face nearly glowed and her eyes shone like diamonds.

"Maybe I shouldn't share this with you now, but I have this indescribable, intense feeling of euphoria. I imagine that it's the earthly equivalent of wanting to surrender to the all-powerful. I just want to follow 'The Way' before me!"

Maria paused, and there was suddenly a loud, but muffled, "Blam!"

Tom's head was filled with noise, searing pain, and the brightest white light imaginable. There was no choice but to surrender to the overwhelming agony.

As Tom faded, and his pain diminished, Maria's words were repeated in the brilliant light, softening with green shadows.

An ethereal face spoke the words, "I am The Way".

CHAPTER 8

TINKLING CHIMES IN A BREEZE...

In Tom's fast fading capacity, he had no choice but to accept the path offered by the ethereal face, presenting itself in the ensuing darkness.

As the green image before Tom continued to darken and became accompanied by tinkling chimes and a light breeze, Tom knew that it had to be the Son giving him one last chance. His mind stretched to grasp the hand held out, hoping it would pull him to safety.

With their hands gripping each other's wrists, there was a dim vision of entering a cave-like access. Sounds of the wind chimes gave way to a rush, as a vortex accelerated their movement through a perfectly round, black tunnel.

During the high-speed excursion, Tom felt like an astronaut. He slowed into a softly colored, misty, zero-gravity destination. He hadn't traveled long or far in distance, but he found himself alone in a different reality and a different body.

His was translucent with no feeling except euphoria. His vision and hearing were perfect, and he could look downward at himself lying on the ground with Maria bent over him. Others joined them, while one called 911. He realized, he was viewing life from the "other" side.

He could discern from the conversations, that he had been bleeding from his right temple which faced up, as his body laid on the ground. Of course, the bleeding had stopped, after his heart stopped pumping. There was no visible entry hole in the bloody wound. There was only damaged skin where hair was missing above the exposed bone.

Maria took a frantic guess as to the cause of the lifeless body that laid at her knees. The only thing that made sense to her was that the muffled pop she'd heard was from a gun with a silencer. It must have made a glancing blow that caused a traumatic shock to his brain. The wound bled profusely until his heart stopped. But there didn't seem to be enough blood on the ground to cause the death, which she confirmed by his missing pulse.

"We've got to start CPR right now!" she commanded to all who gathered around Tom's lifeless body.

Although Maria worked only as a nursing assistant, she had spent many years in the hospital, including the ER. Her lack of credentials didn't stop her quick wits. Here, she was the only one to take charge, and she did just that with authority and alacrity.

Observing in awe, Tom stopped short of cheering for her to succeed. He was happy just the way he was now. He wasn't so sure that he wanted to go back to that inefficient body. His new one had no moving parts to wear out, and as far as he could tell, no duties, obligations, physical or mental stress, or pain.

He watched with ambivalent feelings, as Maria struggled with reviving him. She started breathing with force into his mouth while holding his nose. Jan, whom he had met just an hour ago, started chest compressions. An observer, who Tom recognized as Larry, shouted, "Stop! That's making blood pump out of his head!"

"Put pressure on the wound. Use your shirt for a rag!" Maria ordered between the breaths. Larry did as he was told, and the blood flow slowed to a trickle.

Tom heard sirens approaching. By the time paramedics arrived on the scene, he had lost interest in what was happening to him on the ground. He began to search the scene for meaningful clues. Oddly, he had not grasped, accepted, or cared about the fact that he was now dead.

As he surveyed the surroundings at the marina, all was quiet, besides the hubbub around his body. All attention was focused there. No one except Tom seemed to notice a silver sedan slip slowly behind the palms and ease out onto the road. Tom recognized the driver as an underworld character from Myrtle Beach.

He didn't think much about it, as his reality began to rotate slowly, and then became a dizzying whirl through a dream tunnel.

As his unexplained journey began to slowly enter another realm, Tom became aware again, as if in a dream. His surroundings were unrecognizable but beautiful. The colors were a bit unrealistic, and the shapes, unfamiliar. In all, it was indescribable. Letting go of his inquisitive nature, he recognized his mother coming toward him from a distance. She didn't have the laboring gait of her later years, and she looked like her newspaper engagement picture in an album Tom remembered from his childhood. They approached each other as if walking effortlessly on air.

She warmly greeted him with outstretched arms and a great big kiss, as only a mother could do.

"Hello, Thomas. It is wonderful to see you. It seems like you've come here prematurely, but I'm glad you've stopped here for a visit. This is a heavenly place, and I am so happy. Life is beautiful and peaceful here. There are no real struggles and plenty of love and rewards. I've truly found my home, and I'm blessed to be back."

"Oh Mom, you look wonderful! So happy and well rested! This is fantastic! I think of you so much, and I miss you. I'm truly sorry for all the troubles, I caused you. I think of it almost every day, and I beat myself up over it sometimes."

"Please don't worry about that, Tom. Kids are supposed to misbehave. The first thing we learn here is forgiveness. We were forgiven completely for our mistakes, and to stay here, we too must forgive completely. It's as simple as that. The Holy Spirit fills each of us with Grace, and it's His power that lets us do miracles. It's just a matter of surrendering our meager power. In return, we receive His ultimate power, based on love."

Tom replied with his earthly understanding, "I've heard all about that, but total surrender is hard to do, isn't it?"

"It's much easier here. It's simply the natural thing to do. Without the physical needs and desires, why not?"

Tom persisted, "Do you miss Earth? What is it you do here?"

His mom chuckled, "No, I remember my time there with pleasure, but I can easily do without the strife and drama. By your standards, we probably don't do that much. You see, there is no time here, so there is no hurry. I am abiding in the bliss and the overwhelming knowledge of all time. It's what you are always striving for on Earth, time to relax, enjoy, and learn. Even when you have it, you don't know what to do with it. Instead of just enjoying it, you must do something else to have more. You are always in a hurry to get something done or avoid doing it. Here, it's just natural to live on vacation in the best resort in the universe."

Tom didn't fully understand, and he looked perplexed.

"Don't worry, Son. I don't think you will be staying long. I've heard that you are just here for a little encouragement from the One. You are embarking on a major venture, and He wants to make sure you understand what you are doing. You might say it's a courtesy call. You've asked him for help in what you are doing, and coincidences just so happened that this became the best way for all concerned."

"Coincidences? You mean my death? Did He arrange that?"

"It's what they call an NDE, a Near Death Experience, down there on Earth these days. You won't be dead for long. He saw to that. It was not a coincidence that you turned your head, just as you did. He or One, as I like to call them (or the Trinity, as you sometimes call them), do some of their best work through what humans call coincidences. You are fortunate. He or They love you and want the best for you. He is just concerned that you do it right."

"When you say 'He', do you mean Jesus, God, or whom? Are they in charge here? Is Heaven only for Christians, as they say?"

"Well, yes and no," his mother replied. "They appear differently to different people. You tend to see whom you expect to see. God, who is the same God no matter what name He goes by, appears to everyone, as they are comfortable and expect. Most religions have had the same premise since the beginning of time, 'Do what is right and loving!' It is just presented differently to each culture, as they might understand it."

She dropped her explanations for the time being. A little at a time was the best way to grasp alogical concepts. Pure logic, as we know it, is the surest way to misunderstand Spiritual ideas. Words are inadequate and misleading in that realm. Most words were developed for precise definitions of material and legalistic reasons, and his mother did not want their relationship to be based on such things. She preferred to converse and share on the spiritual plane of love, understanding, and feelings.

"I've actually been expecting to see you here. You are held in high regard by so many here. It seems that you have a gift of understanding the Spiritual. There's a long way further for total comprehension, but you do have a promising outlook. You can grasp the interactive intricacies of material with spiritual interdependence. You will learn much here, but when you leave, there will be even more to reason out for yourself. You will be entrusted with explaining things here to those there. One of the greatest difficulties will be to use the same vocabulary of words to describe two separate realities. The purpose of your visit now is to receive the help and support you've requested. I wish you the best, my son. Most people who attempt this task get crucified one way or another. Always remember that you will return here at the end of your chosen mission. I'll look forward to that point when we'll be reunited!"

Tom was so glad to see his mother. It was overwhelming that he had gotten such attention in Heaven if that's where he was now. If he had his earthly body, tears of joy and mixed emotions would be streaming down his face.

Overcome with feelings of love and wonder, he finally squeezed out a heartfelt, "I love you, Mom!"

"I know you do, Tom, and I love you. We all do. We share such good feelings here," she said with her sweet, little laugh, which Tom missed so much. "There is someone here to meet you. Turn around, Tom."

When he turned, he was greeted by the same one he'd met immediately after his death. "Hello again, Tom. Thank you for coming. I hope you are comfortable and enjoying yourself here."

Tom was shocked to see Him again. He also picked up on the "pseudo-serious" welcome he'd been extended and replied in kind.

"Oh, yeah! It's Heavenly!" They enjoyed a chuckle together.

"There's lots of humor here," He said. "It's all good! Might as well enjoy ourselves. By the way, that other saying everyone likes, got its start here, 'Live, Laugh, Love!'"

What would have seemed corny in the physical, was pure joy and laughter in the spiritual. And they enjoyed each other's soulful smiles. There was total honesty. No need to wonder about someone's motives. Everything was obviously genuine. In that worry-free environment, it was natural to always have a smile that turned easily into laughter.

"Not to pop your bubble, Tom, but there is something that everyone goes through when they first arrive. It's called a Life Review. Perhaps not the most pleasant thing, but you are lucky. Because you will be going back to your life, you'll have a second chance to do things right. It's not us judging you, but a chance for you, as a spirit, to judge yourself in the light of love. Don't take it to heart. No one is perfect. Well, except Me, of course, at least in most people's eyes," He added with a laughing smile.

Tom thought to himself, "Man, you can't help but love this guy."

"I thank you, Tom!" He responded verbally to Tom's thoughts. "Oh, yeah, it's hard to have much privacy with Me around. That's the way it was on Earth, but you just didn't realize it. Hey, don't worry about that either. I won't tell anyone. Your mother already knows."

Tom couldn't help but laugh once he got the embarrassing joke.

Then He shared something a lot of people don't understand.

"I went through a Life Review when I died on the cross. Mine was for everyone's mistakes. It was very intense and most enlightening. That's why I went down to Earth. I wanted to feel what it was like to be human, to understand their perspectives, and to know what it's like to be tested with choices–right or wrong. We knew that temptations presented tough decisions and doing the right thing was often not the easiest choice. We were all-knowing, but we were not all feeling.

"It's easy to make the right choice when you know everything, and feelings are not involved. We know it's much different when you know very little, and you only have gut feelings to rely upon. I had to go there and become as you to experience that for Myself.

"Experiencing is far different than knowing. I lived and experienced an incredible life and purpose. Learning to understand everything through the eyes, ears, and feelings of a man put everything in an entirely new light. There is often pain and sorrow involved in simple decisions. It's very tempting to make decisions based only on personal feelings, instead of doing what is right for all. It's easy to do what feels best for you in that moment, but you often don't realize the ramifications your actions might have.

"Tom, I've heard you say, a lot of the Bible is a metaphor. Spiritual things are hard to explain with earthly language. I used many parables, and its writers used allegories and metaphors. Don't take everything too seriously! Nothing on Earth is, as it is here. 'Live, laugh, and love' will make more sense, when you return home."

He continued explaining Himself and His time on Earth.

"I had a tough time understanding the mixed emotions that people feel, especially when they don't know that doing things through love is always the best option. This is nearly impossible for anyone who wasn't brought up in love to understand. The spiritual laws of nature, such as the Golden Rule or Karma, are not fully understood or even believed by many. People often act selfishly out of their ignorance, more than out of evil."

Then He finished His thoughts from His earthly experiences. "I truly felt what it was like to be ignorant in a complex world. I held so much compassion for people there. Many just did the best they could with what they knew. People and God alike, need to be forgiving of people acting out of ignorance. We don't realize the fog they are seeing their lives through. Yes, they need to be corrected but corrected out of love, not anger.

"Many people believe God, in each of our forms, is perfect, but We realized our mistakes. The big flood for one, and Sodom and Gomorrah, for another. People perished because of our design flaws, yet we learned an enormous amount too. Earth was the first creation for people.

"I felt the regrets of all people, their sadness and sorrows, and their wishes that they could have done things differently. For some, their mistakes were minor and their reviews were learning experiences. For others, there were enormous regrets that came with the lessons. I was devastated by what I learned, knowing our expectations were often beyond human potential.

"Hopefully, we all learn from our mistakes, and the most important thing we learn is forgiveness. We all make mistakes. We must forgive ourselves and forgive others completely and equally. The flood was a horrific one, but We have forgiven ourselves and offered the rainbow as a sign of understanding.

"Unfortunately, there are many who cannot accept forgiveness from themselves, others, or God. They hold onto their feelings of anger, and they blame themselves or others for their mistakes and misconceptions. All they need to do is forgive themselves and accept forgiveness from others. Pride keeps them from admitting that they made mistakes and letting it all slip away. God is not putting them through Hell. They and their stubborn pride are doing it to themselves. Eventually, most turn that around."

Tom was amazed to hear Him explain things from His point of view. It made a tremendous sense. God holds no grudges. He is willing to give all the love and forgiveness that one will accept.

"Your thoughts will be much purer here in this environment," He explained to Tom. "No one can judge you here, except Me, and I'm a little lazy about that. Besides, you have the Holy Spirit in you here. It's hard to get too far off base with Her around."

The One Tom saw as Jesus continued, "You were not really baptized in the Holy Spirit down there. That is something you should check into upon your return. It would benefit you especially with the plans you have concerning representing Me. It's sort of the VIP plan, with perks and direct connections. Well, I won't take too much of your time, not that we have that around here. You'll be returning shortly, just as soon as this Blue Spirit group is finished with you. Have an enlightening time, and don't forget to look up the Holy Spirit when you get back."

Tom was left amazed and mystified after his encounter with The Son. His charisma had immediately put Tom at ease and in awe. He had an essence of love that one couldn't help but love in return. His magnetism and power pervaded his personality, but it was all based on love, causing the universe to bow down in a submission of admiration.

Suddenly, three beings of blue, transparent light approached Tom and beckoned him to follow them into a room of darkness. As they entered, a scene of characters became the only source of light. As Tom's eyes adjusted, the intensity increased, until he became the only member of the audience and the title-role character of the play that was unfolding. He watched intently, as his former-self dominated the would-be stage and documented his life.

Entranced and embarrassed, he watched himself as a spoiled brat. The visuals that he saw did not match feelings he remembered as he manipulated his parents and playmates with tantrums, temptations, and projections of guilt. At first, he thought that he had overcome such childish maneuvers. Then he realized he had simply refined the techniques. His motives remained the same, only more covert.

He watched, as he grew. Tom learned to get the most while giving the least. It seemed on the surface, that he was successful in his tactics. Now he felt the true loneliness of his youth, realizing that while he fooled others on the surface, they had gravitated toward truer friendships. Although he had many temporary victories, he was left behind and alone. Others moved on to more organic love-based relationships, and they thrived in less toxic environments. That was something Tom never learned. With this realization under his belt, Tom would work more diligently at that, when he returned.

When it came to women, Tom was quick to judge on first impressions. Facial features and body types were rated and calculated, before hearts met, mingled, and shared their unique personalities. As a result, Tom had affairs based on negotiations of "pretty" points, power points, financial, and social prowess. He did well in that marketplace, but he got only for what he bargained, people who bargained with the same currency. Unfortunately, trading up—or trading out—were always the next possible moves, but seldom the answer.

Tom continued to watch the highlights of his life unfold before him. He wasn't very happy with the feelings that arose in him, as he watched from this enlightened perspective. He was ashamed that his life had made such minimal impact on the Earth. It was neither bad nor good, just sort of sleazy. He was grateful that this would not be his final epitaph. He planned to change, but then again, he always had plans. The next time, with this help, Tom's life could be far more positive.

He now knew what was needed, an honest plan with a defined direction. He was determined to maintain an honorable and righteous motive with love in his heart. Love was the primary theme in Spirituality that kept coming up.

Love, as expressed in the Golden Rule, is probably the first thing most Christians learn. "Do unto others as you would have them do unto you." Eastern religions have the same philosophy: they call it Karma.

It finally became clear to Tom in his temporary environment. If you do something just to get into Heaven, you are doing it for the wrong reason. The motive should be Love, not greed. The Greatest Commandment that Jesus gave to us is to Love God. And the second commandment is, "Love your neighbor as yourself." And finally, He said, "All else hangs on these!"

Tom realized that if one chose salvation before loving others, it was for selfish reasons and not what Jesus commanded. And not what Jesus did, either. Jesus went through Hell for mankind–literally!

Repeating words in a short prayer that some preacher has made up is not quite the same as making a total commitment and following the vow of loving even the worst enemy. Forgiving and helping one who harms you is the type of love He taught. It's not easy, and we are not perfect, but we must do our best to honor a vow we make to Him.

Love is not always easy, and it takes a lot of effort to change our attitude to always do our best to love everyone. The first step is to stop judging others, especially when there is no reason for it. That's God's job! The Son demonstrated that even He does not want to do it. How can we judge someone else for their actions, when we don't have any idea of the facts? We only need to judge ourselves in advance for how we will respond to a situation. Tom felt humbler now than ever. This was good. He no longer had to support the heavy weight of his ego. Pride was gone since there was no ego to support. People in the heavenly environment could see through each other. There was no one they could fool. He felt exposed but relaxed. He had nothing to hide.

What a difference this acceptance made, unfettered by judgment. There were no false images to project or protect. Pure love allowed each person to completely communicate with others. There were no adversaries. All were one.

Of course, this is much easier in the world of spirit, where there are no physical bodies or tangible possessions. Illusions only exist to help us in transforming to the true spiritual reality, where sight, sound, and other physical senses need not exist.

This need for testing and awareness of sin soon became apparent to Tom. Not everyone could, or would want to exist in a world, where they would not be able to lord their achievements over others. Not everyone could or would want to exist, where there is no competition or strife. Many are far too attached to the turmoil of the world where triumphs over others are their only measure of worth. Too many enjoy their world, where surrender is not an option.

Surrender is the way of Heaven. Not surrendering to become subservient to others, but surrendering to serve and share with others. In a world where physical needs and the concept of time have no importance, serving and sharing among like-minded souls, is a blissful existence.

Those who thrive in competition and strife have the accompanying tensions and turmoil. They are welcome to it! But, they should be cautioned that they will be playing with the big dogs and without all the gentle souls over whom they have ridden herd in the material world.

Tom realized that God was very magnanimous. He is willing to give everyone a choice of their retirement home. It's hard to think of anyone wanting to go anywhere as tough as Hell, but that is how many are accustomed, and how they approach life. It's not easy for one to give up fighting for survival and put their difficulties into the hands of a superior or universal existence. Surrendering is a foreign concept to those who feel they must fight for everything. Pride stands in the way of accepting an easier solution. Most gracious religions have similar beliefs of this, expressed in their own words.

Many feel it's too difficult to lead the life necessary to get through the narrow gate of the "Pie in the Sky" retirement home. Some say that all you must do is to relax and trust Jesus or the universe to resolve your important battles now and take care of your future too. For them, what a relief it is to finally quit fighting and begin to enjoy giving and receiving love! With the love of others and the Eternal, there is less concern and much more peace abounding.

It seemed so crystal clear to Tom from this vantage point. All one had to do is love. We all "miss the mark", a simply-worded definition of sin. No one is perfect. Maybe, if so-called Christians would condemn others less, people could know what Christ was teaching.

Tom felt too many Christians tried to play God and decide who was going to Hell. He laughed to himself when he recalled Christians saying in anger that all Gays were going to hell, while they bragged about their own salvation. As he remembered, God considered braggarts and haters to be sinners too. He surely understood it all now. Just love one another, as He loved all.

As Tom finished his momentary rumination, he recognized his personal Savior's kind voice.

"That's what I like the most about you, Tom. You get It! Love. Unfortunately, many forget my message. Here's a slogan for you, Tom. 'Once you get It, don't forget It'. Oh, and capitalize Love, while you are at It. God is Love. Trust in Me and receive our Grace!

"You will be going back soon, Tom, but you will hear from Me quite often. Don't be afraid to follow inspirational visions that come to you, as long as you let Love be your guide."

Tom saw his mother coming toward him from a short distance. He ran towards her like a little boy again. She had all the beauty and vibrancy from the days of his first recollection of her.

She sashayed toward him as if walking on a cloud. Holding that same goddess-like infatuation for him now, as she did when he was four years old. She was the most beautiful person he knew, and her wisdom and abilities were boundless. Most of all, she was filled with overflowing love. Tom's mother was the same heavenly angel to him now, as she was before he went to his first day of school.

"It's time," she said, just as when she had dropped him off at his first half day of kindergarten. There he had met Miss Holly, his teacher, who would become the second love of his life at five years old.

Returning to his heavenly moment, his mother reached for him, gave him a hug, and looked deeply into his eyes. He could see all the love, hopes, and dreams for him that she had always held. He could also see the concerns and fears for his well-being, as she had shown when he was younger. It was as if she knew the difficulties he was about to face now. There was familiar comfort instilling confidence in him when she spoke to him.

"Just remember, do what you know is right and be quick to forgive and move on."

With that said, he knew things would be okay. As he began to wonder about his future, he became confused, and everything became hazy. Drifting in his thoughts, the haze turned to darkness, and he lost contact with his heavenly bliss.

* * *

Deep in the darkness, he can hear another voice in the distance calling, "Tom, Tom, come back to me. Come back, come back!"

He hears but he isn't listening. It's just noise in the darkness until he detects the anguish in the voice and hears the sobs that ride on the breaths between the calls. A response is being desperately sought from him.

In his darkness, it's hard to gather a thought, until he realizes he is drowning in that darkness and must do something.

"Breathe!" he orders himself, and he responds with a huge inhalation. Like a frantic swimmer, he returns to the surface.

He followed the reviving breath by opening his eyes and saw a blurry sight that resembled Maria looking down at him.

That assured him unmistakably that he had returned to his earthly life. Tom initially reacted with disappointment. He had so enjoyed being immersed in that blissful atmosphere, where knowledge was not only abundant, but it came with the associated wisdom to discern it.

Appreciatively, Tom could now look forward to continuing his life plans. He was buoyed by the confidence expressed by the One whom he wished to emulate and illuminate. What more could one struggling with questions of faith request? While there wasn't much in the way of religious fact, there were buds of wisdom bestowed upon him. He expected to watch them unfold, exposing the pollen for producing seeds of the fruit. Could this be from the Tree of Knowledge of Good and Evil (Judgment) or the Tree of Life (Grace)? The buds of Wisdom seemed like the link between the two! We became mortal beings when God separated us from the Tree of Life, and Jesus restored our eternal life through His Love and Grace.

Those deep thoughts occupied his mind only a few moments before the ensuing pain interrupted his mental process. Promising himself to return to them soon, Tom was forced to focus on his present predicament. He acknowledged Maria with a wincing smile. He weakly thanked her for performing CPR. Only he knew that she had called him back from elsewhere.

She couldn't have known the joy that he experienced before being called back. It did seem like his sabbatical there had ended anyway.

No more thoughts for now. Tom allowed himself to release the pain by drifting into his darkness again, being gently reassured that he would remain on this side of the Divine curtain.

Maria rode to the hospital with Tom in the ambulance. He was still in shock from the blood loss. Then, the monitors alerted them that his heart had stopped again, and cardiac stimulating drugs were pushed through the established IV line.

Immediately he was administered fluids to replace the lost blood volume, and the CPR was resumed that Maria had begun. Now Maria, out of love and a desperate desire to help Tom, lovingly massaged his exposed foot, while the EMT continued to keep the pressure on his head wound. Tom had not been pronounced dead since there was no doctor on board, but the absence of his pulse and breathing certainly suggested it.

After the drugs were administered to Tom, the EMT performing the CPR compressions loudly commanded the other applying pressure on the wound to press hard. It was a little unconventional, but they couldn't let up on the wound to use a defibrillator.

He quickly gave Tom several very hard chest compressions to awaken his waiting heart. It was an act of desperation, but it must have been their lucky day. Or, was there a little help from above? It worked. Unknown to them, Maria's knowledge of a heart-brain nerve link, in the foot she massaged, was another key to their success.

Tom resumed life and made a short communication with the living before he passed out again. But, his earthly brain began an internal correspondence with the heavenly realm.

* * *

Fresh, white snow covered the ground in his mind, while a thin layer of ice caused the thick, but bare, forest branches to sparkle with refracted rays of light from the bright, winter sky.

Tom's eyes followed a snowy country path up a steep hill through the trees. As his mind wandered up the slope toward the light, there came Jesus, zipping down the path on a sled with his long hair streaming behind him in the breeze. Only His joyful whoop of "Yee-haw!" broke the snow-muffled silence of winter. He maneuvered his Flexible Flyer toward Tom until it stopped at his feet with a squeak of moist snow beneath its runners.

"This is great!" He exclaimed. "Come on, let's go for a ride."

Before Tom could answer, he found himself walking beside Him, as He pulled the sled toward the top of the mountain. They trudged effortlessly up the snowy path without speaking. Tom felt like a young boy with an older brother, whom he admired and wished to emulate. The sights, sounds, silence, and love overwhelmed his body and forced all thoughts from his mind, leaving him feeling like a snowflake on the breeze.

When they approached the top of the hill, the light bending over the horizon became noticeably brighter. It was so intensely white, Tom couldn't go further without squinting. Jesus said, "That's far enough for now. You'll see it all later," and they turned around.

Tom couldn't help but ask, "Why do I feel so comfortable and fulfilled with you?"

His companion replied with a smile, "That's simple. I don't judge you, anyone, or anything. That's not my job. Judging crowds the thoughts together and we really need that space between the thoughts as a path to our souls, creativity, God, and childhood. And, one other thing, judge yourself seldom and gently."

With that, He sat down on the long wooden sled and put his feet on the steering board with the rope held loosely in his hands. "Give me a push and then jump on!"

Tom gladly obeyed. Suddenly he felt like a child, without a worry or a care. Beauty, love, and fun not only surrounded them but were part of them. They quickly picked up speed, laughing and screaming around every turn with the trees whizzing by them. He headed for a huge snowdrift at the bottom of the hill, as they screamed with delight. When their sled stopped abruptly beneath them, they flew into the pile's pillowy softness.

* * *

Tom opened his eyes, as he was being unloaded at the hospital's emergency dock. He thought he heard Him taunting him in the distance. "Unless you become like a child, you can't ride my sled!"

Tom finally understood what "become like a child" meant. He had to humble himself and realize that he knew very little about the workings of the universe. Yet, if he would surrender his heart, he could understand on a level far beyond science or philosophy.

The wisdom of the millennia would be available to him. What did he have to lose except his worthless ego?

CHAPTER 9

NO BLAME FOR THE BOOKIE...

Tom regained consciousness as he was being jostled around the emergency room. He opened an eye every time his gurney moved. It wasn't what he wanted to see. The few days Tom had spent there earlier, before meeting his Maker, were enough to satisfy him for a long time.

Although Tom hadn't memorized many Bible verses in his life, he readily remembered one from his short afterlife: "Now I know in part; then I shall know fully, even as I have been fully known. (1 Cor. 13:12)"

That was his first complete thought since being literally *reborn*.

Flagler Hospital wasn't wonderful, but it was all he knew as home for the present. He needed to pull together the pieces, as to how he'd gotten here.

The last moment he recalled was lying dead on the ground. Maria and strangers were working hard on him. He didn't have a clue, how it happened. He remembered noise and pain. Slowly it came to him that he'd been shot. Tom was certain that he had died, but now he was back.

His questioning was soon answered when one doctor, looking down on him, began to explain to another.

"The EMTs with him said he might have been nicked by a bullet to the temporal artery. When they arrived, he didn't have a pulse, and bystanders were administering CPR. He did briefly regain consciousness in the rescue truck. It doesn't look like we can do much more for him now. Make certain that wound doesn't open. He's lucky to be alive. Hopefully, the CPR was enough to prevent any brain damage."

The doctor realized his patient was looking up at him. "How are you feeling?"

"I can't see you very well, and my head hurts," Tom croaked. "So does my throat."

"How about your jaw?" The doctor followed up.

"That's killing me too."

"Anything else hurt?"

"No, I don't think so. You said I was shot? How bad is it?"

"Looks like you were shot, yes. Some arterial blood loss, but fortunately, it's clotted now, so we're going to continue watching it and assure that it heals properly. The pain and vision issues should be temporary. You seem to have a slight concussion, too. We'll take some X-rays and follow up with a scan, but you are lucky to be alive."

"It was far more than luck, doctor. Don't worry though, I'll be all right. I've got a lot to do," Tom softly replied.

The doctor nodded. "That's the perfect attitude to have, but you must take it very easy for the next few days until this heals. We'll let the police know that this is a probable gunshot incident, so they'll be asking questions. Do you know anyone that might have done this to you?"

"Not really. I was just minding my own business."

"Well, that's between you and the police. We'll need to file a report and take some pictures. Rest up, and we'll follow up with whatever we find from the diagnostics."

After he left, Maria slipped into the room. "How are you doing? I am so worried about you. Are you feeling awful?"

"My head hurts so much, and my jaw too. I can hardly see," Tom added. And then, in a quiet, sincere voice he said, "I want to thank you for what you did to keep me alive. You took control, and you kept my stopped heart beating. If it weren't for you, I never would have made it."

"Who told you what I did?" she asked softly.

"I was watching you. You amazed me how you figured out how to keep my heart pumping without me bleeding out. I watched until the EMTs arrived. Then I moved on."

"What do you mean, you *watched* me?" Maria said on an exhale.

"Somehow, I left my body and was hovering over you and me. I saw lots of good people who ran to help us. In most places, people would avoid getting involved. I was truly impressed by everyone who did exactly what I needed. Especially how you led the efforts. Thank you for saving my life."

"Seriously, you mean you died and watched? What else did you do? Is there more?" Maria pressed. "Did you transcend? You know, go up above?"

"Yes, I did. I talked with God. But I just need to rest right now. I'm really hurting. I promise that we'll talk about it later."

At that point, Tom closed his eyes and let things go. He couldn't stand the pain and tried to divorce himself from it. Maria watched his chest as his breathing slowed to a sleeping rate, and the expression on his face relaxed, freed from the pain.

* * *

It had been quite a day for her, too. She'd become very close to Tom in the recent days. Today's events bonded them even further. She had protected and held his life close to hers. Pondering her mental video, it was obvious someone had attempted to kill him.

She was thankful that he'd called her because he needed to talk. Despite the fears that were growing, it was genuinely nice to have someone who needed her, someone who was in need, like she was. There was already someone in her life, but the relationship wasn't like this.

Just as she sank into the chair by his bed, the doctor came in with a local policewoman.

"Is he asleep?" he asked. Then looking at Maria again, he continued, "Don't I know you? Don't you work here?"

"Yes, he just drifted off. He's in a lot of pain and just wanted to sleep. And yes, you do know me. I'm Maria, and I'm an aide on the fifth floor."

"You came in with Tom and the rescue crew, didn't you? Weren't you with him when he went down? Perhaps you could answer some questions for this detective. Rochelle Hinkley, isn't it?" The doctor introduced Maria to Rochelle.

Then he turned his attention to the detective, "Tom really needs to sleep now. Perhaps Maria could answer your questions until later."

Detective Hinkley responded, "She might be of help for now, but we'll need to get a statement from Tom when he's awake and able."

"I'll have to ask you to get my permission before you speak to him, and he shouldn't be upset. He is in fragile condition now," the doctor politely stood firm.

Maria told the detective about hearing a muffled bang in the distance from the direction of the road, just before Tom dropped. From that moment on, her attention was focused solely on Tom, as he laid there bleeding out.

The detective asked numerous questions about the incident and Tom's life that Maria couldn't answer. She did share about his sailboat wrecking under the bridge and meeting him in the hospital. Nothing seemed to be of much help.

The detective also asked Maria far too many personal questions. She felt intimidated as if she was a suspect but then realized that everyone is a suspect in the initial stages of an investigation. Still, she was embarrassed by revealing details about her new relationship with Tom and about her lover.

Relieved when the conversation ended, she was then allowed to go home. Maria desperately needed to get some sleep before her graveyard shift, since Tom had interrupted her daytime slumber. She knew that sleep would be elusive, and now the police would be following up with the other love in her life.

* * *

As Tom tried to sleep through the interruptions, he received a transfusion of two pints of blood. As soon as possible, a CT scan was obtained.

It determined that he had sustained a concussion, but nothing worse than an NFL quarterback got on any given Sunday. There was slight, internal bruising, but nothing that wouldn't heal in short order. Some residual problems were always possible, but nothing to be overly concerned about yet unless symptoms arose. The doctor recommended no head banging music for a month or so, and grinned broadly at his own joke.

Now that he was more awake, Detective Hinkley could see Tom for a short interview. She was very polite, yet businesslike, in her questioning. She began by getting particulars for her report, such as name, legal name and aliases, date of birth, Social Security number, marital status, etc. She immediately narrowed the questioning to details about his estranged wife, Claudia.

Next, the detective asked him to explain what happened to him. Tom said that he wasn't certain, but he'd been told that he was shot. He wasn't prepared to tell her all that he heard and watched while hovering above the crime scene. Nor did he mention Tony, Tony's wife, or Armando. He was weary of her presence and tired of her questions. Tom purposely closed his eyes and ignored her.

There was much for Tom to ponder first. He woke up in the hospital with the full knowledge of his death. He knew he had been shot by a henchman of Tony, his old bookie from Myrtle Beach. Tom keenly heard the muffled rifle shot, a split second before he felt the horrendous pain in his head. His brain was rattled, and the rapid hemorrhaging from the wound had ended his life.

He peacefully passed over to the Other Side, bringing the knowledge of the muffled gunshot with him. It wasn't a deduction or a guess about the bookie's henchman. It was the simple knowledge of the truth, available to him in that realm, and now, a vivid memory which he brought back from there. He didn't mention that to Detective Rochelle though. He figured that only the evidence from this world was relevant to her.

Tom typically would not have felt dishonest by withholding that information from her, but he was feeling guilty about it now. He'd just come from a meeting with the CEO of the Universe! Amazingly Tom felt no animosity, no grudges, only forgiveness toward his shooter. There was no desire to have Tony and his henchman in trouble or to stir up problems for anyone else involved.

There was no blame for the bookie, who had found out about Tom's month-long affair with his wife.

True, Tom was a little confused about forgiveness and ratting someone out. The only thing that came to him was his mother's words, "To forgive is to forget." It might have been rationalizing, but that was all his aching head could offer now.

He'd told Detective Hinkley that he didn't know of any enemies. That could have been a big can of worms. His bookie had already killed him once, sending a message that he didn't take kindly to anyone absconding with gambling debts. Even more importantly, he didn't take kindly to anyone messing with his wife.

Somehow, Tom would have to arrange a truce with Tony and quickly. He had to let Tony know that there were people who knew the details of his attempted murder, making it best for all concerned to call it a draw right now.

Tom would make the affair with Tony's wife known to Maria, along with the gambling debts. She would only disclose this if anything happened to Tom. That way any investigation should blow right over.

Otherwise, there would be plenty of known motives that would quickly lead authorities directly to Tom's killer. In his fuzzy mind, it would work out well. They should even be able to forget about the debt and resolve the situation as if nothing ever happened.

Tom had already closed his eyes, and let Detective Hinkley's questions roll around in their own echo, outside of his mind. He preferred his new thoughts and figured that he should take advantage of the head injury, while he could. As Rochelle continued to question him, Tom drifted back into sleep, only to dream about his money belt and Maria's sweet smile.

* * *

Maria was exhausted physically and mentally. It had been an endless, strenuous day. Her daytime rendezvous with Tom had cost her valuable daytime sleep, but even worse, had almost cost him his life.

Maria knew after that kiss and just before Tom hit the ground, that she was making a connection that happened only once in a lifetime. Bells rang, birds sang, her knees weakened, and she wanted him. She had sighed—and then Tom died.

Her mind continued to replay the day. Miraculously, he'd come back to life in the ambulance. Now there was an investigation of attempted murder. The only thing missing was the bullet. What if it had been her? Would she be recovering in the hospital as Tom was or would her lover be planning a funeral? Maria's head spun.

Her lover. She was utterly exhausted, but she still had one difficult thing to do.

Maria had to tell her lover about her involvement with Tom and that wasn't going to be easy. Madelyn, the same RN that cared for Tom in the hospital, was a possessive lover. She was a highly charged, emotional, and jealous woman. Maria and she had been together for a few months, but Madelyn's anger had shown itself more than once. Madelyn wasn't violent or abusive, but she'd let her feelings be known.

Maria didn't like confrontations, but she was secretly flattered by the deep feelings Madelyn expressed for her, even in anger. Maria was certain that she didn't feel the same way about Madelyn, but at least she intuitively understood her.

Madelyn, blonde and shapely, had the temperament of a redhead. Her passions ran hot in love and hurt. She breathed fire in both. Flames flared fast until the emotion was consumed.

Madelyn dealt with her own emotions. She didn't cast blame, but let guilt take root where it might. She let it be known how she felt, and then she was done with it. Maria had experienced a few hairs singed by the heat, but when the flames were finished, she hadn't felt burnt.

After her anger had been unleashed in the past, Madelyn became silent and introverted, as if she felt spent from the outburst. Then, she'd sobbed as her anger left, and her love returned. She didn't speak, except to whisper an apology. Then tearfully, she'd reach out a weak hand to express a submissive surrender.

Maria had always felt compassion for her hurting friend and received the peace offering reluctantly. Only after realizing that she had not been accused of any wrongdoing or targeted for reprisal, did she surrender her understanding to whom she sometimes thought of as "Mad Madelyn".

Two such incidents came to mind. Once Maria had innocently misinterpreted advances by a former lover of Madelyn's as innocent, and Maria responded far too friendly to what were inappropriate come-on lines.

The second time was when Madelyn had seen her with Tom at the hospital during shift change. She told Maria that she felt betrayed by her flirting with her patient. Maria had stood up for herself by stating that Madelyn had never expressed any desire for a commitment. Maria then added that she didn't want one anyway, as she already had feelings for Tom. The flames had since encouraged each to reassess their situation and desires. Those desires remained unresolved.

In earlier times, the heat of the rage led to tender apologies and deeper understandings of feelings. Their ensuing embraces led to compassionate surrender. With each encounter, the affair that began with lust on Madelyn's part and loneliness on Maria's took another step towards love.

Maria had to admit to herself that she was entranced with Madelyn's body. Madelyn's fair but bronzed skin and long curly blond hair contrasted with Maria's dark complexion and jet black, straight hair, worn in braids at work. Madelyn's limbs were long and taunt, while hers were soft and supple, fitting for her curvaceous body.

Even though Madelyn was thin and her breasts moderate, her body language always excited Maria. She had never thought of herself as lesbian, but she had to admit that she was at least, "bi". Madelyn was the only female Maria had been with, and Tom was the first man Maria had felt desires for in a long while. Her thoughts digressed in avoidance of what she had to do.

Madelyn was probably unaware that Maria had met with Tom that afternoon. That thought scared Maria. She dreaded a full-blown meltdown and the possibility of having to decide between Tom and Madelyn.

Pushing herself off the sofa, she remembered why she had opted for the reclusive, lonely life in which she had dwelt so long. Life was complicated when it turned exciting.

Nevertheless, Maria called Madelyn to fill her in on the situation, so she wouldn't be surprised by a detective visiting her at home that night or at the hospital the next day.

As her friend, the least she could do was to give her fair warning. She knew that Madelyn should hear of the date with Tom from her and not from the police. Not that there was any reason for them to question Madelyn. Yet, television shows began to run through Maria's mind, where the jilted lover became the prime suspect.

After Maria told Madelyn what happened, she was surprised by her calm reception of the news.

"Thank you for calling to explain, but I've got a confession to make myself. I flirted with Tom, too. I don't know what it is, but he's got something that peaks my interest. I don't usually get strong feelings for guys, but he's got something that excites me. I gave him a massage and my card the last time I saw him. I really do understand where you are with him, and I have no reason to complain. But, I want you to know, that I really enjoy all that we have together, too."

Maria didn't respond to that last statement. She was much closer to the heterosexual end of the "bi continuum", while Madelyn was much closer to the other end. That could be dealt with later. She was just glad to have the conversation behind her. It had gone much better than she had expected, but one thing bothered Maria, though. What would Madelyn's play for Tom mean to her own budding relationship with him?

Then Maria's concern deepened. She was very fond of Tom. He was the first guy she had dated in a long time. Not only did his touch make her shiver, they both seemed to be spiritually on par; a rare combination. Tom and Maria were both Christians with questions.

Although they were reluctant believers, they wanted to discover the truthful workings of God.

Maria suspected that Tom and she might not always agree about everything, but they both approached spirituality with a similar hopeful skepticism. At the same time, they both considered religion as a means of packaging a set of spiritual beliefs for marketing to confused crowds. Each sect guaranteed salvation, but only if their particular advice was followed.

Comparatively, Madelyn was anti-religion and almost occult. Although she believed in a god, her vision was more amorphous than any major religion could tolerate. Madelyn sometimes attended a Church of Religious Science. Jesus was often referenced there as a great teacher, but they proposed a power of positive thought philosophy. Consequently, they upheld the universal spiritual laws, rather than Divine personalities. Hence, Madelyn sequentially placed her faith upon every philosophical belief that was proposed.

Maria looked out the window that overlooked the backyard. No, life was not simple at all, right now. She cared for Tom more than she had a reason too, yet she couldn't help sending up a prayer that they might continue to grow closer.

"And Madelyn will not be happy with that!"

CHAPTER 10

IN HIS IMAGINATION...

Tom opened his eyes, ever so slowly, one at a time. He really didn't want to answer any more questions for Detective Hinkley. But, he knew she'd be back.

He saw no other way to free himself from the possibility of a second attempt on his life. If he told all he knew, he would become too incriminating as a witness to let live.

If he shut up, without a suspect and without a bullet, there would simply be no case. It wasn't murder if the victim lived, right?

Tom's knowledge of all that had happened was revealed to him on the Other Side, but surely that would be inadmissible in court. It would also make him an unbelievable witness, even if he stated it under oath. Why then, did he feel so guilty about his silence?

During his Life Review, he always had a good excuse cooked up for whatever he did. He often managed to fool himself about his intentions, or maybe he didn't. This time he needed to be silent to save his own skin. He didn't want to lie. Tom now knew that motive was just as important as *what* one did.

He knew that he was totally forgiven for all he had done in the past. The question was, could he forgive himself for lying now? He realized that he couldn't. He could avoid answering the question, though. That was the only answer he had.

If I were going to stay there, would I still need to do the same review? That in and of itself could be hell.

Maybe what he'd just experienced was like Purgatory, where one could review previous choices. Was that part of the cleansing process? There was so much more he had yet to learn. He wished he could have stayed longer on the Other Side, where knowledge was apparent everywhere. He'd only had the chance to learn the answers to the questions that he had while there in that heavenly realm.

The opportunity was like a smorgasbord. You could have all your questions answered, but you couldn't take that opportunity with you. Maybe your questions could be answered here too, but you'd still have to discern the reply through a haze. He preferred the clarity. The easy way.

Tom couldn't get hung up on his guilt trip. He would learn from it and move on. So much had happened, while he was there. Amazingly he even saw his mother who had passed years earlier. She was happy and radiant. And what was it that Jesus had said?

Tom remembered. "Check out Baptism in the Holy Spirit!" Tom reminded himself to make sure he did that immediately!

He was only there for such a brief time, but Tom's understanding had grown exponentially. Still, all that he had learned was only the tip of knowledge inside the curtain that had been opened to him.

Time meant nothing *there*, but he'd better get busy *here*. Tom muttered his last thoughts to himself.

"God would not give me more than I could do in the time available to me. I simply need to take constant, deliberate action in the direction I am led, and I will arrive where I need to be at the appropriate time. There is no need to hurry or worry. Selah!"

The word, Selah, from the Psalms, finished his sentence. With no exact translation from old Hebrew, he loved the word.

He enjoyed reviewing the knowledge he'd gathered during his absence from Earth. He wondered what else was now in his brain.

Then, another piece of the puzzle, one he would prefer to forget, surfaced. He had a sharp vision of the license plate of the shooter's silver car, Florida, 811-BL5. His vision was not blocked by the trees or any other line-of-site obstacle. Like the hovering view he'd had of his body, those sights did not come from his eyes, but through some spiritual portal.

It didn't stop there, either. That means of visualization followed the silver lines of the car to the driver's window to yield a clear view of a man named Armando.

Tom recognized him from Myrtle Beach. He didn't really know the guy, but he had seen him often at Ocean Annie's, Tom's favorite beach bar just north of town. Armando was there almost every afternoon, but he'd acted too important to acknowledge Tom. He was more occupied trying to buy the young girls overpriced drinks. Tom now knew how he could afford the drinks and girls.

* * *

He had been in St. Augustine just a few days, but he had spent most of his time in the hospital. Tom desperately wanted to get on with his life.

He wanted out! When his thoughts slowed, he realized that the Lord would do what needed to be done, when it was time to do it. He had just encountered God himself, and he should certainly be able to let his stress go. "Give it to God and trust. Selah!" he said aloud.

Tom calmed his mind and relaxed, drifting into a fog separating dreamland from consciousness. Where the mist turned mystical, his vision cleared to see Jesus sitting on a large rock with his feet dangling in a carefree manner. He wore a mischievous smile, knowing that He would surprise Tom.

"Wow! that was quick," Tom exclaimed. "I usually have to go much deeper to find you in a dream."

"I'm always here," He replied. "It's just that you are too busy with your thoughts to notice me. You become so serious about things, that you forget to check your imagination. That's the easiest place to find me."

"You mean that I've been imagining all these conversations we've been having?" Tom asked, somewhat disappointed.

"Well, yes and no," He explained. "I'm alive within you. Remember, you asked me to be here. So, when you think about things, I will always put in my two

cents worth. Guess you might say, we are in this together. I'm your direct link to the cosmos, or My Father, or whatever you want to call it. Like a navigator with an intergalactic transceiver, I'm here to guide you."

"That's cool, I guess," Tom said. "But, why do you hang out in my imagination? What about the other parts of my mind?"

"Oh, I'm there too, but you are much too serious there to notice me. Besides, isn't this place more fun? We can do anything we want in here. It's like a giant playhouse."

"Okay, but how do I know when it's you talking and not me imagining things that I want you to say?" Tom asked.

"Oh, you'll know! If it's about treating others and yourself with love and respect, then that's us working together. If it's about hurting yourself or others, you are obviously off track. Hey, I just take credit for the good stuff!" He laughed, leaving Tom to think about the rest for himself.

Tom finally said, "I like the way we think together, best. Besides, we have fun together, too."

"Great! Do you want to try my imagination skateboard? It's an incredible way to cruise your mind."

"I was never any good on a skateboard!" Tom said.

"You are as good as you want to be...with Me!"

* * *

Tom remained in the hospital for a few days. Although he had come close to death, to say the least, he was healthy overall.

The artery that was damaged clotted very well and was on a natural recovery. That would take time. He didn't want to disrupt that process. It was important that he not do anything to elevate his blood pressure. That included becoming excited or doing anything strenuous.

If he wasn't homeless, he probably would have stayed only a day or two. Since he was, a few more days in his hospital room might be required.

St. Francis House guests weren't typically allowed to stay in bed all day. They might make an exception for Tom, but his doctor wasn't comfortable with that move right away. It seemed that a few more days at Flagler Hospital were in order.

Although Tom would have enjoyed strolling the streets of his new town, he did find his hospital stay enjoyable the last time and was willing to do it all over again. The main objective was to get started on his new calling. With his new phone in his possession, he had no excuse to delay any longer. Tom liked his fifth-floor room and began to resume his work.

He quickly found quotes inscribed over beautiful pictures that said exactly what he needed to say on his new Facebook page. Everything he placed on it had an alluring, inspiring image with a strong spiritual message.

He avoided anything religious, as he wanted to have a wide appeal. Anything too Christian, or otherwise affiliated, would send out a discriminating message. Most spiritual people were seeking goodness that supported their beliefs. Tom just wanted to meet them on common ground. He could always narrow things down later if he thought it fitting.

With several enticing messages pasted, he began searching for 'Friends' to add to his page. He did that on the spiritually oriented pages he visited. The dual motive technique seemed a natural way to find both friends and content. He would share pictures from the pages of potential new friends.

Within a few hours, he'd requested twenty friends, and he'd shared nearly twenty pictures with text on his page for visitors. Thrilled by his progress, he set twenty new friends a day as his goal.

This would be a most manageable schedule. Just a few hours a day would build a growing following for himself. Tom had even more faith in his calling now since he had basically been endorsed by The Man Upstairs. He'd post carefully and not be a pest which in turn would allow him to gather more Friends and become recognized by others.

He realized that he was smiling. The muscles in his face were beginning to ache. Tom went into his tiny, hospital bathroom just to see his face in the mirror. He was sporting a Mister Potatohead-like grin that made him burst out laughing uncontrollably.

The only thing that stopped him was the thought that he might rupture that blood vessel. Calming it down to a smart smirk, he barely contained his giggles. He had to leave the mirror to break off his laughter. Even then, it took a while for the hysterical sputtering to completely stop.

Tom knew he was on the right path to receive guidance from Above. McDonald's market research and corporate oversight had nothing compared to his connections. He had one of the finest franchises in the world. All he had to do was stay connected to Headquarters and follow the master plan. 'Just obey and benefit. Then he realized, that was already his plan! He'd been trying to make it work, but he always screwed up.

That word, *obey*, had always gotten Tom into trouble. He had to be honest with himself and face the truth. He had a resentment of authority.

He'd always questioned teachers, parents, police, and bosses. Maybe he should have been a lawyer. He incessantly challenged their right to have power over him, as well as questioning their knowledge and logic behind their opinions.

Yes indeed, he carried a chip on his shoulder throughout his youth. He could keep it hidden for the most part, but he still resented anyone telling him what to do, how to do it, what to think, and how to think it. That included religious people and ideas. He always felt that he had the better idea.

Now, it seemed he was dealing with the absolute supreme authority. Having met Him, Tom had no doubts about who the head honcho was.

So far, they'd gotten along fine, but he figured he ought to be ready to swallow his pride. It was time to start asking for—and listening to—heavenly advice, as rationalizing his own interpretations of divine things, could well be the forerunner of pride leading to a subsequent fall.

His phone rang and his smile grew wide again. "Hello, Maria! I'm glad you called. I just woke up a few minutes ago, and I'm lying here thinking about all that happened yesterday. I can't wait to share it with you."

He heard her chuckle. "Me too! I'm excited and so anxious to hear about it. It was certainly powerful for me from a different perspective. How are you feeling? Still hurting?"

"The pain in my jaw has lessened, but I still have a headache. I don't know if it's from the blood loss or the concussion. I guess it doesn't really matter, but they must have me more medicated now because the pain is dulled.

"But, hey! I am really excited about everything that happened to me after I was shot. It's too complicated to share on the phone. Can you please make it over this evening?" he pleaded.

"I've got to work a shift, so I'll just come earlier to spend time with you. I'm so glad you're doing better! I really worried about you yesterday. You do realize that you were dead, don't you?"

He was silent a second and swallowed hard. "Of course, I do—and that's part of the reason that I need to talk to you. I can't wait to see you! My mind is swimming with thoughts. Details keep coming back to me. I'll tell you everything when you get here! Wait, I want to thank you again for saving my life. Come now! I can't wait to see you!"

She promised to be there as soon as she could and disconnected the call.

Tom felt considerably better, but he knew it was best to just lie quietly. Closing his eyes, he needed to let go of everything. At least that was his intention, but his mind roamed, fully awake and aware.

His thoughts pictured the scene of him hovering over his own body lying on the ground. Maria. Jan. The silver car pulling away, Armando at the wheel, satisfied that he had done his job well.

Evidently, his mind recorded everything, regardless of whether he'd noticed it at that time. When he replayed it in his mind, every action and aspect was repeated for him, including stored knowledge of the entire experience.

Tom somehow knew Jan's thoughts in those moments. She suffered from the guilt of answering Armando's questions after he'd showed her a picture of Tom and pretended to be his cousin. She'd told him that Tom was walking around on the docks.

Tom sensed her surprise, when Armando took only a quick peek at the dock, turned around, and headed for the parking lot. It occurred to her that the information she gave might have contributed to the shooting, but how could she have known who Armando really was? When Jan was interviewed by the police, she would certainly mention Armando, wouldn't she? He sighed. To tell or not to tell the truth? Only Tom knew Armando, where he hailed from, who probably hired him, and what his motives were.

He closed his eyes and relived the euphoric feeling of no longer having any physical responsibility for his body's actions. That was an intangible, freeing feeling, but as his mind drifted, that sensation drifted with it.

The sweet bliss of his out-of-body experience was tarnished by the possibilities of what could develop if he did or did not give all his information to the police.

He hated making major decisions, but the future of his life probably depended on whether the investigation continued. Alternatively, did his new spiritual relationship require that he make the right decision about withholding information?

The hospital sounds around him faded away. Could he work out things with Tony the bookie? He'd call from the hospital lobby payphone tomorrow and see what he could do.

For sure, he wasn't using his new cell phone to do it.

CHAPTER 11

CRACKING UP AND GIGGLES...

Tom had far too much on his mind. He was struggling to remember what was where and why. So much had happened between Earth and the ultimate destination, as though files on a hard drive had been scrambled. He knew how to unscramble the hard drive on his computer–if only he could do that with his memory.

Taking a deep breath, he eased down into his thoughts and encountered an allegory in progress.

It was in the middle of nowhere in particular. An old, green garbage truck pulled up with its air brakes squawking and horn blowing.

When he looked through the window, there was Jesus behind the wheel wearing a big smile on his face and shouting, "Come on, let's go for a ride, Buddy!"

As Tom climbed up into the cab, he asked, "What are you doing in this rig?"

The driver replied, "Hey, this is what I do. I guess you never really saw me working before now. Don't mean to disappoint you, but I love this job!"

Tom muttered, "Well, you always were a humble guy."

Jesus began to explain. "People tend to hold onto a lot of trash, and they just need someone to help haul it away. That's my job. A lot of them won't even put it out to the curb. That's when this comes in handy." He laughed, reached up and tugged twice to blare the powerful air horn, long and hard.

"Usually I have to go knock on the door, though. If they will answer, I'll even go in and clean house. Some people hold onto stuff so long, they have a huge pile taking over their whole place. No light can get in, and they end up sleeping in the corner. I love it when they let me haul all that stuff to the dump. I especially love watching the smiles return to their faces, as they become renewed with light pouring through their windows into clean homes. After I organize everything they can finally think straight and even enjoy their music."

"Wow!" Tom finally understood. "No wonder I sometimes have a tough time finding you. I've been looking in all the wrong places."

Tom asked Him, "Could I help?"

And he heard the answer, "You just did!"

"Huh?"

Tom was amazed at how such encounters popped into his mind. He was sure there was a rational explanation for his visions, like the non-smoking patch. He was also sure that there was a spiritual reason for them, too.

Just because something had a rational or scientific explanation, didn't mean there wasn't a spiritual connection behind it. Tom remembered that God did most of His miracles through coincidences.

Those thoughts led him to wonder whether that was a natural occurrence or a supernatural one. Instantly he thought, *supernatural* just means extra-natural. God is so natural, that He's extra-natural. Carrying that one step further, Tom reasoned that nothing natural could exist without that extra-natural or pre-natural existence.

Tom had always considered God's existence as very natural, but supernormal, meaning greatly exceeding the normal or average, but still obeying universal laws. Tom now realized differently. God was supernormal, beyond the range of normal and often scientifically unexplainable. Maybe it will be explained in the future, as lightning has only been explained in recent centuries.

Tom didn't intend to become introverted with this philosophical discussion. It was just planted into his head naturally. He couldn't understand it, much less explain it, but it made sense to him. He didn't care to be thinking about it. He just wanted to drift off into a healing peace. He closed his eyes and gave thanks for the logical construct, he'd somehow received. Relinquishing it for the catacombs of his mind to ponder, Tom allowed himself to give up his thought pattern to sleep.

It seemed only moments later that he heard his name being softly called through thick clouds that separated his awareness levels. As his consciousness surfaced, a smile began to form on his disengaged face. Tom's eyes opened enough to catch a glimpse of Maria, causing him to complete his smile with a welcoming sigh. Thinking, *she is always there with a smile for me*, he became awake and aware, responding with a warm, "Hello."

Returning his grin, Maria could recognize his chi, despite his condition. "I hope I'm not interrupting your sleep, Tom. It sounds like you have a lot you want to share. 'Feel well enough to talk now?"

Tom responded, although a bit groggy. "I feel good, I think. You never know what kind of drugs they are giving you here, and how you really feel. There seems to be a pleasant haze all around me." Tom chuckled. "Yeah, I've got lots to share. Just don't know what to say first. I know that I was dead and that I definitely went to Heaven." Looking deeply into her eyes, he continued excitedly. "I met Jesus, or I think it was him, and I spoke with my mother. Jesus and I reviewed my life, and it seems that I have a vote of confidence to work in this calling. He even gave me several hints to help me do what is needed!"

"Really! This sounds incredibly wonderful! What was it like? I mean, it had to be fantastic! Did you meet The Father and the Holy Spirit?" Her voice softened. "I'm sorry, you tell me. I'm just so excited for you. Please go ahead, I'll be quiet."

Tom took over the conversation and tried to explain. "Realize that I was only there for a short time. Amazingly there really is no concept of "time" in Heaven. I know that I couldn't do all that I intended. They felt that I had a purpose here, so I had to come back. I had no choice."

Tom continued with Maria in total awe. "First, I spoke with my mother, who was waiting for me. She looked like the pictures that were taken when I was a baby. Beautifully radiant and elated to see me. She was completely content to be there. I was only with her for...hmm...no, there isn't any time there. We talked only briefly, but we communicated everything! We shared feelings of love so deeply that I can't explain it. We shared hopes, some of which I know will be fulfilled. While I was with her, I just knew this. I no longer had any unresolved questions.

"And Jesus, He was exactly as I imagined him. He didn't have a long robe, but He might as well have worn one. He was majestic. I guess it was like a loose fitting, hippie style, white gauze shirt. You know, with the three-quarter sleeves. His luminous, blue-green eyes looked deep inside me, and his smile let me know that everything was all right. Charisma, that's the word. Yes, the Word! He was charismatic. He was Love. I never felt so loved and free. As I stood with the Lord, all the things I ever worried about, were gone. I had no guilt or sin, I guess. It was like I could read His mind, and the things I had worried about were not there. We looked straight into each other's eyes and talked like best friends. Perfect in each other's minds. I'm probably not explaining this well enough, but it was perfect.

"I don't think we spoke in words. At least not in English. Maybe it was some universal language, but there was no need for translation. There were some things expressed without words. Yet I remember what was said! Although I would have some difficulty putting those thoughts into words.

"I did have an opportunity for lamentation though. I experienced a review of my life. It wasn't pretty. I've made so many mistakes. I was ashamed of what I had done in the past, but now I have the knowledge that it was only in the past. All that had led up to that moment was part of the plan, every detail.

"I reviewed my life, not as punishment, but as preparation. Life is learning. My life had been a lesson of trial and error."

Abruptly, Tom came out of his soliloquy, hearing, "Excuse me. I couldn't help but listen to your story about your Heavenly excursion." Madelyn had been listening, as she stood in the open doorway to his room. "I hope that's alright. It was wonderful listening to you! Maria told me you were back in the hospital, and I thought I should stop by for a visit."

The air in the room suddenly felt cool. Maybe it was the air conditioning that they had been ignoring. Tom and Maria had drifted to another plane and hadn't noticed that they had been joined by a guest.

Maria spoke first, "You startled me! What are you doing here?" Her voice betrayed her dismay at Madelyn's arrival.

Madelyn quickly apologized. "I didn't mean to interrupt. I only thought it would be nice to see Tom. Hope you are feeling better, Tom. I'm sorry you had to come back, but it'll be good to have you around again. 'Hope you enjoyed your one day off, and welcome back to the Fifth Floor!"

"Thank you, Madelyn! It's good to see you again too." Tom acknowledged Madelyn extending his arm, with effort, for a hug.

Maria had a tough time internalizing that. She knew that she didn't have exclusive rights to Tom's attention, but they were sharing such a wonderful intimacy, and she did just save his life! Somehow, she felt those things should carry more emphasis than they did right now. The worst trait that she could exhibit would be to show her jealousy in front of him.

Instead, she abruptly returned to Tom's story. "So, what about God, the Father? Did you see him?"

"From what I understood, you don't see him. We didn't talk about it, but I felt that God is a spirit with way too much energy to observe. Like electricity, brilliant, blinding light, superior knowledge, colors, and energy. You know what I mean, lightning bolt type stuff. Very powerful!

"I could readily feel the presence of the Holy Spirit though. This can't be put into words, especially in the English language, but this is how I understand it. God, the Father is like the power, of knowledge, and the laws that govern the universe. The Son is the expression of this power, or The Word, or Voice. Ultimately the Holy Spirit is the breath that carries the Word of the Father or Son to us.

"Realize that they are really all one, like the three leaves of a clover. We hear a lot about the Father and Son, but not too much about the Spirit or Ghost. Jesus sent the Spirit to us to continue our relationship with Him and the Father. I haven't seen this in scripture, but I do feel the Holy Spirit is the same spirit that is in both of them and can be ours too.

"Jesus told me emphatically to study and receive the Baptism of the Holy Spirit! He was so serious about that, that I am definitely going to pay attention. Would both of you like to join me? That would be great. I could use your help and company on this journey."

Tom could sense the jealousy being repressed by Maria, but she quickly said, "Yes!"

Tom thought he detected a hint of gloating in Madelyn's voice, when she followed with, "Hmmm, sounds interesting!"

* * *

The next day things began to happen quickly. First of all, when his doctor came in, he told Tom that he was making exceptional progress, far beyond anyone's expectations. If things went well, he would be released the following morning, even if he did have to go to St. Francis House to live.

Tom tried to call Detective Hinkley to finish up with the questions she still wanted to ask. She explained that the case had been closed, at least for now, because there was no evidence to substantiate that a shot had been fired. No one had seen anyone with a gun, and no bullet had been found. It was just as likely that Tom had been hit with a sharp limestone rock kicked up from the recently graveled parking lot.

When she asked if he had anything to add, Tom simply said that he was knocked out before he could see anything. He didn't mention his near-death experience. They wouldn't believe that he was hovering over his body anyway.

A few minutes later, Larry called to explain that he'd arranged for Tom's boat to be moved to her new dock on Sunday morning. That was the last day that the insurance would pay for storage. Tom was excited! He was confident that he should be in much better shape by then to participate. Had it really been only four days, since his boat had wrecked under the bridge?

Maria worked a little later that morning and stopped by his room to see him after she was done. "Here's a little surprise for you. It's what every patient in the hospital really wants."

Tom opened the gift and found a set of flannel pajamas to replace the gown with the slit up the back. He went into the bathroom immediately to try them on. When he came out, there was a matching robe on the bed. Tom's jaw dropped when he saw it. A tear rolled down his cheek, as he spoke through heartfelt sniffles. "Thank you so much. That was the worst part of my last stay. You don't know how much this means to me! Laughing through his tears, he gave her a big hug and a kiss on her forehead. Understandably, as she was an employee, and he was a patient.

After he shared all his good news about his speedy recovery, she asked him out to celebrate at the hospital's restaurant on the top floor. He could wear his new PJ's and robe, and she would wheel him up there. So, after checking at the nursing station, they did just that.

Tom was amazed at the beautiful views. It overlooked the Intracoastal Waterway to the east with a sliver of ocean showing above an island. They watched the sailboats heading South for the winter and the crab boats en route to tending traps. A few cabin cruisers were also pointed toward different destinations. Smaller fishing boats carried guys with lots of rods and presumably the appropriate amount of beer to go anywhere they wanted for the day.

For a hospital setting, it was quite a romantic spot. Maria suggested they order Eggs Benedict to celebrate Tom's recovery and triumphs. He could hardly refuse, after eating off the more mundane hospital menu lately. The breakfast was worth the wait and excellently prepared. Sitting almost silently, he sipped his black coffee and she, a cup of green tea with honey. They had just met a few days ago, but it seemed that they had been through so much, that it was comfortable just relaxing together.

Maria had a couple of issues festering in her mind. She didn't know how to present them, or in what order. She only knew that she had to somehow get them out. If she and Tom had a future, he needed to know.

She began abruptly. "I've been having an affair with Madelyn." Watching for his reaction, she continued. "I just want or need you to know. I'm not sure what it means, but I have feelings for you, too. I told her last evening that I had spent time with you and that we shared a kiss. I just can't be dishonest with anyone. I think that you need to know this and understand the situation."

Tom was quite surprised and at a loss for words. Thoughtlessly, he blurted out, "What did she say?"

"She told me that she really wants you, and I suspect that she may be jealous. I do know that I'm jealous of her interest in you. It's important that you understand something. I am not in love with her. I was lonely for quite a while, and we shared some really good times. She knows how to please me, but I don't want to get into this with you at all. I just had to let you know." Then, Maria whispered, "You are probably thinking that I'm a sinner now." Her voice trailed off into sobs. She sat silently and wept. Her tears dropped to her napkin, as Tom sat there not knowing what to say or do for her.

"Look," he said quietly. "I don't know how I feel about all of this. It's a lot to comprehend at one time. I can assure you that I don't judge you in any way. Everyone in this world is guilty of something every day. It certainly isn't my job to judge anyone." And with the hint of a smile, he whispered, "I'm a sinner too, and that is exactly what Christianity is supposed to be about, forgiveness.

"No one needs to be a judge. That's His job, not ours. I know I don't like someone taking my job!" Tom looked around and simmered down. He was passionate about this, yet he didn't see too many stares in the dining room. He continued in a more quiet and calmer voice, "All you did was to love someone. There is no reason to be ashamed of that."

Then Tom started laughing. "I better watch my blood pressure. I'm liable to pop my blood vessel!"

Maria joined in his laughter. "I was feeling the intensity too. I'm so glad that you feel the same way. Sometimes things just aren't simple." She reached for Tom's hand. "I'm truly grateful for your understanding. I agree with you too. That's why I don't attend church often. Usually, people want to put others down to make themselves appear better or something. Then they solicit you to join them against others. I wish they would go back and read those red letters in the New Testament again! But here I go, putting others down," and she began laughing with Tom again.

After the giggles subsided, they looked at each other and cracked up again. What a great relief after what could have been a tense topic and game changer!

Tom switched the subject, as Maria paid the bill with her credit card, "Could we go to a pay phone before we go back to my room? I've got a private call to make, and I don't want to use my cell phone."

"There are some down in the lobby, I know. Pay phones are almost extinct now. Hop aboard, and we'll go for another ride," and away they went.

As they walked, Maria asked, "What do you think about Madelyn joining us to study the Baptism of the Holy Spirit? Can we do it without it being uncomfortable? She is far from being a Christian, you know."

"Well, we might all learn something. The guy who told me to look it up wasn't a Christian either. He was a Jew. Remember too, that I'm new in St. Augustine, and I want to make friends. I do like you very much, and I don't have anything against Madelyn. I think it might be enlightening for us all. 'Alright with that?"

"I just don't want to lose anything that we share. You are a rare find."

"Well, thank you, but I'm not perfect," Tom warned.

Seconds later they were in the main lobby with activity bustling in every direction. Maria stopped Tom's wheelchair in front of an empty pay phone. He dialed his bookie's number from memory, then listened to it ring. A familiar voice answered.

Tom spoke up, "Hello, I got your message, and it hurt. I just called to let you know, that I know what you mean. I don't blame you, and you are totally forgiven. Tell Armando that he is forgiven, too. I haven't mentioned anything to the authorities about who was involved, but several people here have all the pieces to the puzzle including names, locations, motives, license number, etcetera. But, they have no reason to say anything, because I'm okay, and the case is closed.

"It's probably best for everyone if it's left that way. I apologize. I was wrong. I will take care of my obligation as soon as I can, but it will take time. I want you to know that I respect you, and your message is well taken."

"I don't know who this is, or what you are talking about," Tony said. "Don't call here anymore. Thank you."

Tom was hopeful that his honest and respectful reply to Tony's attack would satisfy him. Tony was a businessman, and he did what had to be done until he got his point across. Anything more would just be counterproductive. Tom would pray that it was over now. He would also have complete faith that his prayers would be answered. That was the best he could do.

Tom also gave Maria an envelope with the details that he knew. "If something happens to me, see that the police get this. Just mail it.

Don't get involved personally. You don't know anything, and you don't want to know."

Then he grabbed it back. "Never mind. I don't want you to be involved at all. If I am dead, it won't do any good to pursue this. Besides, I have faith that my prayers will work." He tucked the envelope securely back into his pajama's pant pocket.

Maria was impressed by Tom's respect for her safety. She wheeled him back to his room and gave him a warm hug and a kiss that she wished was reciprocated more passionately. She felt that Tom held back because of the inappropriateness of the location and the employee-patient relationship. She respected him for that, but she still wanted more.

Part of that was true. Tom did want to be considerate of her job restrictions, but more than that, he did not want to mislead her. He didn't want to imply a promise, that he wasn't ready to give or keep.

CHAPTER 12

INSERTING...

Alone now in the solitude of his hospital room, Tom began to work on his Facebook presence.

First, he checked the reactions to his posts from the day before. He had received twenty-five "Likes", ten "Comments", and six "Shares" of his posts. This was far more than he expected from the limited number of his new Facebook friends. He was thrilled! Perhaps more importantly, he was intrigued with the attention he was receiving from people, mostly women, whom he didn't even know. Immediately he was spurred back to mining for more "Friends".

He diligently requested friendships through his new friends' lists. If he got just one friend acceptance from each list, he could triple his online presence in a day. By concentrating on residents of St. Augustine, he hoped to someday sponsor a gathering to unite and consolidate his local band of friends. Tom was always thinking. For friends that didn't live locally, he was already dreaming about an Internet broadcast which excited him even more.

He quickly scanned the pages of his Facebook friends and others with low privacy settings. He was hoping to find spiritually provocative pictures with inspirational, spiritual, or positive non-sectarian messages to share.

He liked that word, "share", as it surreptitiously side-stepped the copyright laws. Copyrights still existed, but with the massive infringements happening on Facebook and other social media, they were blurred and nearly impossible to protect. It wasn't quite stealing or plagiarism. It was *sharing*.

The first quote that caught his eye, adorned an artsy picture of Gautama Buddha. "Silence is an empty space, space is the home of an awakened mind." ~ Buddha.

Next, he found, "Be positive, because your body hears all your mind says." This was prominently displayed on an image of a ballerina doing a soaring leap, in a vignette with a pale and dreamlike blue veil.

Finally, Tom paraphrased an interesting quote and edited it onto another picture he had found.

"You begin to pass your test when you applaud another's success while enduring your own failure." ~ Tom Porter.

He figured that he needed to personally contribute something to the mix. As a bonus, Tom added a link to YouTube for "All You Need Is Love" by the Beatles. It seemed to support the main theme of his page.

Busily, he prepared posts for that morning, noon, and early evening, plus a bonus to keep them singing about love. That only took a few minutes, or that's what he thought until he looked at his watch. He had been online for hours. He'd have to pay more attention to his time, and surely he'd get quicker with practice. Facebook just seemed to suck time away, but at least it was free. That would have to become his daily routine if he were to steadily grow his constituency.

Tom felt many spiritual people were migrating to eastern religions, such as Buddhism or Taoism. He needed to brush up on those to be able to reach out to them.

Hare Krishna, whose devotees danced and chanted in airports, was thriving now. Fifty years after George Harrison's song, My Sweet Lord, the sect has quadrupled to about one-hundred-thousand. The Hippie Hindu Sect built an elaborate temple, called New Vrindaban, in West Virginia to which many withdrew. They later welcomed immigrants from India and fostered temples throughout the states. Tom remembered visiting the temple long ago. When he asked if they worshipped the same God as Christians, their tour guide told him, "God is God is God." It was something Tom would ponder for years.

Many other sects were flourishing everywhere.

Judeo-Christian religions still dominated the country. Tom had a lot to learn there, too. He was studying scripture, predominantly the New and Old Testaments, including Jewish texts. He regarded the Old Testament as a good history. It would clarify how the Jews, including Jesus, culturally developed. He understood that it was a covenant between one group of "Chosen People" and God. Alternately the New Testament revealed a New Covenant, or agreement, between God and all mankind who accepted the teachings of the Christ.

The way Tom viewed it, the laws of Moses were superseded by "Love God with all your heart," "Love your neighbor," and "Everything hangs on these two commandments." Tom felt that the New Covenant put the responsibility on individuals to determine the right things to do. The main criteria was to act in a true spirit of love, without the burden of consulting over six-hundred rules, as imposed on the Jews.

"Then one of them, which was a lawyer, asked him a question, tempting him, and saying, Master, which is the greatest commandment in the law? Jesus said unto him, Thou shalt love the Lord thy God with all thy heart, and with all thy soul, and with all thy mind. This is the first and greatest commandment. And the second is like, unto it, Thou shalt love thy neighbor as thyself. On these two commandments hang all the law and the prophets." (Matthew 22:35-40)

Tom thought that The Golden Rule said it simply enough when Jesus shared the ancient rule in Mathew 7:12, "Do unto others, as you would have them do unto you." It wasn't complicated, but it did require the right motive, some thought, compassion, and practice. *Enough said.*

He continued thinking, "I ought to become a five-minute preacher. Get to the point and get off the stage. So many of them just beat a subject to death, until you fall asleep and miss the point altogether." Tom did like to pat himself on the back. A moment later, he thought again!

It was as if a bolt of wisdom struck him from above. Was that the New Covenant! Was he missing the point! Then he heard the voice of the One he had met in the world beyond: *"I am the resurrection and the life. Whoever believes in me, though he die, yet shall he live, and everyone who lives and believes in me shall never die. Do you believe this?" (John 11:25-26 ESV)*

Tom exclaimed to himself, "That's the New Covenant!" Then he began writing it down.

If we believe in Jesus and follow his teachings about loving God and others, we shall be forgiven and be saved from death. It is all about placing our faith and trust in Him. What's more, we will be set aside and be considered reborn and belong to the body of Christ, and officially be regarded as disciples or followers.

It is not through good works that followers are saved. Because of their faith, they receive a gift from God known as Grace. At that point, they see life very differently and begin to understand things from a spiritual point of view.

Perhaps the biggest change for those who are saved through faith is that they are no longer under the law but under Grace. The laws of Moses, of which there are over 600, are not governing them. Instead, they are expected to do things out of Love, as Jesus would.

Tom found the Bible verse he needed and added it to his writing. It was time he started saving highpoints.

"For it is by grace you have been saved, through faith—and this is not from yourselves, it is the gift of God— not by works, so that no one can boast."(Ephesians 2:8-9)

Tom continued to fall back on the Judeo-Christian tradition that he was brought up in. Yet he knew he had to branch out to meet the needs of the world today. Maybe that Hare Krishna guide was right when she said, "God is God is God." He reasoned, "It's time for religions to stop fighting each other. They all need to join with the common theme that Love is what it is all about! We don't worship different Gods, only in different ways. There is only one God, but many religions.

After struggling with the idea, he finally inserted a link to "My Sweet Lord" by George Harrison on YouTube.

Tom felt that was enough of an accomplishment for a sick guy. He lowered his phone to his side and drifted off to sleep.

* * *

Early the next morning, immediately after the usual scrambled egg breakfast, Tom's doctor walked in. He was amazed at the rate that Tom's wounds had healed. At the end of his evaluation and consulting another doctor, he decided that Tom was well enough to discharge. This suited Tom just fine. He had spent almost his entire St. Augustine stay in the hospital. It had been uplifting after spending days alone on the boat. He'd made several good friends at Flagler Hospital, and it was now time to move on to the real world.

He would have to make some quick plans. He didn't have any place to go. He could probably stay with Maria, but he didn't want to be presumptuous. Instinctively, Tom needed to have a look around his new hometown, before his existence was put at the mercy of someone else.

Speaking of whom, Maria came into his room almost immediately after the doctor left. Tom had only enough time to think that one thought before Maria strutted in with the question. "And, what did the doctor say?" It seemed, she was always watching, waiting, and listening. "I just got off work and was coming to see you, when I saw the doctor go into your room. I waited outside your door, so you could have privacy. Is the doctor happy with your progress?"

Tom was always taken aback by the coincidence of her timing, but he wouldn't let his mind follow that thought. Instead, he answered, "I can go home! That means that I could be discharged this morning. I'll give St Francis House a call in a few minutes. Hopefully, they still have room."

As expected, Maria extended her invitation. "You could stay at my house. You wouldn't have to go up and down the stairs there. Seriously, I've got an extra bedroom, so you could have your privacy. Most importantly, I'd be there to help, if you need anything. No strings attached!"

"That does sound great!" Tom started with enthusiasm. "I just don't like to impose on anyone. I've always been able to take care of myself, and I don't like to take handouts." Pausing, he added, "I'll tell you what. I'll check with St. Francis House. If I can, I'll stay there. If it doesn't work out, I'll take you up on your offer, until my boat is ready in a few days.

"I honestly appreciate your offer," he continued, "I hope you understand how I feel about handouts. I'm not too proud to take them, but I do like to take care of myself first. I already owe you my life."

"Actually, I do understand and respect you for that," Maria responded. "I just want you to know that you are welcome."

As if on cue once more, Madelyn waltzed in. "So, what's happening? Throwing a party again, and I'm not invited?" She led off with a smiling laugh and then continued towards Tom. "Seriously, how are you doing? Feeling any better?"

"The doctor thinks I am. He's releasing me this morning. I'm going to hopefully stay at St. Francis House if there is room. If not, Maria said I could stay with her, until I get my boat back in the water. I'm excited! 'Looking forward to some freedom. This place has been great, thanks to both of you, but it would be nice to be at home again on my boat."

Madelyn had her say, "I'm glad you have it worked out already. Sorry I missed my chance. But if things don't work out, just know that I have room at my house on the beach." Her generous offer switched from joking to jealous. "Guess I need to be a little quicker on the draw."

Tom pretended not to notice, but he was enjoying being the center of attention. "I love the hospitality in this town. You both represent 'God's City' well! I'll have to refer to it now as the City of Love."

"God's City? Where did you get that name?" asked Maria.

"Haven't you seen that purple billboard on US1? The one that says, 'My City, God's City'. It's just a little south of the hospital."

Madelyn chimed in, "Yeah, it was founded in the name of God, by Pedro Menendez in 1565. That's why they call that beautiful park with the big cross, Nombre de Dios, meaning 'In the Name of God" in Spanish. If God is Love, I guess this must be the City of Love. Hmm...I really like that name!"

Maria was finally able to insert her opinion. "There does seem to be an air of love in this town. Its slogan could be 'Love in St. Augustine'."

"Good one, Maria!" Madelyn exclaimed. "I've got to get to work. Have a wonderful day, and let me know what is happening. Later!" She gave Tom a meaningful hug, as she left.

"See you later, Madelyn," said Tom, as he glanced back at Maria.

"Boy, she certainly infused herself into our conversation again," Maria said quietly to no one in particular.

Tom let it pass with a little laugh, feeling it was better not to take sides. He liked them both, and he didn't want to get in the middle of anything. At least not in a negative way. Then picking up his phone he said, "Let me call Shane down at St. Francis to ask if there's room for me."

"St. Francis House!" Shane's voice answered the phone.

"Hey, Shane! This is Tom Porter. Sorry I didn't get back to you the other day. I got shot. At least that's what they say. They haven't found the bullet, though. I'm wondering if I could stay there a few days. The doctor is discharging me this morning and I need a place to go."

Shane gave Tom the unwelcome news. "Miss Roberta already told me that since you didn't show up the other night, you were listed as a 'no show'. You won't be eligible to stay here for three months. I think she's worried about the shooting incident, too. Since she was in law enforcement, she hears all these things."

Tom was going to give it his best try. "Do you think if I talk to her, that she might change her mind?"

"I doubt it. Once she makes up her mind about something, she rarely changes it. My advice is to just let it blow over. Believe me, you don't want to get on her wrong side."

"Okay. I've got other options anyway. Thanks just the same!"

"Wait a minute, Tom. I think we still have those clothes you picked out the other day. They are in the clothes closet, and if you need any food, we have lots of that. I could make up a big box of it to help out."

Tom knew that he could use some more clothes, and it would be nice to bring Maria some food. At least he wouldn't feel like he was totally dependent on her. Tom had a fear of being considered a player or a taker. He didn't want to take advantage of her financially or emotionally. He wanted to contribute something to their relationship, and food would be a good, financial contribution for now.

Emotionally, Tom enjoyed Maria's company, and they seemed compatible on the spiritual and intellectual levels. He wasn't in love with her and was somewhat afraid that she already had plans for him. She was certainly insistent that he stay with her which was convenient.

He could at least stay a few days until his boat was ready. He figured, "What the heck! What good are friends, if you can't use 'em?"

Tom quickly backpedaled on that thought and sheepishly explained the situation to Maria. He correctly identified an icy look from the recently rejected girl, but he rewarmed her heart with an appropriate apology and a soothing smile. The fact that he would be bringing food, at least assuaged the thought that he only wanted to take advantage of her generosity.

* * *

Tom's discharge was ready in a few minutes. He gathered his minimal belongings. He was wearing a thrift store shirt, that Maria had bought him to replace the blood-soaked one he had on when he was shot. It had a palm pattern that Tom really liked. It lent an island mystique to his personality.

His shorts had been freshly washed, and their loops were laced with his all-important money belt. Maria had seen to it that his clothes were readied before his release. Tom realized that he didn't know what he would do without her.

She went to get her car, while a volunteer was on the way to his room with a wheelchair. Clothed and ready, Tom rode with his discharge papers and instructions in his lap down the halls toward the exit. He did a quick study of all the art on the walls, as he passed. Flagler Hospital truly was a wonderful place. When he caught himself getting nostalgic, Tom immediately replaced those thoughts by reminding himself that he didn't want to return, at least not as a patient. Admittedly he was a bit worried about going out into the real world, based upon what happened last time.

When the elevator dropped them in the lobby, he saw the glass-enclosed offices of the social workers straight ahead. The doorway to Suzanne's office looked invitingly open with the warm, yellowish-light shining through it. "Could you push me over there? I just want to say hello to one of the social workers for a minute."

The volunteer responded agreeably and Tom saw Suzanne sitting at her desk studying some paperwork.

"Hello, Suzanne!", he said in a cheery mood. "It's good to see you again."

It took a few seconds for recognition, but she happily responded, "Goodness, hello! I heard that you were back in here. What happened?" She obviously was worried that somehow, someone had found him through hospital information that they had tried to keep quiet.

"Well, I'm not exactly sure, but I'm still alive! Don't have much time to talk now, but I'll get in touch with you soon and fill you in on what I know."

"That would be great! I was meaning to get up to visit you. I'm glad to see you're being released so soon. Are you feeling all right?"

"I'm doing fine, I've really got to go now, but it's good to see you again. Let's stay in touch! Later!"

Tom was brief, not wanting to leave Maria waiting. Probably because he didn't want to incite any further jealousy, a bigger worry than inconveniencing her.

* * *

He was soon out the door and in Maria's car. Tom reminded her that he had to pick up some clothes and food down at the St. Francis House. She was tired but gladly obliged him, knowing he had nothing, but what he had on him. She had never gone there, but fortunately, Tom remembered the way.

When they arrived, about ten people sat around a large, outside picnic table. They were of all ages, from late teens to early seventies. Some were a bit scary, but most just looked poor. Their clothing, of course, had something to do with it, but their hair and skin mostly told the story. It was obvious that it was a long time since the hair had seen professional help. Their skin had endured far too much inclement weather.

While Tom went inside to get his goods, Maria sat outside in the car at the curb. Her window was rolled down an inch or two, so within a few minutes, she had learned a lot. Several told stories about being in shelters across the country, and St. Francis House was considered one of the best. Others either listened or ignored them.

Those that boasted were obviously pretending to know far too much, to be able to work for one person very long. Generally, bosses don't appreciate employees who pretend to know more than them. Those that listened either wanted to emulate the talkers or placate them to stay out of trouble. The quiet ones who ignored the boasters had probably heard it all before. One couple had to be local because they were called upon to confirm local stories.

Inside, Shane helped Tom pick out more clothes from the donation closet, showing him things in his size. Shane then filled an extra-large box with canned goods and dry goods, enough to last a week or so. Tom carried the clothes out to the car, as Shane hefted the heavy, assorted food box. Shane's size and strength generated respect with the residents. They looked up, nodded, and continued telling their stories at the table. Tom was politely reminded to break the load down into smaller bagfuls before carrying it inside.

Tom thanked Shane while getting into the car, and Maria beamed a thankful smile at him, as she pulled away from the curb. "It would be nice to help this place out somehow, sometime. They seem to do so much for people who need it," Maria said compassionately.

Tom agreed. "Maybe we could organize something when we get our ministry going."

Maria was surprised and grateful that he had included her in his future. Of course, Tom was more focused on making plans for his future, than including her or being altruistic. Maria took it as she wanted to hear it. It just added to the pleasant smile, she wore now. She continued driving up King Street, left on US1, and then right on State Road 207.

It was a new view for Tom, as they headed out of town past the St. Augustine Record newspaper building. Continuing a few miles west on State Route 207, they turned right onto Lightsey Drive disappearing into a development of manufactured homes.

Maria had a modest, but charming home with a pool inside a fenced backyard. It wasn't an expensive place, but it sure seemed comfortable with four bedrooms and two baths. Maria explained later that she had been fortunate enough to get it during the economic slump for half of its original value.

"You can put your clothes in here," Maria told Tom, pointing to a bedroom with a full-size bed and chest of drawers. "Make yourself at home. There's a bathroom across the hall. If you need anything else, just let me know." After she finished showing him around, Maria slipped into her room to get a good day's sleep.

Tom decided to use his time checking out the day's social media. He logged onto Maria's Wi-Fi connection to investigate Twitter. It seemed that celebrities dominated Twitter, and who is more celebrated than God! Since he had met God personally, Tom figured that he might speak for Him. He wasn't sure how He would feel about that idea, but Tom did have an "in" now with the world's greatest celebrity. That and a few insightful quotes should give him a leg up in the new media.

Tom was not coming from his ego. He knelt for an earnest prayer session and soulful talk with his Heavenly Father. If the new venture was to be a success, he knew that he would need blessings and guidance from Above.

For several minutes, Tom let the hot air out of his ego. He wasn't negative about himself, for he was God's creation. He knew in his heart, that next to God Almighty, his own wisdom and power were nothing. In truth, he relied on the power and glory of the Universe to provide him with wisdom.

People from his old life wouldn't recognize him. When he totally humbled himself before the Almighty, he did so without showmanship. He did so in his proverbial "prayer closet". He asked questions without presupposing a particular answer. Tom knew that if he wanted to receive truthful guidance, he had to be able to listen with an open and welcoming mind. All he needed would come into him if he gave it a home in his heart to abide.

When Tom finished praying, he meditated, clinging to his meaningless mantra, until all thoughts were gone. Only then was he ready to receive the requested wisdom of his Father. Tom felt that to pray was to ask, and to meditate was to listen. Most importantly he knew that listening to the Universe speak required his undistracted attention.

During his meditation, he left his question in a quiet space, that existed between God and himself.

"May I represent you on Twitter?"

Only when he felt a pure and clear affirmation, did Tom act by simply Tweeting what he felt should be his theme, #tomnodoubt, "God is Love".

Tom felt a familiar childlike-enthusiasm as he heard his old sled buddy yell in the distance, "Come on! Let's go for a ride!"

CHAPTER 13

WARM BEER AND COLD WOMEN...

While Tom was recovering at Maria's house, she was working the graveyard shift. Awakening mid-morning after his first night there, she was already home and asleep. He decided to quietly work on his Facebook page, while she slept through the afternoon.

Breaking the silence, a light rap on the front door interrupted his work and solitude. He was surprised to see it was already four o'clock. Glad for the excuse to get up and stretch, Tom answered it. He peered through the little view hole and was surprised to find Madelyn with an index finger to her lips.

Tom opened the heavy front door, as Madelyn opened the aluminum storm door. Again, putting up the quiet finger, she softly asked, "Is she still asleep? I didn't want to wake her, knowing she's had some busy days. I have been thinking about you, and since it was going to be a boring afternoon at home for me, I thought I'd bring over a pizza!"

Tom whispered, "That was nice of you. She went to sleep a little after ten this morning. I don't know how long she usually sleeps, so I've just been trying to be quiet."

"I don't want to wake her either," Madelyn pointed to a bench by a nearby pond. "Want to sit and talk there for a while? It's such a relaxing spot with the birds and trees. Let's walk over. We won't disturb Maria there."

"Let's do it!" He began taking steps toward where her gaze had just been aimed. "I just hope she doesn't get upset if I'm not around when she wakes up."

"Why should she? Besides, she can see the bench from here, but I understand. You better not let her see you having too much fun! You are supposed to be under her care, you know." Madelyn finished with a good attempt at sarcasm.

Tom picked up on it. He knew that his best course of action was to say nothing. He only came back with a subject ending, "Yep!"

Madelyn knew how to open him up, "Boy, you are just like a politician! No comment? You simply don't want to incriminate yourself."

Well, she was right. Tom had a growing respect for Maria, but she did tend to take control of situations. Although he enjoyed her company, she acted like he belonged to her. It was easy to sense the obvious jealousy between the girls. If Madelyn were her lover, why should Maria be concerned that he would come between them? Wasn't there at least some sort of team loyalty between them? Besides, he didn't have any obligations to either of them.

Madelyn observed Tom, as the wheels turned in his head. His face expressed everything he thought, right up to when he held back the little laugh that his eyes betrayed.

She hit the nail straight on, reflecting his muted thoughts. "You seem to need some space, but Maria wants to act as though you've been dating for years. She and I've had a nice fling too, but she needed to know where everything was going, including her sexual orientation."

Tom confided, "Maria mentioned your relationship to me, and how she had to explain to you after I was shot, why we were together."

Madelyn picked up the reins of the conversation, "You did share situations that could create bonds between you, but it could give you a false sense of bonding too. It's probably difficult staying afloat with all that's happened in your life lately. You've had some rogue waves hit your life raft in the past few days. Just remember that although she may be the skipper of your dinghy right now, you are still the captain of your ship."

Madelyn made lots of sense with her cryptic analogy. "Thank you," he said, holding onto the premise. "I'm just bobbing and weaving with the waves. I keep trying to swim in a direction, but it takes me where it wants. It's one helluva ride though!" Tom laughed like he was having fun.

Madelyn caught his drift and reacted with an appropriate, "Enjoy it!"

"Are you being sarcastic?"

"No, honestly I'm not. It's like we all must play a part in this big play, and we can't even create our own characters. I'm sorry. I'm not talking about you so much, but Maria is often unsure of where she stands with people and is worried about labels. I don't care much about what others think. I do what I want and spend time with whom I want. I like her, and I like you. Consequently, I hope we can all be friends. We'd be good for each other! Maybe if the three of us could talk it out, we could get past these stumbling blocks that are keeping us apart." Madelyn was finally able to say her piece, letting her feelings express her heartfelt wish.

"Did Maria and you recently break up or something? Am I in the middle of this? I have no desire to interrupt your relationship. I just got into town this week and met you both. I'm not in love with anyone. You are both very attractive to me, but I am not here to cause problems and mess up anyone's life. Right now, I need friends, and you are both that, hopefully. Can't we just leave it there for now?" Tom was adamant with Madelyn about expressing his feelings too.

Madelyn picked up the conversation, "Thank you! Maria does mean a lot to me, and I'd hate to have our relationship destroyed. The romance has diminished recently. I know she hopes to be with you, mostly because it'd be more conventional, and that means a lot to her. Before you appeared, she and I shared a solid relationship. We were friends for a long time before becoming lovers. That was incredible, even though it was only for a few months. I don't know, where we are going with it now, but I'm hoping we can put it back together again. Well, I know it will happen, but I hope it can be without the prejudices and labels that the world wants to put on us."

This was almost more than Tom wanted to hear, but it was good that Madelyn and he were sharing their feelings and communicating. She was doing most of the talking, as he was holding back. Maria wasn't there, and he held a certain amount of loyalty to her. As he reflected upon this, he vowed to himself that he would fully release his feelings at the proper time and not keep them restrained, as he usually did.

Standing up, he said, "I think we should go back to the house and see if Maria is awake now. She should be a part of this conversation since she is part of the topic. I'm certainly glad you brought this up though, and I hope we can get it all out in the open."

Madelyn arose too and held her arms out offering a hug. Tom fell into them without hesitation. As he drew her close, Madelyn lifted her lips, as she whispered a message without words with her seductive, green eyes.

Tom turned his face, denying himself that pleasure, but he held Madelyn close for a long, warm hug. He was in no position to deny receiving a tenderly passionate kiss on his cheek. As Tom slowly released Madelyn, he spoke in a soft voice, "I just don't want to burn any bridges. Let's go."

They walked down the quiet road together, heading straight toward Maria's house, as if they were on a mission. Tom felt a new closeness to Madelyn and had a desire to hold her hand. It was so close to his, he could feel its warmth. Instead, he restrained himself, not wanting to violate any unwritten code of honor between friends.

Tom had to remind himself that he just got out of the hospital and was supposed to be resting. He needed to keep his blood pressure within reason. The slow walk wasn't worrying him, however, the vast possibilities of relationships in this town could be fatal in his condition. It was time to rein in and slow down his thought process, before his blood boiled with passion. It was true. In St. Augustine, love was in the air, everywhere.

As they crossed the road back to Maria's house, Tom noticed the emotional sky above them. It was gray and grayer with a few touches of blue. The clouds swirled and curled together without hinting of what was to come. It could be sunshine or storm, or it could remain gray and blasé. There was no telling what was going to unfold today, and tonight was only hours away. It could be clear and warm with stars sprinkling the sky, or it could be darkly ominous and raining until dawn.

Tom still didn't have a clue. He asked for peace, as he walked forward, knowing that what was to happen, would be exactly what should happen. The next hour would depend on the next minute, as the script was already written. Tom would play his part, not knowing what his lines would be, until they came out of his mouth.

As they approached the brick front stoop of her embellished, austere home, Maria appeared in the doorway. "Hi! Sorry I slept so long," was the unexpected greeting.

Madelyn, who knew her moods much better than Tom, was quite surprised to encounter the warm welcome. "Hope you don't mind that I stopped by. I thought you might be up about now. I brought some pizza!" she exclaimed as if pizza solved all problems.

"Great, we could have it as an appetizer, while we cook some burgers by the pool. It's cloudy, but it's warm. With winter coming, why waste the night!" Maria shocked them both with her mood. "If the pizza's cold, we could warm it up in the microwave, while Tom starts the hibachi."

The girls stayed inside, while Tom poured charcoal into the old-style hibachi. A good soaking of lighter fluid and a tossed match ignited a strong blaze on top of the coals. Tom hadn't used a hibachi in years, but the nostalgic, powerful scent made him wonder why he'd ever switched to a gas grill.

Gas was quicker than he remembered. But, now he realized that the time spent watching the fluid's blaze, and the anticipation of it burning off and leaving a red glow on the embers, were just as important as the burger or steak that was grilled. That memory made him want a cold beer in his hand while he waited.

* * *

Meanwhile, inside, the girls spoke about patching their relationship. Each realized they had feelings for Tom and still had feelings for each other. They had to get that out front before everything went up in smoke. They were confused for sure but they had only known Tom for a few days and everything was already going topsy-turvy.

In an attempt to settle their dispute, they began making confessions.

"I liked Tom from the beginning, but I don't let too many guys get to me," Madelyn told Maria. "Then, one night, when I raised the covers to straighten them, I was astonished when I accidentally discovered his 'manhood' that was outside of his gown."

Maria nodded. "Well, I've noticed a big lump in the covers too, and I've actually felt it against me in the pool. Very impressive, but he doesn't flaunt it."

Madelyn joked, "Maybe he's just playing hard to get." They both laughed at the double meaning. "Let's go see what he's up to now!" They laughed again.

* * *

Magically the back door opened, and Tom saw Madelyn with a cold Yuengling, America's oldest and his favorite beer. "You didn't think I'd bring pizza and not bring beer, did ya?"

Tom was impressed. "You wouldn't have a guitar in there I could strum on, do you?"

"Hang on, I'll ask Maria."

Just as the flames began to subside, Maria brought out an old acoustic guitar with a pick stuck beneath the strings on the neck and a battery-operated tuner. "Here, it probably needs tuning. I didn't know you played."

"There are lots of things, you don't know about me yet," Tom teased as she closed the door. The girls exchanged knowing looks and smiled.

Tom couldn't figure it out. All the tensions Madelyn and he imagined before never materialized. In fact, Maria smiled more than he had ever seen. Something must have happened.

But if it made everyone that much happier, he didn't care about the reasons. He was starting to have a really good time.

Madelyn came back out with turkey burgers and a spatula on a plate. "Here, these are for you, when you are ready. We're working on the fixings."

Just then Maria handed Madelyn the pizza box. "Here's the appetizer. Don't get yourself too full," Madelyn said, as she passed it to Tom.

Tom sang a few songs, eating a slice of pizza between each. Maria and Madelyn listened during their trips in and out of the kitchen. They enthusiastically expressed their admiration for his playing. When he mentioned that he had written those songs, they reiterated their praises.

Tom delayed putting on the burgers until the flames were gone. Hot coals and slow cooking gave him more control over the process and allowed him to flip burgers during his breaks. It was his ideal barbecue; playing music, flipping burgers, sipping beer, and entertaining two, beautiful women.

After they ate and finished their drinks, the trio took a dip in the pool. The water was chilly at first, but they soon adjusted while splashing and playing. They relaxed and talked a bit, eventually getting a little more familiar and solidifying their friendship with hugs all around. The tensions of jealousy and mistrust subsided leaving all three feeling much closer than before.

Cold beer and warm women brought out a more sensual side to Tom. The women let their defenses down, too. Group hugs and kisses warmed them in the water, as it became a contact sport. They each revealed an unseen side of their personality as they reached out to each other with a new and easy agenda. They all seemed to be enjoying themselves as they gently reached new bases.

Tom backed off a little and Maria sensed his nerves tensing and his mood withdrawing. "Are you okay?" she asked him.

He answered thoughtfully. "I just don't want to get overstimulated with my condition being as it is."

The girls understood and reduced the excitement. They had pushed the envelope a long way for someone just out of the hospital. Everybody's blood was boiling.

Tom climbed out of the pool and sat on a chaise. The girls casually joined him, and all relaxed quietly for a while. Maria finally passed around giant beach towels as the evening cooled, and things became quiet.

It was then, that Maria brought up the subject of their different opinions toward the Deity. She broached it very diplomatically letting each of them feel at ease to explain their own personal beliefs and orientations.

"It seems that all of us are looking for our own way of worship. Granted we are each a bit different from the norm and from each other too. "I know you have different doctrines, Madelyn. Where do you find yourself now?"

Madelyn, usually sure of herself, felt a bit intimidated. "Maria, you know you're right. I've flitted around, investigating many religions, and I've found faults with each of them. I like the Eastern religions like Buddhism and Tao because they search within for answers and are accepting of others.

"I also like relating to a personal God. Jesus brings love to the table, but Christianity, as a religion, has been very hateful over the centuries. As a woman, most of their sects treat us as second-class citizens. However, the United Methodists have many women ministers and are appealing with their slogan 'Open Hearts, Open Minds, Open Doors.' I love that outlook, but it has accompanied a declining membership since the late sixties. I guess it's hard finding enough Christians that open-minded."

"I have a really enlightening book that both of you would enjoy reading. It's "The Power of Positive Thinking" by Dr. Norman Vincent Peale. I guess they call it New Age. He presents powerful concepts that I can grasp. Of course, a lot of Christians pooh-pooh his techniques for miracles, even though they are straight from the Bible."

Madelyn continued, "Only a small percent of Millennials are affiliated with a religion. I don't blame them because religious don't even follow their own teaching! Love and forgiveness seem to get lost when they are put into practice. I see believers spending more time judging than behaving as they should."

Tom felt he had to respond. "Yeah, the old hypocrisy complaint. It is true, but it's hard to avoid. You just did it, and I am doing it now. Maybe we all should realize that we aren't perfect and be forgiving of each other. As the Beatles said in the song, Let it be, let it be."

With those simple words of wisdom, the three friends followed the melody, as it echoed in their minds. Those "simple words of wisdom" set them free. Each of them let their minds relax. Letting it be, they settled into a quiet bliss. The silent love that surrounded them filled their hearts.

As the sun slipped lower on the horizon, sunset colors took over the sky. Maroons and blues blended their stripes beneath the red sky and behind orange clouds. The beauty of the sunset quickly lost its priority, as the December breeze chilled their skin. A quick look at the sunset and they retreated into the tepid water. Tom brought the cold beer, colas, and warm pizza poolside as the girls watched and then nodded to each other.

"Do you like your pizza cold, Tom?" Madelyn teased.

"I'm used to warm beer and cold women, so this is definitely an improvement!"

"After a comment like that, it's got to be your turn to tell us about your views on re...Oops, I almost said *religion*. I should say, spiritual things, Tom. What do you have to say?" Maria smiled with her question to him.

"You already know me well, Maria. But to catch Madelyn up, you are right! I don't have much use for religion. There are so many sects with so many individual rules, and they all claim to be the one true religion. With each pointing a finger at the others, I think they're all wrong," Tom spoke with conviction.

"You both know that I had a Near Death Experience a few days ago. There was no suggestion of religion on the Other Side. Oddly, I think that may be the reason, I was called there. In fact, I know it is. I know that it is all about love! 'His love for us, our love for Him, and all our love for each other!" Tom grabbed a piece of pizza, took a bite and a quick swig of beer.

Then he resumed, "The All Powerful is not an egotist, as so many expect Him to be. He doesn't need us to praise him. He's not that insecure. Praising is just our way of humbling ourselves and releasing His power into our lives. He doesn't want to punish us, and he doesn't. He just tells us that life would be so much easier if we lived in love and kindness instead of hate and greed. By accepting or rejecting His teachings about love, we accept or reject Him. If we accept the Spirit of Love fully and live in that Spirit to the best of our ability, then we will continue to live in that spirit eternally. Some are too proud to accept or believe that, and instead, they choose to live with hate, crime, and chaos, both here and Beyond.

"In other words, if people believe in love, God, and goodness, they will find it and live with it. If they believe in God, He will exist for them. After their death, they will have continued peace with themselves throughout eternity and be even closer to Him.

"If they do not accept His Love, His teachings, or His existence, He does not exist for them. They will live with the chaos and hate that they chose to believe in, forever! Their hatred will compound itself in that chaotic environment through pride and create even more resistance to accepting the love that is offered to them. As you might imagine, that would be hell, and that's a choice made by many."

Madelyn had a serious and puzzled look on her face. "Tom, how do we know all this lasts for eternity? You know, Heaven or Hell?"

"That is really simple. There is no concept of time in death or eternity. It's just forever. Whenever you die, that's forever. If you die with good, pleasant, peaceful, loving thoughts, that is what you will experience, as you pass over. Whether it takes a second or a billion years, that's your eternity.

"The same is true if you die with hate, guilt, and resistance in your heart. Those will be your last thoughts, and they will go with you into your afterlife. This could be your hell, trying to find your way out of your nightmare forever."

They huddled closely together in the tepid water, seeking comfort and warmth from one another. It was like ghost stories being told at summer camp, only real.

Maria had a question. "What if a person was good for the most part, but didn't have their 'born again' stuff in order? What then?"

Tom came back immediately with an answer for her. "That's an iffy question and deserves an iffy answer. I can only speak from experience. I was in that situation.

"I hadn't been a churchgoer, so there were lots of questions about God. Even after serious reading, studying, and thinking, I hadn't made my commitment to Him or His way. Almost immediately after the gunshot wound, I was dying. Those were my last moments, and I called out in earnest to God. 'I haven't done everything right, but I wasn't that bad either!' Fading fast, I began to see the incredible image of my Savior's face with his hand reaching out to me. I grasped Jesus' wrist as He pulled me into a voyage that I'll never forget.

"You see, I don't think God wants anyone to go to Hell. He loves us far too much. When I saw Jesus' arm reach toward me, I knew it was my last chance. We grasped each other's wrists, and I was pulled into eternity. At least that's the way it appeared to me."

The girls were hanging onto Tom's every word. This was the good stuff, this was the important stuff. Tom could see the girls holding each other closely, when Madelyn asked, "What about Purgatory? I've read that you can go there instead of Hell and maybe get out."

Tom thought for a minute before he answered. "That's a tricky, complicated subject. Theoretically, if you ask for another chance, you would be reconsidered. There is a good chance though, that if you were too proud to accept help before, you would still be too proud and angry to ask for it."

Maria and Tom had made their choices, but Madelyn still had a question. "So, how does Jesus enter into all of this?" she asked looking at Tom.

"Jesus is known as the Word because He is the voice of God. The Bible is also known as the Word. Although He is all knowing, He came here to identify with us. He came humbly, so he could experience everything as people do, without the resources of the rich and powerful. As a man, he experienced the moral and emotional dilemmas of the people. He realized the weaknesses and limitations of all mankind and our vulnerabilities with sin. That's why he is glad to forgive those who believe in him and accept His gift of Grace. His Grace gives us a wonderful feeling, knowing that our future is secure, and we can feel confident that the strides we make are supported.

"Christians will say you can only get to Heaven through Jesus. I don't know if that is exactly true. He might have shown up in many forms and by many names. It's egotistical to think He only spoke to a few people in the world. Think of it. 'Jesus' was only the name of the human body that housed the Spirit of God. When He said, 'You can only get to the Father through me,' He probably wasn't talking about his body, but about the Spirit. The Holy Spirit that is, no matter what you call God."

There was silence after Tom paused, until Madelyn finally spoke up, "It's your turn now, Maria. What is your take on all of this?"

"Goodness, where do I start? First, I love what you both have said. Next, I guess, is that I don't consider myself a leader. In many ways, I would prefer to comfortably go to church and listen, instead of becoming involved. I would like to sit in a church pew, sing some songs, listen to a sermon, and feel good about all that's happening.

"Then I'd like to enjoy the social aspect of sharing in the Bible study. Then go and do some nice things for people. Unfortunately, that seldom happens for me."

Maria wanted to gather her thoughts before continuing. "One issue that angers me is that I don't like being considered a second-class citizen because I'm a woman. Most churches have rules against women being equal with men. Either we can't be preachers or officers, or some other sexist rule surfaces. Thousands of years ago, when the Bible was written, lifestyles were much different. Very few women could read, and most women had little experience outside the house. Women stayed home to take care of the children because men couldn't breastfeed! Thankfully, life is different today. Women are on par with men, except in places like the church, where men prefer to keep women subservient.

"Sorry, Tom. I don't mean you. I just had to say it. Many women feel this way, and many of us don't go to church because of it. They don't bring their children either. Ironically some men don't go to church these days because of the same reason. It is no longer the place, where they are apt to meet a mate!" Maria finished up with a head of steam.

"You go, Girl!" Madelyn agreed. "I've gone to several spiritual meetings with groups other than churches, and they are composed of predominantly women for that exact reason. It's been over fifty years since the Civil Rights Act of 1964 made discrimination illegal based on race, color, religion, national origin or sex. Churches don't have to honor it, and most don't. Therefore, many women don't honor churches."

Tom jumped into their discussion. "I don't blame you. I guess churches don't have to obey that law, and women don't have to obey churches. Disrespect works both ways."

He continued calmly, "That is one of the reasons I have been drawn to this cause. I do agree with you. I've heard too many feeble excuses offered by churches to overlook the abilities of women. Even Jesus and God used women in many capacities."

Maria followed up on Tom's statements. "I don't blame you, Tom, or most other men. I know there are men with good hearts. It probably comes down from the top of the religions, where the leaders are afraid for their jobs. If they don't do something about it, soon there simply won't be any church jobs. The Internet has almost wiped out the Post Office, and it could wipe out a lot of churches too. I'm sorry this upsets me. I really don't care to talk about it anymore."

She changed her tune, "Why don't we enjoy this time in the pool, while we still can. St. Augustine gets really cool in January, so let's have fun now. It's nine o'clock already, and I have to be at work by eleven. You're it!" Maria suddenly yelled, tagging Tom before making a quick dive away from him.

They spent the next half hour frolicking, cavorting, and joking. All the time, they were growing closer, as their personalities intermingled. Finally, Maria said briskly, "I better hurry now, or I'll be late for work!" She briskly climbed the four steps out of the pool. Tom and Madelyn followed but at a slower pace. By the time they got into the house, all they heard before Maria closed her bedroom door was, "Goodnight, Madelyn! See you tomorrow!"

Madelyn took the hint and got dressed in the hall bathroom. When she came out, she heard Maria's shower running, and Tom walked her to the door. As they reached out for a friendly hug, Madelyn placed a well-aimed kiss on Tom's lips. Her lips were warm and passionately lingering, with Tom sensually reciprocating. Immediately she placed her index finger softly on his lips before he could speak.

"That was just a friendly peck. And only the beginning!"

Madelyn gave him an alluring look, another quick kiss, and then walked entrancingly to her car, while Tom watched with his mouth agape.

CHAPTER 14

A TRANSCENDENTAL SKI TRIP...

The next afternoon, Tom was becoming weary of quietly doing his Twitter and Facebook maintenance all day at Maria's house.

Again, she was "sleeping off" her midnight shift. Having 'Shared' and 'Liked' enough pictures for the day, he moved on to check to see what kind of 'Comments' and 'Likes' he was getting on the fluff and flowers that he had posted on his Facebook page earlier.

He was thinking that while it presented enough food for thought and good vibes, it might lack the addictiveness of an antagonist in a good novel. He knew people can only stand so much sugar before they are ready for something bitter to cleanse the palate.

That's when he saw a post from Madelyn, who had 'Friended' him yesterday. In response to a pretty picture post suggesting that Christians be more loving, Madelyn commented, "That would mean being less judgmental."

Just as Tom was replying with a diplomatic comment, a faster-typing Friend chimed in. "Are you doing something you're afraid to be judged on?"

Madelyn quickly replied, "Are you playing God today?"

The respondent fired back, "Are you siding with the devil today?"

Tom finally got a chance to hit the enter key after he'd typed, "Love, Love, Love!"

To Tom's great surprise, Madelyn commented in response to all the above: "I apologize. I responded in judgment rather than in love."

Equally amazing was the other response: "Thank you for your apology. It made me realize my error. We all see things from different perspectives. I apologize to you, too."

Tom chimed in after a few moments of inactivity. "That was one of the most graceful interactions I have ever seen on Facebook. It showed immediate growth on both parts. Thank you for your openness to humility. That is a true demonstration of love."

Another commented, "Love is born in humility."

A couple of minutes later, the comment came, "So that is why Jesus was born in a stable!"

For a little while, it was almost like an old-time chat room. Tom was glad to see the lively exchange. The people responded positively to each other, even after the rocky start. After all, this was St. Augustine! And this was only his third or fourth day online. It was a humble beginning, but Love was in the air!

"Third or fourth day?" Tom surprised himself by talking out loud, but he just remembered that he was supposed to get his boat out tomorrow. He'd have to get in touch with Larry!

Just then, a 'Share' came. It took its rightful place at the top of the page. Tom recognized the profile picture and name as one of yesterday's new Friends. The individual shared the logo of a relatively new group in town with the Facebook name, Compassion of St. Augustine. When Tom clicked on the picture of the logo, he was overwhelmed by what he found.

The group was connected worldwide. Its sole intent was to enlist people, businesses, religious organizations, and people to join to foster compassionate thought and action with everyone else in the world. Finally, an organization with the single purpose of putting the Golden Rule at the top of mankind's priority list.

Tom loved it at first glance, and let it remain on his page. He would research it more before he endorsed it. Sometimes something too good to be true requires due diligence to ensure its authenticity. If it seemed legit, he would be glad to sign the Charter for Compassion. With that in mind, it was time to sign off Facebook and go to Google.

There he found that the City of St. Augustine had just endorsed an initiative to become one of the first Compassionate Cities in the world. That added more fuel to his fire and quest for compassion. He put in his notes to contact Karen Armstrong, a St. Augustine resident and world-renowned author on compassion and religions.

Before he went offline to call Larry, he checked his Facebook page once more. Some joker had posted a picture of a cow with the caption, "I don't go to church. I get blessed more for less at Chick-Fill-A!"

Tom had a good laugh and clicked "Like".

* * *

Tom reached Larry, and they arranged a time for retrieving his boat. Larry suggested that a couple of extra hands might be helpful, but they shouldn't expect any problems. The mast would be strapped down to the deck, out of the way as much as possible, until it could be repaired or replaced later.

Larry smiled when Tom mentioned that he might bring Maria and Madelyn along. They could park at Edgewater Marina, by Hurricane Patty's. Larry lived there and had an eighteen-foot skiff they would use.

Tom's boat was on the land at St. Augustine Marine, so they could watch as the thirty-foot sailboat was moved into the water.

Tom quickly called Madelyn and asked if she wanted to join them. She loved boats and was thrilled to go since she was off the next day.

Next, Tom knocked on Maria's bedroom door and asked if she wanted to help with moving the boat in the morning. She was groggy and grumpy, but nine worked for her, and she wanted to join them.

Tom promised that he would take them out for breakfast before they moved the boat.

Tom called Larry back to confirm that all was arranged and invited him to join them for breakfast. Larry suggested Tammy's Cafe, where the food was good, fast, and cheap.

That's what Tom wanted to hear, so the plan had legs. He was apprehensive, considering how his last voyage had ended, but hey, that was a week ago! It was time to get his sea legs back and the boat wet.

Reviewing his plans, he appreciated everyone's commitment. Larry would be in his skiff, ready to tow the 'New Covenant' if needed. One of the girls would go with each of them. Tom's much-delayed plans would be in full swing finally, and he would be living on his own boat again. Time to plan his next steps.

* * *

In retrospect, he had just arrived at Maria's a few days ago. Their arrangement in her home was cozy, but Tom couldn't afford any long-term commitment. And, he was still married, too. Another thing to clean up.

A need for reflection called him to the backyard to meditate, while Maria finished her day's rest. Sensing an obligation, he started a pot of coffee and jotted down a note leaving it on the kitchen counter.

"Here's some coffee for you. I hope it's to your liking. I'm outside meditating. I should be done in about twenty minutes if you would like to join me."

Tom slipped out the door and into the bamboo-rimmed yard. There was a chair next to an umbrella that he opened for shade. Feeling the warmth of the late day, Tom relaxed into a prayer of thanksgiving for all the blessings he'd received. He liked Psalm 100, verse 4's idea of "Enter into his gates with thanksgiving, and into his courts with praise: be thankful unto him, and bless his name."

That always put a smile both in his heart and on his face. He could feel his objective: "...the kingdom of God is within you" of Luke 17:20.

He delved within himself to commune. Once within, Tom would rely on the repetition of his mantra to replace the less-worthy thoughts that monopolized his mind. If he wasn't too preoccupied, he would often, but not always, have what he considered a *Godly* encounter.

Sometimes it was thoughts of a Divine nature that Tom attributed to the Holy Spirit. He could tell because the thoughts were ideas or solutions that he had been praying about or thinking about in a continual state of prayer in his mind. Tom got in that "zone" when alone. He felt that pure thoughts ran through him in that state. Although he had never tested the hypotheses, he felt that he might have access to heavenly powers in that "zone".

Other times, he had a realistic vision or dream, where he could participate in a conversation or activity that always had some sort of important meaning.

He found himself in that empowered state in Maria's backyard. That was so special that Tom wouldn't talk about it with anyone. In fact, he tried very hard to not feel special about it. He knew that pride could lead to a fall. He knew that all too well. He also knew that he had to have faith in order to use his gifts.

The powers weren't really his, he only became the medium for them, when he was balanced. That, he knew, to be the most important way to use the gifts to affect changes in himself. Listening and allowing advice from the Holy Spirit to change him was all that he needed.

As those thoughts began to unfold visually in his mind, a white light flickered, and a quick series of quiet clicks gave him the sensation of watching an old-time movie in the theater of his mind.

In that movie, Tom was the main character. It began when he awoke on a Monday morning to the promise of a beautiful and sunny, winter day. Only a few, puffy, white clouds were present to give depth to the crisp, blue sky. It was the perfect day for skiing, but he had no one to go with him.

Then he thought, why not ask Jesus? Everyone is always asking Him to do this or that for them. Maybe He would just like to have some fun for a change. It seemed like He would be glad to come along and enjoy the wonder of the beautiful creation from the vantage point of a mountain peak.

The mountain was covered with packed powder and glistened all around them, as they rode high above it on the lift. The immense view of the surrounding hills was unscathed by human development and demonstrated a phenomenally artistic touch. Leaving the lift at the top, the two stopped to share the awe-inspiring view, before they started down a gentle, warm-up slope. The forgiving conditions let Tom's rusty body get reacquainted with the sport and develop unusual confidence in his inept style.

They skied almost every trail on the sparsely crowded mountain. Only the expert slope, marked by triple diamonds and covered with moguls remained. Feeling his oats, Tom followed Jesus down, putting faith in His coaching. Jesus gracefully began the arduous task of weaving his way through the countless large bumps of snow. He had perfect balance, and Tom tried to follow his lead. He knew that leaning too far back with pride and overconfidence would give him speed, but take the weight off his ski tips and lessen control. However, leaning too far forward with fear would dig the tips in and cause his over-weighted front to stop, while his lighter rear end would spin him into reverse.

Tom was doing well three-quarters of the way down the hill until a large mound of snow put fear into his mind and caused him to over control. As he leaned forward, his tips slowed, while his rear end spun around in front of him, leaving him skiing backward and picking up speed. He ended up landing hard on his back. While Tom was laid out in a huge snow bank from a fear-forced overreaction, he listened to his coach chuckling. Tom nodded with an embarrassed smile.

"You're right. I should have kept the faith!"

That was a great lesson in Tom's life. Listen to the voice that's inside you, the one that you know is right. Keep the faith without pride and maintain balance, but if you stumble a little, laugh it off and get up to try again. Life is a great sport, and you can always have a pro share it with you.

* * *

As the vision vaporized, Tom returned from his Heavenly Zone. Slowly he opened one eye and then the other. It could be too big of a shock to his system to waken too quickly, almost like having icy water thrown on you as you slept.

He had learned the one eye technique back in 2005 when he was in college. Tom dated a wealthy coed, who sensed a spirituality in Tom. She practiced Transcendental Meditation, which she loved, and wanted Tom to benefit from it too. Even the student price was in the thousands, but she just put it on Daddy's credit card.

LeeAnn was her name. Her family had old money. Eventually, she was whisked away from Tom and sent to an Ivy League college. Tom's heart was broken, but he knew that their upbringing was far too different for them to share their lives. He always felt grateful to her though, for opening his eyes to so much.

Transcendental Meditation, TM as it is known, was not a religion, but rather a technique allowing one's being to be temporarily released from the attachment of earthly things.

Through relaxation and silent repetition of a meaningless mantra, the mind can avoid giving attention to normal thought and thus create space for a God consciousness. TM is well recognized and mostly documented as an aid in reducing blood pressure and instilling relaxation. TM's originator, Maharishi Mahesh Yogi, even mentored an Enlightenment Program costing a fortune, but it was guaranteed.

Tom still used that technique, combined with prayer, to enhance his relationship with the Divine. A TM practitioner is suggested to do two sessions of fifteen or twenty minutes a day. Tom wasn't that regimented and would sometimes go months without meditating. Then there were other times when he would do it quite often. He felt that transcendence aided in his understanding of the Other Realm. While he considered prayer akin to asking, he regarded meditation as listening to the Divine.

As Tom reentered the "normal" world, his muscles tightened slightly, and his thought process became more linear. All aspects of his being were ready to respond to the potential circumstances that might arise. As he looked around him, the grace of the bamboo and the peace of the pool's water eased his transition. He let his eyes wander, seeing things in a different context than he had twenty minutes earlier.

His gaze lowered and focused upon Maria. She was sitting near him and blending in with the bamboo. The shadows of thin stalks and long leaves gave her a soft camouflaged appearance. Only the absence of the green colors separated her from the surroundings.

When Maria's image began to appear focused to Tom, he responded with his winning smile. It was too soon yet to communicate verbally. His eyes held a glazed look from the bliss that encompassed him. Maria seemed to understand. While it might not work well always or with all people, sometimes nonverbal communication far surpassed that of a spoken tongue. It seemed that they shared that trait.

Finally, Maria spoke, "Did you have a nice meditation?"

Tom nodded in affirmation, then a few moments later he spoke softly. "Yes, most illuminating."

Tom continued talking about his meditation. "Everyone's meditations are different, and we seldom share the particulars. I feel close enough to you that I want to share. It's more of a personal thing. Since my NDE, I've had visions elucidating moral principles of the Bible. It is common for me to encounter Jesus who enjoys teaching with visual parables. In my mind and my imagination, this is the Word coming to life."

Tom then asked Maria, "How long have you been here?"

She moved closer into the chair next to him. "I came out quietly, just after you did. I didn't want to disturb you, so I just slipped back to my favorite spot. I was meditating, while you were, but evidently not as long. It was nice just to know that you were here. I could sense your spiritual being. It was incredibly comforting!" Maria placed her hands on his shoulders.

After a moment of sweet, reflective silence, Maria whispered in his ear, "Would you like to go for a swim?"

That caught Tom off guard but pleasantly peaked his interest. "That sounds great! I'm about ready!"

"I turned up the pool heater a bit this morning. The evenings are getting a little cool, and I love spending them in there with you."

She followed that with seductively unbuttoning her blouse. She stepped out of her jeans before she said, "I've got my suit on."

Tom followed her to the pool. He couldn't help but notice her well-exercised body in the strappy, black bikini. Trying hard to speak, he gasped, "Are there any towels?"

Leaning over a large woven basket by the pool, she grabbed two towels, dropping one by the pool and tossing the other to Tom.

Before he could recover again, she dove into the deep end. Captivated by her mocha curves and graceful moves, Tom quickly stripped down to his boxers and swamped her with a well calculated, cannonball plunge.

The mood ranged from playful to passionate, as they splashed and engaged each other in the water. They soon began to tire and cling to each other.

Falling into a warm embrace, the water floated away any notions of hesitating. They pressed together tightly, and each body shared the warmth of the other.

CHAPTER 15

A NEWPORT DOCK...

As planned, Madelyn met Tom and Maria the next morning near the docks at Rivers Edge Marina.

Maria suspected Madelyn might notice the subtle change in chemistry between Tom and her. The three chatted as they walked over to Tammy's Comfort Food Cafe.

Being Saturday, the pace was relaxed, and many of the chairs were empty. The waitresses could take their time passing out insults to habitual customers. The tourists got a pass on the friendly abuse but received a free, intimate understanding of a closely knit, small town.

Larry was one their favorite sitting ducks. It was easy to tell that they loved him.

"You all must be relatives of Larry here, 'cause we know, he doesn't have any friends."

"My friends are smart enough not to come in here. I just love the harassment. It keeps me humble," Larry countered. "Guys, this is Tammy. She's been working here forever. She can't find a real job."

"I totally ignore Larry. He means well, but he's socially inept." She smiled at the others. "You look like newcomers. We'll give y'all a pass today, but we're usually mean in here. Where y'all from?"

Madelyn spoke up, "Maria and I work at the hospital. Tom, here, is the one from the front page last week who got his boat stuck under the bridge. Now he's stuck in town."

"I had to make a grand entrance somehow! Like Larry, I needed to be humbled."

Tom was glad he didn't need to hide his identity anymore. He could be himself and interact freely in his new, friendly hometown. "I'm truly happy to meet you, ma'am."

Their coffee, eggs, grits, bacon, and buttered toast came soon after the bantering. Having hungry attitudes, they finished breakfast with the anticipation of beginning the boat relocation. Madelyn offered to pay the bill, while the others continued talking, so Tom gave her the money and a wink.

The plan was that they would make their way down the San Sebastian River in Larry's skiff to Tom's boat. On the way back, Maria would ride with Larry, while Madelyn would help Tom because she was experienced in sailing.

If New Covenant seemed worthy, she would go under her own power.

Tom nodded at Larry. "If not, you and Maria tow us in to her new home. The three miles should go pretty easily."

Larry laughed. "Well, like you, she's endured a good deal recently. Let's be prepared for the unexpected."

Madelyn joined them in time to share in the laughter. With purpose, they walked back to the marina, boarded Larry's skiff, and began their adventure.

* * *

The ride was gentle on the outbound tide. It was cloudy in the western sky, but Larry explained that clouds there usually caught in air currents over the Saint Johns River and rode the breeze up to Jacksonville. The potential rain clouds were over ten miles away and nothing to be worried about. It seemed to be a perfect day for the relocation.

Madelyn quietly shared a little of Tom's medical condition with Larry, as there was a need to keep the ride gentle. He gave an understanding nod.

Larry kept his outboard at an idle with just enough power to steer. There was probably a three-knot current due to the outbound tide. That, added to idle speed, made it about six knots. Just perfect for a mellow morning on the water.

They passed an alert osprey atop a green, navigational sign. Larry explained to Maria that the big, green signs with numbers were called "cans" because they replaced the green can-shaped buoys.

The red pointed ones, he continued, were known as nuns, because the corresponding red buoy looked like a nun in her habit.

She listened attentively to her introduction to navigation. Larry progressed.

"They're markers for the channel, and if you don't stay between red and green, especially in Florida where the water can be shallow, you are apt to hit bottom. The numbers allow you to find yourself on a chart, too. Red should be on your right, and green will be on your left when you return from the sea. Going out, we'll have green on our right. That's all you need to know!"

After pausing, Larry couldn't help but explain further. "If you are on the Intracoastal Waterway though, the red should be on your right when going south. If you're going north, then it's on the left. That's because you could return from the ocean inlet in either direction on the Intracoastal."

When Larry finished his unrequested sailing lesson, Maria was glad that he had taken the time. He'd made it simple, and it was comforting to know how to navigate. She felt fortunate and appreciative to have someone take a few minutes to explain something that she had wondered about.

Larry continued to point things out, like the roseate spoonbills nestled in the marsh grass. Maria already knew about the tall, pink bird often mistaken for a flamingo with a spoon-shaped bill, but it was news to Tom, who was from farther north.

"This southern bird is abundant in St. Augustine's coastal marshlands. In fact, it's the official bird of Highway A1A, Florida's Coastal Highway."

Larry's last point of interest was the former Desco Marine factory, now a boat storage marina, where they stacked boats high with forklifts in a building. They called them boat condos.

"Desco was once the largest shrimp boat manufacturers worldwide. Their motto was 'The sun never sets on DESCO boats.' That marketing slogan hailed between the nineteen forties and fifties when St. Augustine was the shrimp capital of the world and the builder of most of the world's shrimp boats.

"The same property eventually became home to Luhrs, one of the largest manufacturers of sport fishing boats. Besides fishing boats, they produced Hunter sailboats and Mainship Houseboats."

Larry pointed to a few marinas across the way. "John Lures also owned Oasis here. Next is Xynites Boat Yard, another shrimp boat builder. Finally, after that is John Lure's St. Augustine Marine, where Tom's boat is. They used to build shrimp boats there, too. Recently, it's become the home to the likes of the Coast Guard, Homeland Security, DEA, and other government watchdogs."

Maria sat mesmerized by Larry's knowledge of the area. She was mostly interested in his demeanor, as he told stories. He didn't boast of his local knowledge. His stories were products of his passionate love of St. Augustine and its fishing industry. She could see his eyes light up as he brought the colorful past back to life for them.

* * *

While the outboard was quietly pushing the skiff with the current, Tom had a chance to talk with Madelyn. She had grown up in rural Pennsylvania, the only daughter of a natural gas driller, who eventually became the owner of portions of many natural claims.

Her father's job provided a good living, and the gas rights provided her with a good start in life. "I did, however, develop some quirky ways about me though," she said with a wry smile.

Although Madelyn grew up in Pennsylvania, she spent most of her summers with her grandmother on St. Augustine Beach. She attended Flagler College, studied art for two years, but later switched to nursing, in Jacksonville. There was far more beneath the surface, that she wasn't divulging, Tom was sure. It seemed typical of the locals not to quickly bare their pasts nor brag about their successes.

Larry let the boat coast up to the dock at St. Augustine Marine. Then he gently slipped his outboard into reverse to counter the current.

Madelyn knowingly slipped a rope around a dock cleat, letting it grab under tension until friction stopped the forward motion. Larry directed Maria to place the front line around its nearest cleat.

* * *

Tom loved being on the water and happily anticipated being reunited with his craft. As soon as he stood up on the dock, he caught sight of New Covenant.

It was the mast-less, modest sailboat looking a bit forlorn next to much larger craft. It stood propped up straight onshore, third in line from the dock entrance. A blue tarp covered the companionway entrance that had to be sprung for his rescue.

That night seemed decades ago, and Tom's heart began to race when he saw her again. She wasn't anything fancy, but she was his home. Just fiberglass and wood, but she was endowed with spirit as if it was an extension of his own.

New Covenant was a little worse for its ordeal. Obviously, the mast was broken. It was snapped in two about ten feet from the top and joined only by the rope and pulley systems for the sails. The whole mast was laid down, supported by the starboard side of the deck.

A mass of sail cloth was tucked in where possible. The mast had to be taken down because the extreme torque under the bridge had weakened the bottom supports. Also, the stays or diagonal cables that supported the mast at its top were useless. His smile faded to a frown and suddenly he smiled again.

This isn't an end, but another chance. He ran to it.

The few surface abrasions and marks could be easily fixed. Of course, the companionway needed repair, but Tom couldn't see anything that would stop her from floating.

The next step was to inspect the inside. Larry got a step ladder from a marina mechanic he knew and propped it up on the port side. Madelyn was quietly explaining to Maria the difference between port and starboard sides.

"Starboard comes from 'steer board' and is on the side where Europeans usually drive. Port is the side where the passenger pours port wine and waves to those still in port," Madelyn joked, while Maria took it all in.

Larry talked, as he climbed. "I took all the cushions out and put a fan in the doorway for a few days when it was sunny. I threw them back in a couple of days ago when it threatened to rain. It's a real mess in there, but it's beginning to dry out."

Tom, directly behind Larry, began to talk as he climbed down the companionway steps. "Yeah, I can feel the dampness."

"I'll open the front hatch. It's going to take some time before you can stay here. You'll have to open it every morning and close it at night. Put the fan in the hatch, and keep tarps over the openings in case of rain. This is going to take a lot of your time and attention, but I think you'll be all right. Finish drying it out as fast as possible. Listen, you'll have to use bleach to eliminate the mold and wear a respirator." Larry sounded like the voice of experience.

Tom was immediately overwhelmed with gratitude. "Larry, I owe you big time for helping me out so much! This seemed impossible a few days ago."

"Don't worry about it. I love boats, and I hate to see one go to rot when it's salvageable. This should be just fine if you take care of it! You could even plan to live upon her, even without the mast. I'll take you over to Sailors Exchange and introduce you to the right people. I know that they can find you a used mast for a fraction of the new price. It might take a little time, but we do have a great boating community here, and everyone will help you get what you need. That's the way boaters are around here. I know. I've been helped many times and just like to pass it on."

The foursome was quiet for a long minute. Tom battled back tears. Another amazing gift just for him.

"Well, let's see if she starts!" Larry yelled. "I didn't want to mess with the engine without you here, but it doesn't look like it got too wet. I did charge the battery earlier, though. It should be all right if we start it and then turn it off right away before it gets hot. If she does start, we'll be in great shape. If not, you might want to figure out the reason before you leave here. That's up to you, but at least you'd know. It does cost close to a hundred dollars a day to dock here."

"Let's not worry yet." Tom was praying, as he turned the key. *Dear Lord, let her start!* It cranked, coughed a few times, and then started up. The old motor ran smoothly and responded instantly when he revved it.

A few seconds later, Tom shut it down. "Sound good to you? She sure seems ready to me."

With a wide grin on his face, Larry nodded.

"All right! Let's do it!" Maria cheered.

"Go for it!" Madelyn screamed, pumping her fists in the air like pistons.

"Okay!" said Larry, obviously thrilled that it worked so well. "Let's go over to the office. You can finish up with the paperwork, and then we'll get them to put us in the water."

* * *

Dan, the service manager, explained the charges. "The insurance paid everything, except for us to take down the mast and lash it down. We charged you a hundred for that because you're a friend of Larry's. It's usually twice that amount. If you can pay that now, you'll be good to go."

Tom happily paid the small price to get his boat back. The service manager picked up the radio and called for the Travelift operator to head towards Tom's boat to launch it. The happy group left the office patting each other on the back.

The large, diesel, smoke-belching lift began to rumble ever so slowly towards New Covenant.

Larry suggested, "Check out all your gear, so you'll be ready to go when he puts her in."

Tom agreed, and they all climbed aboard to make sure the required Coast Guard safety equipment like fire extinguishers, life jackets, buoys, lights, horn, etc. were there and ready.

Anchors, ropes, bumpers, boat hooks, radio, and everything else needed were located, too. Tom was immediately impressed with Madelyn's familiarity with the nautical items that she found and called out.

Maria quietly suggested to Tom, that they pray for a safe voyage. He responded by holding out both hands.

"Let's say a little prayer about this."

When all four had joined hands in a circle, Tom began. "Dear Lord, thank you for being with us on this beautiful day that You have made. We are here to put New Covenant back into service. We pray that You will lead us and guide us up this river to her new home if it is within Your plan. In the name of Christ Jesus, we trust and give thanks."

Everyone said, "Amen!" together.

Tom and Maria were happy to have Madelyn and Larry join them in prayer. They weren't sure if Larry was a believer, but they admired his obviously loving heart. They could never gauge where Madelyn stood with religion. She still flitted among all the beliefs, picking and choosing traits that she could accept in her heart at that given moment.

Just about that time, the four I-beam legs of the Travelift straddled them. Centered properly about them, the diesel idled down. Two sets of three long, heavy, fabric straps about two feet wide were lowered to the ground. The lift operator's helper dragged them underneath the vessel and between the skinny support tripods. They were secured with high grade, steel pins to corresponding cables hanging from the other side of the lift. At that point, the crew was asked to leave the boat.

The winch was engaged, and the powerful diesel revved to meet the power needed to lift the soon dangling, thirty-foot, sail-less sailboat. The snail-paced machine gingerly progressed onto concrete bulkheads and straddled a rectangular launch site at the river's edge.

Stopped and secured, it then lowered the mini-yacht into the water. The fabric straps were also lowered, leaving the boat to float and rock in the water, while it waited for the crew to board.

Tom and Madelyn climbed on quickly to ready for the shakedown cruise, while Larry and Maria boarded his skiff.

Tom easily started the engine. With all the bravado of an ocean liner readying to cross the Atlantic, they hollered to their friends left behind. Tom slipped the transmission into reverse. It backed out slowly and smoothly into the brackish river. In a few moments, he attempted to put it in forward gear, but it remained stuck in reverse.

Tom frantically kept attempting to shift gears, but it kept backing and turning on the inexperienced captain, who was paying more attention to the shifter than the ship's unintended course.

"Quick! Turn it off!" commanded Madelyn. "Grab that boat hook," she ordered and pointed.

Befuddled, Tom looked around and saw an eighty-foot, multi-million-dollar yacht that they were approaching much too quickly. Madelyn had to turn the key off herself to slow their rearward motion.

"Grab the boat hook and start pushing off! Do it now," she ordered again in a full shout. She moved forward nimbly to the bow, where she turned and placed the rubber tip of her hook against the shiny fiberglass hull, that they seemed to be approaching sideways.

Tom finally realized what was happening and began pushing with all his might. The current and coasting remnants of the reverse thrust of their boat continued to propel it towards the docked mega-yacht. It took their combined strength to keep the two crafts from colliding. Madelyn could hear Tom's prayer, as she quickly searched about the boat for a more tangible solution.

Madelyn saw the Bruce anchor lying near her on the forward deck, attached to a short chain and neatly coiled rope. She surmised the situation quickly and hopefully correctly. If she could throw the thirty-two-pound Bruce far enough forward and to the left, it could give them enough leverage to pull away from the yacht.

She had always been taught to lower an anchor and not to toss it. Anything caught in it could go with it, including a finger or a foot. Judging by the neat coil, Larry had made, she trusted it would fly unimpeded and safely. She did a fast check of her position and calculated that she was safe enough.

She heaved it a good twenty feet before it splashed. She wrapped the line once around a pulley designed for controlling sails and began tugging with her body tilted, and her feet braced next to a porthole against the cabin. Tom was so impressed he could only stare.

What started as a last-ditch effort, miraculously worked. The rearward motion stopped with inches to spare. However, the boat began to blow sideways. Thankfully, Tom seemed to be able to handle the pushing needed to keep the boats from colliding, while Madelyn was able to pull them far enough forward to allow a few feet of swing room between the two hulls.

Larry and Maria arrived in his skiff, just as Madelyn exhausted the rope, and the chain reached the foredeck. After Larry saw that they were out of trouble, he joked, "I thought you guys were going to buy yourselves a big boat!"

Madelyn countered, "That yacht is a real beauty, but I didn't want to buy her today!" Everyone's eyes fell on Tom who was being awfully quiet and sheepish.

"Oops," he said. "I don't think my insurance would cover sinking that one. Thank you, Madelyn, for turning off the key. I obviously don't think well in reverse."

Larry interrupted. "Let's move this boat more before we give Tom a really hard time. You're still way too close. Here, Maria, hand this rope to Madelyn. Hook that on the bow, Madelyn, and I'll pull you a little forward, so you can get that anchor up. Boy, you did a fantastic job throwing it. See if you can pull that up, Tom, she's got to be exhausted."

Tom was chagrined by the near disaster and thankful that things worked out as they had. He went forward and started pulling in the chain, as Larry tugged their boat ahead with his. The anchor was well sunk into the mud until the forward motion pried and popped it out by tilting it in the opposite direction that it dug in. Then Larry relaxed his towing tension, and let Tom redeem his manhood by hoisting the heavy anchor with its not-so-light chain.

"I couldn't get it to shift into forward," Tom informed Larry, panting as he pulled and lifted the anchor to the deck.

"Do you want to check your linkage now? You might as well see if it's something simple before I tow you. You'll have to do it sooner or later."

Larry hid his advice in the form of a question. "The transmission should be right at the rear of the engine, at the back of the engine compartment."

Again, Larry tried to give Tom a hint where the problem might be without causing him embarrassment.

Tom responded to his gentle nudging, "Yeah, let me take a look." Then he opened a hatch in the floor and stared. Puzzled for a moment, he found a cable connected to a lever on a conical shaped cover behind the engine.

After wiggling it, he hollered, "There's a bolt stuck where the cable attaches to the shifting lever. It's binding on the transmission." After wiggling a little more, he got excited and yelled, "Hey, I just got it out! The shifter moves now!"

"It's moving up here too!" Madelyn hollered back. She watched the lever in the cockpit move back and forth. "I bet you fixed it!"

There were smiles all around! "That bolt looks awfully familiar," Tom said. "I bet that's the same one I lost from the bilge pump that I replaced. It must have bounced around last week with the wreck and then got stuck in there. Oops again!"

"Good news," yelled Larry. "Start her up, and let's see if she'll go now! This is a shakedown cruise and it just got shook down in there. Let's see what happens next!"

The boat started readily and shifted easily into forward, taking Tom and Madelyn slowly northward up the rather short San Sebastian River.

There were several "Manatee Warning" signs posted, as the homely but cute, lumbering creatures were sometimes seen in those waters. That day just happened to be one of the lucky ones. Tom pointed to one up ahead on the port side.

Madelyn told the Northerner about them. "Manatees are gentle mammals, often called sea cows. They weigh around a thousand pounds when fully grown and can be up to thirteen feet long! They almost look prehistoric, don't they? Some say they are evolved from land mammals. That and their slow grazing on greens reinforces the sea cow image. They are herbivores and no threat to people. Unfortunately, they are too slow to avoid fast boats!"

Tom couldn't help but smile, as several came close enough to see clearly. "This is the first time, I've actually seen these!" Tom exclaimed to Madelyn. "I wonder, are they always this friendly?"

"They're certainly not shy around humans, but I've never seen them approach a moving boat this closely," she said. "They prefer the shallow waters, where they can feed on weeds. Oh, they enjoy fresh water from a hose, but it's illegal to give it to them. If they become overly friendly with people, they can be injured or easily killed by boat propellers, either deliberately or accidentally." Madelyn explained that she'd seen too many scars on their backs from propellers. "It's a shame that people don't behave more responsibly. They are so gentle.

"They are somewhat like dolphins in intelligence, but they aren't too smart about motor boats. Dolphins get out of the way, manatees don't. You should be at least three hundred feet from shore to leave a wake. In other words, to protect manatees, don't make waves!"

"I love all the whiskers around their mouths!" Tom proclaimed as they left the manatees behind to stay in the navigation channel. Tom reminded himself, "Red, right, return!"

Madelyn stood behind Tom in the cockpit, so she could see the manatees or potential dolphins on either side. She remained behind him after the manatees were gone and gently slipped her arms around his waist. Tom was pleasantly startled, as he gently maneuvered the tiller to stay in the channel. He twitched when she broke the bucolic silence.

"I was impressed how you handled that situation. We almost wrecked back there!"

Tom recoiled, "Huh? I panicked and almost wrecked us. I'm still embarrassed. If it weren't for you, we could have been hurt and both boats damaged too."

"Well," she said, "I saw it happening differently. At first, I was upset that you weren't doing enough to rectify the situation. You were just praying, as you pushed off. Then I was astounded how fervently and confidently you asked Him for help. Suddenly it was as if a bolt of energy filled me, and a clear view of what and how I was to act appeared in my mind. Honestly, I was being led by a higher being to do everything precisely, as it needed to be done. Please know that I wasn't doing it by myself. It was being done through me! This sounds wild, but I am telling you the absolute truth."

Tom's head and voice shook, as he tried to sort through the events. "I don't take credit for anything, but sometimes prayers come true in the strangest ways. It seemed like you instinctively knew how to save the day, and you had the confidence to do it."

Tom continued. "I truly believe that most miracles are done through coincidences. I like what Einstein once said, 'There are only two ways to live your life. One is as though nothing is a miracle. The other is as though everything is a miracle.' I choose to believe that everything is a miracle!"

Madelyn nodded, "I like that, too." Then after a reflective pause, she spoke softly. "I know it was a miracle! Suddenly everything changed. I didn't even feel it happening. What's more, I think it changed the way I will look at things and at you now."

"What do you mean? How will you look at things?" Tom asked quietly into the wind.

"Well, for one thing, I see you differently now. I was never one to see auras like Maria. I don't know how to explain it, but when you were asking Him for help, there was a bright light around you. You were lit up with a white glow."

She leaned into him, "I've been reading about various religions and their workings. You know, the magic, the miracles, the supernatural, the power of God, or whatever you want to call it. Their basic beliefs seem to be all the same: think positive thoughts, be humble, do good, do things in love, give, and you'll receive. They're really all about the same."

After a moment, she continued. "But Tom, a few minutes ago, I felt God's power come through me! I watched as you spoke to God the Father in Jesus' name, and I know that it was answered directly through me. It was one continuous happening, and I was just a conduit for what was needed. It was exhilarating! And I loved it!"

Madelyn still pressed closely behind Tom, as he focused ahead on the water. He was remembering all Larry had taught Maria on the ride down the river after breakfast. He was listening to Madelyn over his own thoughts. She so wanted Tom to share her joy in that Divine intervention and celebrate it with her. Smiling, he felt truly happy for her and blessed to have shared the incredible moments with her.

Immediately he was compelled to tell her more about himself. "I have more to share with you now. After I was shot this week, I did die, and Maria brought me back to life. I remember visiting Heaven and speaking with Jesus. I not only have marvelous memories of it, but I also have acquired a miraculous power, the ability to believe with certainty."

He turned to look directly into her eyes. "I have been in Heaven and experienced the all-encompassing wonder of God. It is truly beyond hope and faith. It's the supreme, absolute knowledge that I will receive *all* that I ask of God if it is within the realm of His plan.

"I can tell you, Madelyn, you have that power too. Experiencing His power coming through you is not a myth. Hold onto that moment in your mind and in your heart." Returning his gaze forward, he continued navigating and sharing his findings in faith. "You can draw on it whenever you pray, and I suggest that you pray without ceasing. Keep God in your thoughts. Always! Do everything in love, because God is love! Know, as you do now, that His power is your power, whenever you ask in Jesus' name."

Madelyn had big questions. "I really don't understand the Trinity concept. What's the difference between talking with God, Jesus, or the Holy Spirit?"

Looking steadily down the river, Tom listened for a moment, then began to explain. "The Father is the Creator, Jesus is The Savior, and The Spirit makes us sing. But that is just me and my silly thoughts, from a song I wrote a while back."

Getting serious, he expanded the thought. "There wasn't any mention of the Trinity in early Christianity, although Paul and some others mentioned the Father, Son, and Spirit, but they weren't all one or equal back then. It wasn't until 325 AD, that a duality of the Father and Son became equal at the first Nicene Council under Constantine the Great. He unified all different Christian sects in the Roman Empire and had the priests see to it that all scripture jived. They left out many of the previous books of what was to be the New Testament.

"The Second Nicene Council didn't really take place in Nicaea, but in Byzantium about 380 AD. That's when the Trinity was added to the Nicene Creed, probably as an effective way of explaining everything. After that, Christianity became the official Roman religion, and dissenters were terminated. The Trinity wasn't established to explain the Godhead, but to bash any competing ideas.

"Trinity is basically a concept that is seldom fully understood or agreed upon by scholars. If you should disagree with their teachings, you can be thrown out of many churches though, such as the Baptist Church."

Tom tried to explain more about the Trinity, "They are all one, as the three leaves on a clover, but they have different attributes. It's like a father can also be a parent and a doctor." Tom went a little deeper, "The Father is not visible or personable. He encompasses all power and the laws of the universe and the knowledge of all things: time, physics, chemistry, other physical sciences, mathematics, arts, etc. The Son translated all that into language and feelings that we can understand. Known as the Word, He spoke everything into being, and having lived as a person, Jesus continued to feel and understand us. He sent the Holy Spirit to us as a comforter, when he left. The Spirit is in the Father, in the Son, and in all the believers. It is the enthusiasm of love that we share and crave. The Spirit provides us with comforting love, understanding, and faith."

Madelyn nodded and pushed her windblown hair back from her face. "Thank you! Now I can at least grasp their differences and the oneness too!"

"Well, that's the basics. Don't worry about it too much. There are plenty of ways of looking at it, but if you can feel this, you get the idea. I need to talk to you and Maria more about the Holy Spirit soon. It's important for us all."

Madelyn found it easier to speak about her spiritual ideas and issues now. With indignation, she took a deep breath and raised her voice. "I find it extremely difficult to understand what so-called Christians have done with the Inquisition, witch hunts, and manifested destinies, and so on. Do you realize that many things that Christians have done, go directly against their own beliefs? Tom, isn't that appalling to you too? I don't think that I could ever join a Christian church for those reasons. Somehow though, I know something miraculous happened to me today that demonstrated incredible strength and power over and through me." Madelyn's expression softened, and she laid her head against his back.

Tom understood and pointedly began to address her issues. "I feel the same way. I don't consider myself a Christian. If I must use a label, I am a Follower of the Way, like His original followers referred to themselves.

"Most religions, sects, or philosophies have good intentions, but I cringe at the thought of calling myself a Christian with the continuing issues today. I realize most Christians are good, loving people though.

They have faults, but we all do. It's just the corruption of some and the negative judgments of others that give that religion such a bad name. That's why I am not religious, and I don't adhere to any specific sect. I feel that visiting churches and their groups might allow me opportunities to point these negative things out to them. It would not be easy, but someone should do it.

"One important thing to remember is that most of the people that were used by God to move his plan forward were far from perfect. Moses and David were both murderers, and all the others had their own limitations. We need not worry about us or others not being perfect. It is not possible for humans!"

* * *

Meanwhile, Larry and Maria had fallen in behind them with his skiff. Quietly Maria had watched Madelyn with Tom from a different vantage point.

She saw what happened, but only imagined their intimate conversation. Mistakenly she felt betrayed by her supposedly best friend. She couldn't blame Tom because he still had his back to Madelyn. Ironically, Maria was jealous of the attention Tom was receiving from her former lover. Her only response was to cross her arms over her chest in disgust and indignation. Larry and she had no idea of the celebration taking place ahead of them.

Suddenly Larry zoomed by in his skiff, waving for them to follow. When Tom saw Maria's face, he remembered that Madelyn was still standing closely behind him with her arms wrapped tightly around his waist. He also remembered last night's watery tryst with Maria.

No, Maria probably would not believe what they were discussing. Tom made a silent prayer about it and let it slip out of his mind. He had no control over Maria's thoughts. Instead, he paid attention to Larry's visual directions to his new home.

* * *

There were several open slips amongst a dozen at the docks situated neatly behind an old house on the river. It was a short walk on a dirt road to Highway US1 and about a mile or two into the heart of town. Just enough exercise to keep healthy and get where one needed to be.

Larry had been on his cell phone to the dock owner when he passed them. As they slowed down and pointed their bows toward the docks, a stocky man came out the back door of the house, giving Larry a wave. He pointed to the last slip on the dock. Larry then hollered back to Tom and pointed to his new home.

"Bring your boat around here."

Tom allowed what little current there was to cause him to drift past his target, until it was time to push the tiller fully right, causing the bow to come all the way around with only a little throttle.

Just as the bow entered the slip, he edged the engine into neutral and let the tidal current halt the boat. He was a bit proud of his docking as he reached out to the stocky man's welcoming, strong grasp.

"'Bobby Horton, and you must be Tom! Glad to have you. And this young lady is?"

"Madelyn," she said, reaching out her hand to the owner who pulled it toward him, guiding the boat alongside the dock for tie up. He held it tightly and spoke with her, while Tom set the bumpers and tied his lines to the cleats.

Bobby's warm, honest, and giving mannerisms impressed Madelyn, who prided herself on being able to read a personality. She could feel the positive energy in his touch and noticed the difference when he let go.

"Sorry to hear about your accident, Tom. You can keep your boat here, while you fix it up. Let's say for three months right now. Come talk to me about that time. We'll see how things are going, and how we are getting along. If you need anything, let me know, and I might be able to point you in the right direction. I know quite a few people around here who can give you a good deal."

Bobby obviously knew how to deal with people in a generous manner, but he also let them know there were limits.

"Oh, and stop by the house, if you have a problem, and bring this young lady, when my wife, Lynne, is around to meet her!"

Then he gave him some particulars. "There's thirty-amp electric here, and water over there. You can run a hose to fill up your tank but don't hookup directly. If you spring a leak in your plumbing, your boat will end up on the bottom and may pull down the docks.

"You'll see me out in the garage quite a bit. Stop by and say, 'Hello'. I'll let you be about your business now. Hope everything works out for you. Take care."

Bobby went to talk with Larry, as Tom, Madelyn, and Maria gathered, stowed, and secured their belongings before leaving the boat.

When they met up with Larry, Madelyn surprised everyone by saying, "Lunch is on me at Hurricane Patty's. Let's celebrate Tom's new home!"

CHAPTER 16

NOT THE OPPOSABLE THUMB...

Maria watched nervously as Larry's boat approached Rivers Edge Marina. The marina shared the parking lot with Hurricane Patty's.

The last time she was there, her greatest first date turned into the most heart-wrenching moment of her life. She had fallen for a guy who dropped dead in front of her. Only quick thinking and valiant efforts allowed her to save his life.

Looking back, she was amazed at her own actions. "Miraculous" was the keyword. She could scarcely believe that she had acted so precisely and taken control so boldly to keep him alive. It wasn't until she thanked God for His help in her prayers that night, that she realized it truly was His help that prompted her decisions at exactly the right moments.

Tom shared the same uneasy feelings about Hurricane Patty's. For him, though, it was obviously miraculous. It was in those moments of his death that he literally met his Maker. His death meant nothing to him, except for the fantastic voyage into his life Beyond. Most of it still pervaded his being and thoughts.

He knew for certain, what so many people believed merely through a leap of faith. His death was actually the most wonderful time of his life!

If only he'd had the opportunity to ask more questions. Everything he'd ever thought or questioned there became immediately clear to him. Knowledge was omnipresent to all there. He could still ask his questions now, but replies seemed to come back much less clearly. Be that as it may, today was the time to celebrate getting his boat back in the water. And to having great new friends.

The three of them rode with Larry in his skiff to the marina. He adeptly pulled alongside his white sailboat not much larger than Tom's, but in pristine condition. Larry had obviously spent a fair amount of time maintaining the exterior. There wasn't a mar or scuff on the shiny, white surface. Even the non-slip deck had no trace of mud or sand on it. Bristol condition was the nautical term.

All four of them went through the lot and up onto the restaurant's deck, where they found a table by the water, under an umbrella. The breeze was a bit cool, but the warm, Florida sunshine balanced the temperature perfectly.

When the waitress greeted them with a stack of menus, her face lit up at the familiar sight of Tom and Maria's faces. They flashed back to the recent encounter under much worse circumstances. After a short, awkward silence, Tom interrupted the quiet.

"Jan, isn't it?"

"Yes, and you are Tom, aren't you? Man, it's so good to see you up and walking around! The last I saw you, they were placing you into an ambulance and whisking you away. I didn't know if you would make it. I called the hospital the next day and was told that you were doing okay. They wouldn't tell me anything else, but that was enough for me."

Then Jan turned to Maria. "You were amazing! You saved his life!"

Tom didn't mention that he had watched the whole scene. "I want to thank all three of you for being there for me. I would never have made it without you."

Maria knew that even though Tom mouthed gratitude profusely, he would have been happier staying on the higher plane. She was also aware that he was still adjusting and enjoying his second appearance on Earth.

Still, the fact that Tom felt he was on a mission from God inflated his ego so much that she worried what any setback might do to his fragile pride.

Suddenly, Maria understood her feelings. She was jealous and jealousy made her small and vicious. Once again, she reminded herself that she held no claim on him. Even though they had become much closer the night before in the pool, no commitments had been made. Their relationship wasn't consummated, either. Yet, Madelyn's gaze told Maria that she was out to play catch-up.

Maria needed balance and took a deep, silent breath. She first thought of those who judged everyone and every action, real or imagined. Those actions had no impact on their lives whatsoever. Then she realized that she was doing the same thing, herself. She didn't really know what Tom and Madelyn were thinking, only what she *thought* they were thinking.

Maria's thoughts reeled back to the question of original sin. That bite into the fruit of the Tree of Knowledge of Good and Evil caused considerable consternation that continued today. The moment Adam and Eve began using that knowledge of good and evil to judge the actions of others, they differentiated themselves from the nonjudgmental animals and became human.

It wasn't the opposable thumb that differentiated them. It was the haughty knowledge of good and evil. They were beginning to act like God, so He threw them out of Eden. God didn't want them to eat of the Tree of Life and live forever. "...He placed the cherubim and a flaming sword that turned every way to guard the way to the Tree of Life."(Gen. 3:24)

That moment still reverberated in the minds of Christians. They used that knowledge to judge themselves in every action, judge others with minimal evidence, and then judge themselves for judging!

Although Jesus gave them forgiveness two thousand years ago, humans still judge whether He's judging them as worthy of being in the group that is beyond judgment. Maria laughed under her breath. *The real spirit of Jesus probably inspired Bob Marley's song, "Don't Worry, Be Happy!"*

As Maria looked up, everyone's eyes were on her. She started to react, when the lyrics sang in her head, "Don't Worry, Be Happy!"

Larry spoke up, "Are you still with us, Maria?"

"Oh, yeah! My brain just took a little side trip." She smiled and was in a much better mood than a moment earlier.

"What are you having for lunch?" Larry pursued.

"I don't know yet, but I'm hungry!" Maria acted like she hadn't missed a beat.

Jan came back with the drinks. She asked Maria, "Do you want something to drink now? You seemed a little distracted earlier."

"Yeah, I'll have a glass of Chardonnay," she said, taking advice from the repeating lyrics still dancing in her thoughts.

"I'll get everyone's order in a minute," Jan said. Then she leaned towards Tom and spoke quietly. "I need to talk privately with you. Give me a minute to put her drink order in, then meet me inside."

Of course, everyone was wondering, but no one said anything. It was obviously not their business.

Tom shrugged his shoulders and said only, "Hmm..." Then he laughed and rolled his eyes. After an appropriate amount of time, he excused himself and slipped inside to find Jan.

* * *

"What's up?" Tom asked when he caught up with her at the end of the long bar.

"There you are! You should know that the lady detective who was questioning everyone here about your incident, came by this morning with even more questions. I found out yesterday that Ron, who lives in that sailboat with the bubble hatch, found a bullet in his wooden mast the other day. I guess that stirred things up again, and she is back on the investigation.

"I didn't get to tell you earlier and I didn't think much about it at the time, but about a half hour before you were shot, I told a stranger that you were outside looking around the docks. Now it seems like a huge coincidence that you'd be shot just a little later, and then he would disappear. I remember seeing him leaving in a silver car, after you went down, too."

After a thoughtful moment, he sighed. "So now the investigation is back on. I'm sorry about all this. Just be careful what you say to anyone. These things can get messy. Seriously, thanks for letting me know. Did the detective say anything else?"

"She asked me if I could identify the guy. I told her that I remember what he looked like. Do you know who he is?"

Tom shrugged. "I didn't see anyone looking for me before I was shot. But, I've got a past. Who knows? You can let me know if you hear anything though. Here's my number." He ripped off a piece of paper from his pocket pad, wrote on it quickly, and handed it to her.

Then, always thinking in business mode, he asked, "Are you on Facebook?"

When she replied, "Yes," Tom asked for her last name. "Court, Jan Lee Court. Friend me!"

More than happy with her response, he winked and promised to do just that.

Back at the table, everyone was still looking at the menus and talking about food. Larry, who lived at the marina, was making suggestions.

"The hamburgers are fantastic, big and juicy! I love the crab and artichoke dip, too. It's an appetizer, but it's made in a big, round bread bowl, so it's a meal in itself. I'm addicted and I crave it at least once a week. The Minorcan Clam Chowder is incredible if you don't mind that it's spicy. It's won several awards in the Chowder Cook-Off at the Conch House."

"I love clam chowder, but what's Minorcan Clam Chowder?" Tom interrupted to ask.

Of course, Larry was glad to explain. "It's like Manhattan Clam Chowder, tomato-based and red, but it has datil pepper in it. That's a very hot pepper supposedly brought to St. Augustine by the Minorcans."

"Minorcans?" Tom asked.

"They were indentured servants down in New Smyrna, who were enslaved by their plantation owners. The British, who owned Florida for twenty years, freed them in 1777. This town still has an influential Minorcan population. Lots of their influence in the foods." Larry smiled and finished his free history lesson.

"Okay, Larry, you convinced me. I'll have a bowl of Minorcan Clam Chowder," Madelyn said with a laugh. The others joined in too.

Undisturbed by the good-natured razzing, Larry still defended himself. "We do have a newbie here, and I thought he might enjoy the history." Larry nodded with his firm affirmation, more laughing than serious.

Tom said diplomatically, "Thank you, Larry, but I think I'll have their Mushroom Swiss Burger today. Still building up my red blood cells, ya know."

Maria added, "I decided to have the Crab and Artichoke Dip. I've had that at other places and really liked it."

"They have the best here," Larry approved. "I'll have the Fish Tacos, myself. They're delicious!"

"You didn't mention the tacos earlier, Larry," said Madelyn.

"I got way too much flack on my other recommendations, so I just shut up." Larry laughed as if to say, "That'll fix all of you!"

Everyone gave their orders when Jan returned. While eating, they decided to go to Maria's later that afternoon to grill salmon and swim in the pool. All the razzing suggested they would become good friends.

* * *

Tom and Maria went back to her house, while Madelyn and Larry went their own ways after eating.

Larry mentioned that he wouldn't be able to stay long, but he was happy to be invited to Maria's. Everyone seemed to like him. He was a truly genuine person and happy to help others in any way he could. He said that he could find Maria's house from the address she gave him and would meet them about five. Madelyn would arrive then, too.

Maria was anxious to talk to Tom on the ride home. "I had an actual epiphany back at the restaurant. I've admittedly been uptight about Madelyn and you. I see that she continues to come onto you, even though she knows that I have feelings for you. She's been my best friend, and I know that I have no hold on you. Still, it rubs me the wrong way.

"Then love suddenly filled my heart, and started singing, 'Don't Worry, Be Happy!' It was magical! All my stress disappeared. I honestly had no more worries, and I was singing in my mind and in my heart. It felt wonderful, and I hope it stays this way. I'm accepting that I don't have power over everything. If I just give these things to Him, I am free!"

Tom nodded that he understood. "I noticed your mood change back at the table. That's when Larry said, 'Are you with us, Maria?' The tension suddenly disappeared from your face, and you looked so relaxed.

"This isn't easy to explain, but I had just lifted you up in prayer when we were coming in on the boat. I had seen the jealous expression on your face. I don't want to sound like I have any special powers, but it seems that my prayers have been answered frequently and regularly since my near-death experience last week. Just my thinking about something seems to initiate a cause and effect."

Maria offered her spin on it. "Perhaps your faith is that intense now, that the ball automatically starts rolling whenever you begin to think about something."

"Yeah, I've considered that too. I don't even have to form a request in my mind. It's like unintended prayer. The time that I spent with Him was incredibly powerful. It seems that I'm in a constant state of prayer now. Sort of scary. I'm not sure if it's even me doing it. Things just happen, when I think about them. This plays constantly across my mind. It seems that I'm always in prayer, just as Apostle Paul recommended. Although it is totally fantastic, it may also become a burden. I have an obligation to spread His love now. I realize that He is totally forgiving, but I feel guilty if I miss an opportunity. I guess that I'm part of His plan, and He probably expects me to screw up occasionally. Surely, I'll find my balance sooner or later, but for now, I'm just finding my way."

Maria listened closely to Tom. He had a life event that few have ever realized. Every near-death experience is somewhat different, but there are also many strong similarities. People encounter the Divine from their own cultural orientation, yet there is a universal code of behavior in which Love is the key principle.

Maria suggested, "Why don't you join me in my 'Don't Worry, Be Happy' trick? You know—let go, and let Him!"

"Thanks, I'll do just that!" he replied with his endearing wink. Then they sang a couple of verses together, as best as they could remember and ended up laughing and giggling together.

Maria redirected their conversation a little. "How is your web work coming along? What's happening?"

"It's going well. I've only been working on it for a few days, yet I have close to a hundred friends. The best part is, I'm getting lots of 'Likes' and 'Shares' for the limited number of friends I've acquired. Almost half 'Like' the pictures and quotes and several of those pass it on by sharing. With enough Friends, I might have a few things go viral!"

"Do you need any help?" Maria offered.

"I'm sure I could use some, but it's hard for me to delegate responsibilities. I'm accustomed to doing things alone. It would really be nice to have someone to bounce ideas around with me. It gets lonely doing everything by myself. Do you know anything about Twitter? We need to get on there soon. Right now, I'm just getting started, and my schedule is manageable.

"Eventually, I expect I'll be much busier. You could be helpful just stimulating conversations by commenting on my posts and others'. 'Likes, 'Comments,' and 'Shares' help build enthusiasm. When it reaches 'Critical Mass or Critical Energy', there should be enough stimulating content to intrigue minds, and coax them to learn more about His love."

Tom continued in a softer tone, "I need you to be in my life. I need you to stimulate conversations with me and keep me on track, especially when I'm wrong. This cannot be done by one person. Both Madelyn and you have encouraged me with your different viewpoints, and I need that! There's a large, overlooked population of spiritual individuals that are sailing without a rudder. It's going to take more than just my efforts in the background fanning out enough thoughts to encompass those lost and looking for a path."

* * *

Maria cherished Tom's request for her to engage his thoughts and supplement his work. Ecstatic inside, she was thrilled that he needed her encouragement, too. In her next breath, she knew she had to be honest with herself. Her jealousy of Madelyn could always reappear, but the lyrics, "Don't Worry, Be Happy", would have to override it.

She remembered how close Madelyn and she used to be. Madelyn had even helped her get into her house when she was struggling for the down payment. Maria realized her envy was not because of what Madelyn did, but because of who she was: beautiful, intelligent, open-minded, rich, generous, and free-spirited. Maria realized that she needed to soften her own heart and have more confidence in herself. Madelyn was a wonderful woman and a close friend that she didn't want to lose.

She envisioned how she wanted her life with Tom to be. She wanted to dote lovingly over him, while he did the same for her. She imagined them in their home with Tom being the ideal mate, conforming to all her expectations. He'd be like a puppy on a leash and ready to be the "Best in Show." As she thought, she giggled quietly. How silly she felt for developing a school girl's dream, without her considering the person in her dream! She astounded herself with how much she had matured and changed her self-image and expectations with her "don't worry attitude." She wondered if her changes were from the unintended prayer Tom mentioned, and how long her changes could last.

Maria glanced over at Tom and pulled her thoughts together. "I'd love to be involved in your dream. I think our viewpoints are close enough to work together on the same path, and I'll be glad to alert you whenever you stray. It seems to me that you want to enter the uncharted waters of spirituality, rescuing all those in the doldrums without a religion to guide them.

"Madelyn is in those waters. She is a spiritual being, but she's looking for direction, and a few others to share a lifeboat with her. I think she senses your direction like I do."

Maria continued after a pensive breath, "Your near-death experience has made you an authoritative person that she and others can respect. You're not just a pastor trying to build a profitable church with a tried and true product. You want to recruit individuals who are hearing personal calls, but have no labels to wear or maps to follow."

* * *

Tom detected a marked change in her personality. It was only a few hours ago that she had her arms folded with a pained, tense look on her face. He was amazed at the difference in her since he'd felt her jealous darts directed at Madelyn and him earlier in the boat.

"You have such great intuition, Maria." Tom had already let her off the hook for her previous posturing. "I know we will work wonders together."

Tom believed Maria's change of perspective to be divine intervention. He now had faith that whatever he asked in *His* name would be done, but only if it was His will. Tom was confident that he had gotten His stamp of approval. Now he was encouraged to move on with all that was in his mind.

Tom was hoping and praying that Madelyn had been stirred by her experience that morning. He was deeply thankful that she let a higher power work through her to receive Christ into her heart.

She wouldn't have to follow any religion, and she wouldn't have to join any church. She only had to put her faith in Him to lead her in the right direction. It seemed like the Holy Spirit would become a part of her life soon!

Tom believed that Madelyn would certainly help them if it was within the Master's plan. Madelyn had gotten a Holy nod that morning, but Tom stopped halfway through his thought to remind himself to let it go. Let God do as He would.

Enthralled and empowered by all the recent successes in soliciting and receiving help from Above, he cautioned himself again about being proud or assuming credit for what was happening. As difficult as that was, he well knew the dangers of pride and misappropriation of credit.

Eagerly, but patiently, he awaited seeing Madelyn at the barbecue that evening. The subject would come up when the time was right. It was truly amazing how many thoughts could occur during the short space of a conversational gap!

Maria cleared her throat and changed the subject. "Do you know that your aura is incredibly bright right now? When we first got into the car, I clearly saw the purest green color surrounding your head and shoulders. In just a few moments a brilliant, cobalt blue became more dominant, and then the two colors blended to become a dazzling, sunlit turquoise. As we're talking now, the indigo color of your transcendence chakra is glistening with bright streaks of white energy emanating from within you. It's good we are coming up to my house. I'm too distracted to drive."

After pulling into her driveway Maria said, "I don't see these colors with my eyes, but I sense and view the aura's color and the chakra's energy in my mind. Right now, what is normally very subtle for me, is becoming extremely distracting. I have never, *ever* seen such intense colors! What is happening?"

CHAPTER 17

SURRENDER IS KEY TO...

They continued to sit comfortably in the warm car outside of Maria's home.

Tom could hear Maria talking to him about his aura's colors, as a thickening fog formed between them. His thoughts had risen to such a higher plane, he couldn't be interrupted. If he were to explain, it would be that he was receiving the Word from Above.

In that moment, all he heard and felt earlier was being impressed upon every aspect of his being. He was profoundly lost in the greatness and nuances of the words that held the answer for him.

Surrender is the key! It unlocks the strength of love and humility and becomes the posture of potential. This power is not ours, but it listens to our being, as we relinquish our desire to control it. It follows the adage, "Let go, and let God!'

Tom understood that no one uses the power directly, or takes credit for it. Yet, if we make our desires known, all things are possible. Anyone accepting His words may humbly and lovingly ask and receive His blessing.

Then everything becomes completely different. It's an entirely new reality. A wonderful way to position oneself in humble belief is to express thankfulness for blessings in advance. Tom gave thanks in advance for the wisdom of the Word, that he knew was to come. In doing this, he humbly internalized his faith, as he expressed his gratitude to the Universe.

Only Tom's glowing smile communicated the essence of his experience to Maria. She instinctively knew that she was witnessing his aura in total complicity with the other realm. Brilliant, white light warmly embraced them both, as she sensed the wisdom of his epiphany.

Tom continued in deep, prayerful thought, and Maria didn't want to disturb him. There was no hurry and no worry. The wintery sun of the Florida day was perfect for relaxed enjoyment. The temperature was cozy, and the breeze was perfect. It was one of those few times in life when nothing could be better.

Maria could feel his energy. She likened it to Chinese Chi or Qi, the energy of life. Some people reason that Chi arises from the physical being, while Taoists and Buddhists say matter arises from Chi. Maria didn't know, but she truly enjoyed the exquisite sensations of being within Tom's realm of spiritual energy.

After an indeterminable amount of time, Tom spoke. "Selah," was all he said.

Maria had seen that word used only a few times while reading Psalms. She had even looked it up, but it had no exact meaning. The best she could understand was, "Relax and know God." Evidently, that was Tom's conveyance. It was exactly how she felt, as she basked in his aura.

This feeling was reflected in Tom's smile, as he emerged from a trance-like state. There was a chuckle in that smile that led her to wonder what the joke had been there? She knew from his opening eyes that words could not describe it. Maria was certain, there was something mystical, yet magical, from the Other Side by the sparkles in his eyes. She really wanted to know more.

A barely audible sigh escaped his lips when he recognized her delving and questioning stare.

"I'm sorry, but I can't explain it right now. Maybe soon, but not yet. It seems that you have the right idea though. Some things just don't translate into words easily or accurately, but it is literally lovely."

Without speaking, they got out of the car and walked into Maria's house. Pausing in the living room, they turned towards each other and fell into an embrace that surpassed cumbersome words and allowed them to communicate on a level where words didn't get in the way.

They awoke hours later on the plush pile rug to the door chime ringing. Of course, it was Madelyn. After a shout of, "Be right there," Tom scurried for the bathroom, and Maria opened the door for the early visitor.

"Am I interrupting anything?" Madelyn quipped with an arched eyebrow.

"No! You didn't give us enough time," Maria retorted.

"Good!" Madelyn came back with laughter. "I wanted to be here!"

Maria laughed too and let the comment pass. "You are very early!"

With Tom still out of the room, Madelyn spoke in a hushed tone. "I know, but you are my two, most favorite people! Maria, I realize that things have become strained between us. I've felt like an outsider. I know that you and Tom have gotten closer, and I'm feeling alone and jealous. I guess that it's none of my business, but I sense you don't want me around Tom."

Maria looked down. "I'm sorry. I felt the same way and really threatened by you. It was obvious that you had your eye on him, too. Honestly, nothing has really happened between us. We've had lots of hugs and shared quite a few kisses, but that's as far as it's gone. I know that we've really connected, though. In fact, I'll be assisting him with his spiritual projects. I know he will want your help too if you're interested."

Maria continued, "Anyway, I need to apologize to you. I'm sorry for trying to exclude you. It occurred to me today, that whatever happens, will happen. It's not in my control, and I have to stop worrying about it. Those feelings will only create problems. We need to learn to go with the flow." With a giggle, she whispered, "I've been singing that song, 'Don't Worry, Be Happy' all afternoon. It's stuck in my mind, and I'm feeling so much better about everything."

Madelyn responded by pulling Maria close. "I'm really glad for you. I'm sorry that I was inserting myself between you and Tom. I've been jealous, too. I'm not sure of what, though. I don't know if it's because you like him, or he likes you. Maybe it's both. I miss everything that we shared, but I do like Tom too, a lot."

"Exactly!" Maria agreed as Tom walked back into the living room. Madelyn dropped her arms and faced Tom squarely.

"Did I hear my name mentioned?" he asked, half pretending that was all he had heard.

Madelyn was quick to respond. "Yes, we were both saying that we like you, Tom!" His eyes darted from her to Maria just in time to see her mocha skin blush.

"Well, I like both of you, too," he said softly as if he didn't understand.

Madelyn clarified herself, "No, a lot more than just like!"

Again, Maria's cheeks brightened.

"Hmmm...," Tom hesitated, not knowing quite how to respond. Unsettled, he laughed. "I'm truly torn between you. Seriously, I love both of you." At last, Tom admitted this to them. "Honestly, it's been difficult, not feeling that I could express that to both of you."

They each paused to look deeply into one another's eyes. Magically and magnetically they were drawn together for a much-anticipated group hug. They held onto each other tightly, until they experienced a new feeling of love shared through them.

It was Madelyn, the least abashed, that broke the quietness. "It's all right. Finally, we are honest with our feelings. We need to be true to ourselves and to each other. Now we don't have to hide our feelings from each other any longer! These feelings are occurring naturally to us, so we shouldn't be ashamed of them."

Maria, the last one to ever admit that she could be in a love triangle, broke down. Tears streamed from her eyes. In a flood of feelings, all her emotions that had been stifled and hardened by uncertainty felt resolved. Without judgment, there was no distress. Surrendering to this relationship, she found her peace.

Their balance became wobbly, as they clenched each other. Tom eased them toward the couch. As Madelyn and he sank into the billowy cushions, Maria let herself slip down onto the soft carpet. From there, she watched them calmly share an embrace. She knew the warmth in the lightness of their touch from her intimate encounters with each of them. Maria knew that the three of them shared a circle and a bond that had almost been severed. It would now be complete and strengthened.

Maria's jealousy had been transformed into a gracious and giving love for Madelyn and Tom. She felt genuinely happy for them and for herself. She'd have the friendship of two wonderful people that she could trust and rely upon. Her tears stopped and the calmness in her heart had accepted her new role with Tom and Madelyn.

Madelyn was right. They didn't need to hide their feelings. Although the thought of losing them to each other lingered on Maria's mind, she no longer wished to fight for either of them. With certainty, she loved them both and readily sensed, that each wanted to be with her, too.

Maria could only hope and pray that the love they shared would be a sustained reality. Still, there was no confirmation of anything beyond friendship. It just seemed so intense, lasting, and far beyond any friendship that she'd ever known.

As each of them began to share their thoughts, it was obvious that they all desired the same direction for their loving relationship.

Tom broke the quiet. "Neither of you know that I am still married." He dropped a huge bomb with this revelation.

"My wife and I have been apart for a few months, and I'm fairly confident that divorce papers have been filed. It's just not wise for me to become fully involved in any relationship now. I don't know how I could justify myself right now to you."

Madelyn straightened her back. "I see no reason to justify anything. I'm where I want to be, and I intend to stay there!"

Maria was more shocked. She was anxiously looking forward to the next phase of her life. She instantly wondered, what else she didn't know. She turned sharply to Tom. "When were you going to tell me this, you son of a bitch?!"

Tom realized that he was in deep trouble. Taking a step back from them, he kept his voice gentle and spread his hands out in front of him.

"Look! I met you only a week ago. We have spent very little time together. There have been several, major events in that short time: like being shot, dying, going to Heaven, and meeting two wonderful women. I haven't had time to even think of my past, let alone who might still want to kill me. I promise that this will not stand in our way. I'm sure of it! It's only a matter of signing some papers.

"Meanwhile, nothing has changed. I still love you both. I just don't want us moving too quickly. Today I honestly let both of you know my feelings. In the days ahead, which I hope are short, I don't feel that I should be sexually involved with either of you. Nor is it right to make a romantic commitment now. I'll start working on my divorce tomorrow."

Maria was still hurt, but calmer. "So, now we go backward in our relationship?"

The sarcasm wasn't lost on Tom but he tried to reassure her.

"No, I don't see any reason we should do that now. My marriage is over. She said she was filling for divorce, and I'm glad. I have a new life, and you were in it when it started. And you're in it too, Madelyn. If you still want me. It is, what it is. Let's work together. We are such close friends now, and we can look forward to becoming so much closer!"

Tom held his arms out, hoping to be joined by the others. Madelyn took only a second to join him, as she hadn't lost much ground.

Maria took a little longer to recover. Realizing that she could end up alone, she relented and joined them. All three were burnt from their first upset, but their new, joint resolution would not be so readily destroyed.

At this point, Maria's thoughts were interrupted by Tom's ringing phone. Madelyn and she couldn't help seeing the look on his face and hearing the fearful tone of a woman's voice through the phone.

After a brief exchange, Tom said, "I'll check into it," and hung up.

He glanced at the women. "That was Jan from Hurricane Patty's. She wanted to warn me that there's a major discussion happening on my Facebook page. She feels that I should check on it–says it's getting out of hand." He brought his page up on his phone.

After a deep sigh, he shared the problem with Maria and Madelyn. "It seems that my 'LightPost' article has ruffled some feathers. Looks like I've engaged conservatives with New Age could-be Christians. Here, see for yourselves!" Tom showed them the post and comments on his oversized phone.

Some people on Tom's page were up in arms because he had expressed an opinion about Luke 2:48-52, saying that twelve-year-old Jesus had disrespected his parents by neglecting to tell them that He would not be traveling back with their group to Nazareth from Jerusalem. That caused them about two days extra travel and a great deal of stress by having to return and look for him. Tom said that Jesus had sinned by not honoring his parents. Well, that began a major ruckus. Several Christians started leaving scathing remarks about Tom's post.

Tom's Page
Hello, I'm Tom, and this is my page. I welcome people from all spiritual orientations here to discuss their opinions. Freedom of speech is important. I'd appreciate it if we all could treat everyone respectfully.
Vince Daniels
Tom, if this is your page, then you must be an idiot. Your LightPost is full of crap! Why are you trying to fill everyone's minds

with fake religious stuff? If I find my kids reading this crap, I'll be looking you up and taking care of you myself.

Tom's Page

I'm sorry if you don't like what you are reading here. You are welcome to go elsewhere. If you would like, I could even "Block" you!

Mike Martin

What you'll be trying to block, is my fist from knocking your teeth down your throat! You might think you are in Heaven when you see all the stars. Know that you'll be waking up in Hell!

Tom left the conversation, as it was. He didn't want to add fuel to the fire and hoped that it would simmer down with time. But, he added new comments the next day just to stir the pot.

Tom's Page

When Jesus went home with his parents, the Bible states that he grew in wisdom and stature. He had more to learn to become more like his Father and evidently took the next eighteen years doing it. There is speculation that He might have spent time studying other recent religions like Buddhism and Taoism.

The depth of Tom's thoughts and understandings in his last post fueled the controversy even more. Replies continued to fill his page, faster than he had ever seen before. His page scrolled as he read. People on all sides of the burgeoning debate expressed their opinions. Tom's new insight expanded their formerly static awareness with heightened and passionate emotions.

Several commented with thanks for presenting eye-opening views. Others blasted him for contaminating the Bible's scripture with his questionable, personal opinions.

One response caught Tom's attention more than the others. A person called Pastor Ken posted something that pricked a nerve in Tom's defensive senses.

Pastor Ken

You need to stick to the scripture and keep your personal opinions to yourself, or you might be silenced permanently.

Tom touched the profile icon to bring up the pastor's page. He instinctively checked Pastor Ken's Friends and found Mike and Vince from the day before. Tom printed a hard copy of their pictures and the links to their pages.

The following day, Tom posted his LightPost a week ahead of schedule. Controversies could draw out those who are questioning, Tom thought.

Tom's Page

LightPost ~ Paul, the Appeaser ~

We are told that if we, either Jews or Gentiles, have faith in Jesus, we will freely receive the Grace of God. Yet the Pharisees of the early church required that Gentiles follow the Jewish laws of Moses that never pertained to them. That meant Grace was not free to Gentiles, and it placed a yoke on Gentile disciples that even the Jews were never able to bear. This included Jewish laws against "sexual immorality" and food sacrificed to idols.

Actually, the church elders did not quite forbid these things, but only wrote them a letter saying, "If you keep yourselves from these, you will do well." (Acts 15:29)

As Tom watched his page's activity escalate from the sideline, he recognized Mike, the earlier trouble-maker. The buddy, Vince, was missing from the action, but Pastor Ken had joined in. They added more interest to the heated conversations. They did restrain themselves from fanning the flames, as they'd done previously. Tom was a bit surprised at how mild their tactics were without Vince.

Tom kept inviting comments. Buddhists, Taoists, Wiccans, Muslims, various spiritualists, and others entered the fray regarding those and other topics brought up by others.

After inviting Friends to share his posts on their pages, his party got even hotter!

Eastern religions remained mellow, but Christians and Muslims wished to express their differences in feuds. The anger of the past millenniums appeared with only a light fanning of the flames.

Tom considered that he might have shared and posted ideas too controversial. At that moment, it seemed that to heal the world was far beyond his scope for the next few days.

CHAPTER 18

HACKED AND BACK...

Tom sat down with a steaming coffee mug the next morning to read what had ensued overnight on Facebook. He made several unsuccessful attempts to sign in using his email address and password.

Frustrated, he went to Google for a new Gmail address and then created a different Facebook account. He thought maybe he could access his page from a new account.

Once back on Facebook, he could find no trace of his old page. It really was as though it never existed. Tom's heart sank, as he contemplated the loss of all his hard work. He steadily searched for his online presence, but still found nothing. According to Facebook, it did not exist and never had existed.

Tom remembered that yesterday he had printed out a list of his 'Friends'. At the time, he felt like it was being egotistical, and he almost aborted the idea. Fortunately, something told him to continue. Going to the pages of several friends, he still couldn't find himself in their Friends lists.

Reaching Maria by text, he shared the bad news. Desperate to retrieve his page with nearly a thousand 'Friends' and a reputation that he had diligently built, Tom was focused on his task.

Maria understood his panic and upset but was unable to help him other than to suggest that he contact Madelyn because she knew some top-notch IT people from her internet days.

Tom texted Madelyn with his dilemma. In just minutes Tom received a reply. "I couldn't find you online either. Yeah, something very weird is happening. I mentioned your page to an old friend, Jorge, just a few days ago.

"He's one of the best IT investigators that I truly trust. I'll ask him to look into it. He even has the legal credentials to go in the back doors of most sites to investigate possible hacking. I'll give him your information, and he should be in touch with you soon. Stay on the lookout for a message from him."

After thanking Madelyn, Tom repeatedly checked for new texts, emails, and voicemails. He poured another cup of coffee and celebrated that Madelyn was so well associated on the web.

The word, 'serendipity', slipped into his mind to explain all the wonderful coincidences in his life. It might have been karma, but he doubted he had been good enough for that. His body relaxed, as somehow, he knew things would be all right.

There had to be a reason for the current upheaval. Perhaps wrinkles in life's smooth fabric were needed to allow changes to occur.

As time moved on, his mood deteriorated. Honestly, he was distraught to think that he might have to start over. Maria walked in through the door from work and saw him sitting despondently on the couch. She sat down next to him, shook her head softly in empathy, and offered him her hand and her best advice.

"Let's pray about this and let it go. I'm sure it will be resolved soon, one way or another," she said.

A few moments later, Tom leaned over and said, "That helped. Guess that's the least we can do about it now, but where do we go from here?"

"No, I disagree!" Maria sharply corrected him. "Praying is the most important thing we can do now. Not only will it put forces far beyond our comprehension into action, it will relax our minds and allow us to think more creatively."

"You're right," Tom agreed. "Sometimes I forget. We are under Grace! It not only forgives us and gives us the keys to Heaven, but Grace allows us to receive many blessings right here on Earth. Sometimes I feel that I am sitting in life's sweet spot. I am so glad to have you by my side, reminding me. Sorry I was feeling so negative. And, thanks for your wisdom."

"Everything is going to be fine." Maria was smoothly assuring his efforts. "We should practice a little Mindful Awareness. It will let you relax and live in the now. Without your worries getting in the way and destroying your faith, your prayers are more likely to be executed. Close your eyes and follow my voice. Sit comfortably and relax. Take a deep breath in. Now, let it out. Again, in, and out. Concentrate on the space between your breaths. In. And out. In. And Out. Concentrate on in–out...."

Maria let Tom continue for a while before she continued in a soft, low voice. "You're aware of all you need at this moment. Just breathe. Let life evolve without your control or judgment." She matched his rhythm with, "...in... ...out... ...in... Let your mind ride on the spaces to its natural place. It is not the thoughts you hang onto, but the thoughts you release that allow you to rise. You are free to just ride the light breeze of your mind, while everything else is done for you."

Tom did as Maria suggested, leaving behind his cares. In that state of mind, he found himself floating amidst a triangle of hypnosis, meditation, and awareness. He was completely content. All unneeded thoughts were left behind to join an abandoned excess of knowledge.

When Tom finished the exercise, he became the master of his own mind, allowing only positive thoughts to gain influence.

Good thoughts and warm colors emerged, with his favorite being a soft coral with a creamsicle taste. With this awareness, Tom realized Maria and Madelyn were positive manifestations from the Other Side.

An obvious thought closely followed, "Good thoughts produce good results, as happy chuckles yield uncomplicated relations."

His pattern of thinking created a brainchild, that would eventually turn today's hardship on Facebook into a harvest. Tom's anger at the unknown hackers melted in his state of mind and transformed it into love for his enemy. In just moments, his hate had changed, guaranteeing him a positive outcome for his accelerating avocation.

An hour later, Tom awakened from a restful nap with Maria nestled next to him on the couch. He simply let his eyes close to drift back into the sweet sleep.

He realized that his life was in excellent hands, and he needed to appreciate that. Half asleep he recalled a quote questionably attributed to The Buddha, "There is no way to happiness; happiness is the way." Nothing else made better sense. There was no reason to think it through further.

Tom popped awake an hour later filled with inspiration from within. He realized that his present predicament was really an opportunity to expand into other markets. He could use this time now to get Tweeting on his New Covenant Twitter account. He had been devoting all his time to Facebook, and he needed to branch out.

Tom excused himself, extracting his body from a sleeping Maria's arm wrapped around him. He had ideas and needed to pursue them, while they occupied his mind. He got up, moved to the kitchen table, and searched Google for tutorials for using Twitter. It was time to start tweeting with the big boys. He felt that Facebook was great for modest personal audiences, but Twitter could potentially reach a much larger group.

Discovering the differences between hashtags, cashtags, tweeting, retweeting, and "followers" as opposed to "friends", intrigued Tom. He found that if he tweeted brilliantly in response to another tweet, he would get requests from followers.

When he got his Facebook page back, he'd ask friends there to follow him on Twitter. The 140-character limit would require him to change his style, but it would be fun to expand his outreach with new followers.

Already Tom was making great strides toward another beginning for his cause. He skipped lunch and plowed on until supper time. By that time, he was following almost a hundred tweeters of repute, and he was already being followed by a small core who shared his interests.

By the time Maria stirred, Tom was a new man with a new direction.

* * *

As Tom and Maria were discussing what to prepare for dinner, Madelyn appeared at the door with a bag full of moo goo gai pan, egg rolls, and a plum wine called Meijiu. It was her way of celebrating the good news she wanted to share.

Her friend, Jorge, had found the amateur culprit, who'd hacked Tom's page. The computer that originated the hack belonged to Pastor Ken. The actual hacker left a Facebook login signature, as the Mike, that Tom had also encountered that day.

"By the way, your old page will be restored by tomorrow. Jorge just has to get in touch with a friend of his at Facebook," she reported with a grin.

Tom was amazed at the speed that she had worked, and he was interested in hearing more about the hacking. "May I get Jorge's email address to find out the details?" he asked her.

"I'm sorry," she replied. "He does things for me as a favor, and he doesn't want any information about himself revealed. If you have specific questions, I could ask him. He's the best, but a certain amount of secrecy goes along with his work."

Tom thanked her repeatedly. "At first I thought about having the hacker prosecuted or taking some other steps. Now I realize that would take out Pastor Ken. Amazingly though, this works well for me. It got me going onto Twitter, which will be a fantastic venue for what I need to do!"

Madelyn came back, "Yeah, you just need to cut your losses. Jorge probably can't release how he discovered everything. He'd have to charge you a fortune if he were to document everything legally. You haven't sustained enough harm to bother a prosecutor, and no attorney would take it as a civil case. It's no real loss and therefore no foul."

"You're right. I had a better idea anyway! Jesus says, 'Love your enemies.' I'm wondering if there is some way that we could show them a huge expression of love! That's the way we should take care of this. I'm over being angry, and this feels right. I'm enthused about all the incredible changes that their bad prank forced me to make in my strategy. I'm so far ahead of my game plan now, that I've got no desire to get even with them."

Maria stood up from the couch, yawned and spoke. "You could do something for his ministry or his church. He should appreciate any help. Can we eat now? I'm really hungry!"

Tom twisted the metal cap off the plum wine, as Maria gathered three large, plastic wine glasses to match her clear, plastic plates. Winking at them, she emptied the wine bottle into their glasses.

"Nothing, but the best!" Madelyn laughed, dividing up the takeout container's contents with a large serving spoon.

Tom dealt out the egg rolls with plastic packets of duck sauce and hot mustard. It was the perfect meal for celebrating, and the plum wine was a plum-soaked liquor with a high alcohol content that brought out its fun.

It had been a crazy day, starting with disaster and ending on the edge of opportunity. They needed to celebrate and be silly.

Tom's answer was counter-intuitive to most people, even to those who supposedly believed in His words, "Love your enemy."

As the three ate, ideas for an extravagant endowment of love began to hatch. They noticed their moods being uplifted by the thought of doing something positive in response to the negative attack.

Tom felt wonderful about being able to forgive, rather than be vindictive. He thought aloud, "Why, after two thousand years of instruction, do Christ's followers seldom do what He says?"

Tom realized that popular movies, television, and books reverted to the "eye for an eye", the Hebrew law of retaliation, rather than His teachings of "turn the other cheek" and "love your enemy."

Madelyn got more excited. "Let's find out what they need and do it! This is the type of thing I like to do with my money. We could finance improvements for what I imagine is a small church. Maria and I could check it out, and I'll pay for it. I just don't want them knowing where the money came from. And they probably shouldn't know that Tom is involved, until *after* the fact. Maria can head it up, while you stay in the background, until it's unveiled, Tom."

They hoped to overwhelm Tom's detractors with a gift from a most unexpected donor.

Tom quoted his mother, "You catch more flies with honey than with vinegar."

* * *

That Sunday, Maria, and Madelyn went to Pastor Ken's service in a small, country chapel in sad need of repair. It wasn't difficult to find out what the sparsely attended church needed.

The slight pastor's voice roared with authority demanding everyone to tithe, bringing their first fruit to the church. He admitted from the pulpit that their church's mortgage was in arrears. They had to come up with five thousand dollars just to keep their doors from being locked. If that happened, he intimated that they might all end up in Hell for letting the Lord down.

Maria recorded the service on her iPhone and replayed it later for Tom. Each of them had compassion for the pastor whose hopes were failing, and his reputation, collapsing. The pastor even alluded to a Mike, who sat alone in the front row bellowing "Amen!" into every gap, appropriate or not.

No matter what else was missing, the red-faced, middle-aged preacher had faith. His entire service was filled with ranting on how they would overcome their problems if they could act in belief. During his passionate diatribe, he shared that he was a lay preacher without a formal education. He spoke like a dirt-poor southern man. Tom could have easily criticized most everything Pastor Ken had said with his overbearing attitude, but instead, he applauded the ardent faith with which he proclaimed it.

Tom and the girls felt it was the perfect opportunity to bestow love on those would-be enemies. Madelyn led with her surprising ideas for them.

"Let's pay off their mortgage, fix up their building, and pay for Pastor Ken to study divinity at his choice of schools. I'd even like to buy them a new sound system. Let's show them what love can conquer!"

Tom was totally surprised by Madelyn's obvious affluence. He was in awe of her plans, and he was just beginning to realize the extent of her fortune.

* * *

By the following Sunday, Madelyn and Maria had accomplished their goals. Maria had made the arrangements for the presentation of their gifts.

The girls smiled in anticipation until the close of the service. Then Maria abruptly stood up and surprisingly introduced Tom holding an oversized cardboard check for $87,000 addressed to their mortgage bank.

Pastor Ken and their former adversary, Mike, were completely overwhelmed. They flashed looks back and forth, trying to decide if they should smile and be happy. They couldn't deny their beaming eyes with tears forming in the corners.

Next, Maria quietly brought out a replica check made out to St. John's Paint and Repairs written in an amount that would overhaul the rustic chapel. Everyone's eyes were moist, as she presented a photograph of a sound system, complete with mikes, mixer, amps, and speakers with an authorization for the installation.

Pastor Ken and Mike apologetically welcomed their former adversary, Tom, as part of the package. Tom responded congenially, letting bygones rest. He knew making a gift with the wrong intentions would negate the blessings. Tom intentionally didn't use the phrase, "Love your enemy". He instead spoke the words, "With love for our new friends."

All that felt much better than any reprisal, and it would move them forward far faster than any negative act could have done.

Madelyn had arranged for a free hamburger, hotdog, soft drink, and ice cream catering truck to greet the congregation, as they were dismissed.

Balloons and bouncing beach balls enhanced the surprise celebration, as kids and adults alike kept the multi-colored orbs afloat.

Tom, Maria, and Madelyn helped serve the refreshments. Christian music filled the air, rounding out the excitement of the afternoon. Once the food rush subsided, the trio slipped secretly away like God after a miracle. They hadn't done it for thanks, only for love.

As unconventional as their response was, it wholeheartedly embodied the seldom applied, two-thousand-year-old teachings of Christ.

* * *

Later that day, they enjoyed their own burgers, dogs, and vegetables on the hibachi, while delightfully rehashing their love offering.

Tom raised his glass in a toast to the two women. "How did you girls do all this? It was fantastic, but it must have cost a fortune!"

Maria reminded Tom, "Madelyn is loaded. We won't discuss how much because she doesn't want anyone knowing that."

Madelyn spoke for herself, "Let's just call it pennies from Heaven for now. I have been very blessed."

Tom wondered of course but just sat there agog. He didn't have to say a word because they were written all over his face.

Madelyn spoke up again, "I love doing things like this more than anything else in the world. I shouldn't tell you, but sometimes I feel guilty that I probably receive more pleasure giving than others do receiving. I'm just glad that you both can share that with me. I really have been blessed and don't feel like I am doing all this. I really feel it's like I said, pennies from Heaven. Thank you, Lord."

"Well, I am impressed, I have to say. It sure is a wonderful thing to do. A 'Christian' thing," Tom said gently.

"You could say that. It is, I guess! Not to brag, but I have been doing things like this for years. Loving others transcends all respectable beliefs. It does seem high on the priority of Christianity, but it seems to get lost in all the dogma.

"The truth is, I started giving seriously when I began studying Buddhism. Not really the religion, but mostly the beliefs and practices. Gautama Buddha, also known as Siddhartha, never claimed to be God, and many of his followers considered him enlightened, but not a deity. I avoided the religion but loved the philosophy.

Maria, who had heard the story before, flipped the burgers and rolled the wieners. Meanwhile, Tom questioned Madelyn without judgment. "What do you consider yourself now, Christian or Buddhist?"

Madelyn laughed. "I consider myself more of a nudist than a Buddhist. I guess whoever has the label-maker decides. Personally, I would like to follow Jesus without a religion. They all have their own dogmas, and I don't know all the idiosyncrasies. Still, Buddha's ideas make sense. However, I consider him a philosopher, not a deity. So, it's not a conflict."

"I think you are right," Tom said. "But, I don't think many Christians would agree. They don't like anyone messing with the competition. The way I look at it is that Buddha, the Awakened One, was a Man-made God, while Jesus was a God-made man."

Maria spoke for herself. "I'm pretty much the same. I have a faith, but I don't think I could abide by all the rules of any sect. There are many people out there like us, and that's who we are reaching out to now. It's just important to have the freedom to believe what you believe, without someone saying you are going to Hell!"

"I'm glad we got that settled," Madelyn sighed. "I'll be more comfortable sharing some of my weird ideas with y'all, then." She had relaxed into her southern self.

"Everything is done! Time to eat!" Maria said. "Why don't you say grace your way, Madelyn? I don't think Tom has heard one of your prayers, yet."

Madelyn was glad to do that. "Dear Lord, we are thankful for you being as one with us. Let us be mindful of the love abounding within us. May we share that love with the universe, including all who are in it, knowing the more we give, the more we will receive from your unending well. We continually give thanks for this continuous moment."

"Amen!"

"Amen!"

"Amen," they each commented.

"Thank you! Let's eat! We'll talk later!"

* * *

Tom became introspective. Although Madelyn, Maria, and he had made tremendous strides toward their undefined goals. The recent, miraculous events made him doubt his own contributions and abilities. The girls had done more than he had to overcome the last challenge. Tom wasn't sure where his depression was originating, but he could feel tears welling up in his eyes. As he turned reflective, Tom could sense being whisked into a state, where he was in touch with the source of his feelings. Whether it was inside his head or in another realm, it made no difference. He drifted to where he needed to be.

He had originally believed that there was amazing power in a myriad of spiritual beliefs. He didn't reject any group, and he was willing to reach out to all beliefs in hope of further enhancing the acceptance of each group. Still, he leaned upon his Judeo-Christian background and relied on the teachings of Christ.

He felt the main principles of love, honesty, humility, faith, karma (sowing and reaping), and others were basically the same. He didn't categorically reject other beliefs, whether religions of East or West, New Thought, or old. He believed each had its strong points and deserved respect with a fair, individual appraisal.

Tom didn't expect everyone to accept the tenets of others' beliefs, but only to honestly accept their rights to hold individual beliefs. Hopefully, that could lead to the understanding of other people and their thought processes. After all, he felt that was the first step towards loving others, a goal of most spiritual philosophies. Love for others was the necessary ingredient in any spiritual philosophy that he could respect. Of course, good, not evil, followed that oath of love.

That is where Tom became confused. In researching so much in the Christian practices, he felt he was neglecting his original open-mindedness and consequently became too orthodox in his approach. It was this that concerned him most as he entered into prayer.

"Dear Lord of all! Please be with me, as I try to be fair to you and all concerned. I am sitting here confused and needing guidance. I am trying to present you and your spiritual universe to everyone in a way, that each can understand you, your ways, and their relationship to each other."

As Tom let his request hang in the air, he drifted into meditation waiting for guidance. Releasing his grasp of worldly logic, he entered a realm of spiritual wisdom. Peacefully floating in his comfortable darkness, Tom could feel a wave of intensity coming over him.

He found himself on a tropical island floating in the fog of low clouds, with brilliant colors arriving with the dawn. The figure that he recognized as Christ appeared in a long, white robe reflecting the shimmering colors. It was a stage version of Him with a shiny microphone grabbing Tom's attention by echoing, "I am the voice of God...God...God..." He stifled his laughter and waited for Tom's reaction.

Tom laughed, recognizing the humor in His voice. "What's up?" he asked.

"Just thought I'd formally introduce myself. Many call me 'The Word', because I speak for the Father and Holy Spirit, even though we are all one. Got that?"

"Yes," Tom acknowledged with a nod.

"I am also known as The Way in Christianity and many other religions. I have only one thing to tell you, LOVE. It is The Way! No matter which you choose or don't choose. Understand now?"

"I think so, but The Way to where?"
"To Grace and your heart's desires! You'll see very soon!"

Tom knew he had a special treat in store for him. He looked forward to the euphoria of accepting the freely given, unconditional love of the entire universe, as it might surround him in heavenly delight. Yet, he knew there was one thing in his life that prevented submissive surrender to flow easily.

He needed to decide honestly about his marriage situation.

* * *

That evening Tom lay alone in his bed, ruminating about divorcing his wife.

"Should I do it?" he asked himself, not knowing that he was in a dream.

That was when his wife, in her former splendor, appeared before him, wanting to meet with him.

"I miss you. I want to see you. I still lo..." the dream image and voice of Claudia dissolved, as Tom began to wake.

Startled and tense, he sat straight up. It didn't matter what time of night it was. He had to call. He grabbed his phone.

"Hello... Hello?... Who is this?" A gruff voice answered. It was a voice Tom knew all too well.

In the background, Tom could hear Claudia asking, "Who is it, Tony?"

Tom immediately hung up, then reared back to throw his phone against the wall. As his hand followed his aim toward the target, Tom's mind told him it was over!

He dropped the phone to the floor, as his knees dropped him to the bed in tears. He lay there sobbing until he adjusted to reality. He released more than tears, as he let go of his grasp on the past. Tom remained huddled in a fetal position until he eventually opened his eyes willingly to welcome his new life.

A pleasant melody of laughter and giggles wafted in through the window with the evening air. Happily, he knew it was Maria and Madelyn approaching the front steps of the house.

As the front door opened, the sweet sound of Madelyn's voice called out, "I've got pizza!"

"And I've got beer!" Maria echoed.

Tom joyfully hollered back, "And I've got something to celebrate! Meet you at the pool! Suits, optional!"

CHAPTER 19

PATH THRU THE GARDEN...

After the joyful celebration and even more contributions to Ken's church, Tom and the girls learned that Mike, who had instigated the riff and promulgated the hack, died unexpectedly. He was putting up his Christmas lights on a second story balcony when he fell to the ground.

Reports called it an accident. Mike was a large, muscular man, and the theory was that he bent his six-foot frame over the three-foot rail and toppled. Mike flipped midair, landed head first, and snapped his neck, while his body continued through the rotation.

The death sent Tom into a dire depression for days. During that time, he remained in Maria's guest room, only coming out periodically to use the bathroom and pour himself a glass of water.

Maria and Madelyn were concerned about his despondency at first. As his behavior continued, they became even more troubled about his overall mental state.

All Tom would say when pressed, was that he was grieving and that he would be okay. One time he expressed to Maria that it was his fault. When she tried to inquire and console him, Tom resumed his trance-like posture in the wingback chair in his room. He desperately needed a shower and shave but wouldn't listen and didn't care.

After two days, Madelyn arranged an appointment with a psychiatrist. When she told Tom, he responded, "I'll be ready."

On the next day, he came out of his room for a late supper. Maria had left for work, so Madelyn had come over to monitor him. He behaved almost normally and even shared some of the thoughts passing through his mind.

"I knew there was something with Mike before learning of his death. I sensed him wrestling with his guilt over how he'd hacked me. I know that he was a genuinely good person, and he felt bad about the rift. He fell because his negative energy wrapped him in such guilt, it made him careless with his balance. He suffered a classic and fatal Freudian slip.

"I didn't know at the time, but I was the reason for his fall. Regretfully, I should have assured him that I had forgiven him. That could have made a significant difference in his life. It would have been the right thing to do, too. You know, 'Forgive us our trespasses, as we forgive those who trespass against us.' I was holding a grudge, that I should have been strong enough to overcome. It's a shame, that seemingly little mistakes can have such catastrophic repercussions in our lives and others."

"Still want to go to the doctor tomorrow?" Madelyn asked softly. "She has counseled patients with Near Death Experiences before."

"Yes, I definitely think I need to see her. There are feelings that I haven't addressed yet, and some unexplained new powers to understand. I could use her help."

Madelyn nodded. "I highly recommend her. I have seen several shrinks, but she is the only one who seems to understand me. She has uncanny perception. She could easily feel things I thought but couldn't put into words."

"That's exactly what I need!" he came back excitedly. "My thoughts always seem just out of reach. I know there are answers, I just can't find the right questions."

"Then, you'll love her. Her name is Dr. Angelica Gould. I started seeing her a few months ago. I couldn't find where I wanted to be spiritually or romantically, and it was driving me crazy. She helped me rearrange parts of my life, like a jigsaw puzzle, until it made perfect sense. She helped me prepare for what was to come: Maria, you, and other revelations. That's my story, but I don't want to project my thoughts into yours.

"When I saw her the other day, I mentioned you had come into my life and, along with Maria, I had exactly everything I was looking for in love. She'd really like to meet you. That's when I set up a tentative appointment for you.

"Don't feel you have to go for my sake. It's only an offer. You might enjoy and benefit from it. I have a feeling that it will be a key to a door that needs unlocking."

Tom replied in awe. "The last few days, I felt that I was going crazy. I didn't have any answers but just kept faith that outside forces would somehow make sense. You obviously hold the answer to my prayers."

Suddenly Madelyn felt deeply touched and warmly whispered, "Tom, I knew the day I met you that you were my answer, divinely sent."

After his shower and shave, they enjoyed a Madelyn staple, delivered pizza. She complemented this with a robust bottle of Italian wine from the ready stock in her trunk.

She spent that night with Tom during Maria's work shift. Neither was trying to shortchange Maria. They only needed to spend the quiet time together. Tom felt so much better and now he held hope for enlightenment.

The Italian cuisine seemed to spur an amorous passion brought on by the melding of their minds. Together, they cuddled and coddled, enjoying the cozy couch and warm fireplace, while Maria worked through the night.

Their lips touched repeatedly as they relaxed and reclined. While remaining barely within their previously reasoned bounds, they shared each other's breath and body heat beneath an oversized throw.

Awakened by a pink, predawn sky, they left for an early breakfast to avoid questions upon Maria's return. They seized a continued opportunity to know each other better, while they relaxed with their coffee in the South Beach Grill overlooking the Atlantic.

Light chatter between bites yielded pleasant surprises and surface acceptance of each other's character. Although their life experiences differed greatly, their personas were compatible. During their conversations, Tom seemed to return closer to normal.

He felt ready for his appointment with Dr. Gould. Yet, what was revealed while he sat on the doctor's couch opened a window to the possibilities of his new endowments from Above.

Doctor Gould asked pointed questions to uncover Tom's experiences in the other realm. When she became convinced of the sincerity and depth of his observations, she adeptly put together the pieces of his puzzle. Within the first hour, she established a framework to help him make sense of his expanded discernment.

From Tom's answers, she expected that he would have the common difficulty of adjusting higher world expectations into an earthly life. She suggested a couple of simple exercises that would help with his transformation.

"Primarily, you are experiencing a major change in your understanding. After many years of learning from a former perspective, you now know that love is the highest law of nature. It must almost immediately replace years of your fear-based 'operating' system."

Dr. Gould continued. "There are two exercises that I suggest you do at least twice daily. These are designed to help you adjust to the new paradigm that you will strive to live.

"The first exercise is to not judge anything. Start with one minute. During that time, unless something is an immediate threat, do not judge it as good or bad. There is no need. For this minute, do not even judge yourself or others. It will be difficult, but keep trying. Don't judge yourself for errors, either. You will improve. Do this several times a day. Each day, increase it by another minute.

"The next exercise is meditation. You said that you do Transcendental Meditation. Do a full twenty-minute session twice daily using the first exercise. Try to continuously only say your mantra. If you stray, return without judging yourself. If your mind wanders, briefly notice if you are judging something. Then return to your mantra. Don't judge yourself or others.

"Before you go, I'd like to use a little hypnosis to allow you to move into your meditations more easily and deeply. I'd like to implant a post-hypnotic suggestion that will relax you immediately. This will allow your mantra to draw you in toward what is called 'God Consciousness' by quieting any inner noise, as you let go."

* * *

After Tom consented, Doctor Gould led him gently into a light and airy state of hypnosis with his body asleep and his mind awake.

"I am going to give you a suggestion that you may use anytime to return to this heavenly state. You will only respond to these words from yourself or me. When you use this suggestion, you will immediately return to the relaxed feeling you have right now. To do this, simply say, 'Relax. Completely and totally relax.' That's all you will have to say. When it's time to return to normal, you will say, 'Time to wake and return.' You will remember those two suggestions and may use them anytime you need to relax, especially when you want to meditate."

After he fully awakened, she had him say the suggestion phrases to demonstrate their effectiveness. Tom was amazed at how rapidly his whole demeanor changed. He was sure his meditations would benefit greatly from the simple procedure.

"You may use this relaxed state to become closer to your subconscious from which you may forgive yourself and others. Or, if you get anxious, this is a wonderful place to retreat. Enjoy it."

"Come back next week, and we'll review how you are doing. You'll recognize how often you judge everything. These exercises will help you eliminate that habit. Being non-judgmental is a key element in unconditional love. I know that is what you're seeking, and you were sent here to learn it."

Tom smiled and got to his feet. "Thank you so much. Madelyn said you were amazing and I completely agree."

Angelica smiled and went to her desk, then returned. She handed Tom a small book called *The Prayer of Jabez,* by Bruce Wilkinson.

"Considering your near-death experience and new outlook on life, this prayer, hidden in the Bible (1 Chronicles 4:10), will enable you to receive a miraculous increase of spiritual territory," she said. "Be sure you say the whole prayer, or you will leave yourself open to evil spiritual warfare. Warn Madelyn and Maria, too."

Tom nodded. "See you next week!"

* * *

On the way back to Maria's from Anastasia Island, Madelyn turned her all-wheel-drive convertible to enter the 'A Street' ramp to drive onto St. Augustine Beach.

After passing the Beachcomber Restaurant, they could see that the low tide left a wide area of sugary sand between them and the waves. The sea oats and sand dunes separated their vehicle from civilization while adding color and form to the natural seashore.

Madelyn spoke up, "We'll have to take a walk here soon. I love the breeze, the birds, and listening to the waves crash. It makes me and my problems seem so insignificant, like specks of sand within eternity. There's nothing like it, but we should get back to Maria's, or she'll be worrying."

"You're right," Tom replied. "But, let's take a moment here to enjoy the scenery and each other."

Madelyn parked her Jaguar facing the beach and they shared the ambiance of the view and each other's warmth. Tom silently tried his post-hypnotic suggestion as they snuggled together. Embracing, they unclenched their worldly attachments and accepted one another completely.

Finally, Tom spoke. "I haven't been a very good houseguest lately. I should let Maria know everything is going to be okay. My whole attitude toward life has changed. Thank you for taking me to Doctor Gould this morning. I needed to talk. Hopefully, we can catch Maria before she goes to bed for the day. I'd like to share it with you both."

Madelyn respected Tom's responsible inclination and pointed her vehicle onto the next ramp off the sand. They rode directly back to Maria's with only gentle music in the background.

Thrilled to see Tom cleaned up and in a good mood again, Maria grinned. "I'm so glad to see you smiling! You were out of here early this morning. Did you go to the doctor?"

Tom answered, "Yes, after we went out for breakfast. Honestly, I started feeling a lot better last night, after Madelyn got here. I was tired of being a recluse and sulking, so we stayed up most of the night talking. Then we got up early, ready to go."

Maria glanced at the single beige blanket strewn haphazardly on the couch but didn't say anything.

Tom noticed and quickly continued. "We wanted to get back here to let you know that I'm feeling better and had a great meeting with the doctor. She gave me several exercises to aid my meditations. Apparently, what I'm experiencing is normal for those who've had a near-death experience. I go back next week. Everything is going to be much better! I can't wait to try the new techniques."

Maria and Madelyn started talking, leaving Tom out of the conversation. Maria was peppering Madelyn with questions and Tom decided to let them talk. He gave them each a warm kiss.

"I'm going to practice my new meditation technique now, so I'll see you both later."

The girls continued talking, as Tom slipped away into the guestroom and dropped into the wingback chair.

While Maria questioned Madelyn if they had slept together the previous night, Tom tuned it out. It wasn't a conversation he wanted to join. He simply closed his eyes and told himself, "Relax. Completely and totally relax."

On command, Tom sensed his legs, arms, and body sequentially become heavy, warm, and relaxed. His mind followed his body, preparing a void to receive his repeated mantra. Neither worries nor thoughts interrupted. Soon he found himself floating beyond thoughts and mantra. There alone, immersed in transcendental bliss, he gently progressed to Maharishi Mahesh Yogi's state of "god consciousness".

In that moment, a voice invaded his peace. "The fruit of the Tree of Knowledge of Good and Evil causes judging and prevents unconditional love."

Tom recognized the voice of Mike, remembering him inserting "Amen" repeatedly into the sermon before the church celebration.

However, the face of Mike was now warm and projected a smile of heavenly love. Tom knew that Mike was speaking directly to him in the present moment. Tom understood Mike's expression as one of total forgiveness. Tom immediately felt very humbled by the depth and honesty of Mike's entire appearance. Although Tom tried to express forgiveness in many situations, his were only words, and words alone were not real.

Something was different in Mike's ethereal voice. It conveyed a fullness of heavenly radiance that Tom would never forget. He felt its power but knew he could not project such honest fullness while he remained in his earthly body.

There was no need to think. No questions entered his mind. For now, he was content to receive the gift of forgiveness.

After an indeterminable moment, Tom's third eye opened. He could see his guru washing his feet.

Tenderly He massaged and cleansed them. Tom felt his entire body and mind dissipate into the moment, as the nerve endings of his soles were soothed and stimulated. It felt wonderful to have such attention lavished upon him. He also felt unworthy that his Master would lower himself to become a servant to him. Tom raised his head and looked deeply into his mentor's eyes as he heard Him say, "I am so glad that you are my friend."

"Wow!" That was the most amazing thing to hear from someone so magnificent.

Then Tom realized it was exactly what made Him so wonderful. His teacher was always humble and ready to shower love upon all. All we had to do is realize and accept it.

After He dried Tom's feet, they embraced meaningfully before strolling down the beach. Together they looked out over the vast water at the most colorful sunset ever seen. Although Tom felt tiny in such an awesome setting, he was filled with love and felt totally satisfied.

Once again, Tom realized all that this meant. Only by being humble, can one receive and assimilate gifts of beauty, love, and power that are endlessly offered to us. Pride is our problem. Humility, its antonym, is our solution.

Tom looked forward to the time when he would fully assimilate that outlook into his life. New wisdom foretold, that with faith, the time would come when he would blend the powers of humility and love. He knew that phase of his journey would be soon. And, Maria and Madelyn would be there with him.

As Tom awoke from his meditation, it was as if he had just returned from his near-death experience. He inadvertently flipped open his Bible to Jesus speaking in John 14:26: "But the Helper, the Holy Spirit, whom the Father will send in my name, he will teach you all things and bring to your remembrance all that I have said to you."

Tom knew they were to begin an overwhelming spiritual journey because only those who believed could understand the true meaning of the Word: "Whoever has ears, let them hear."(Mat. 11:15)

Fully awakened, Tom reached for his new book, The Prayer of Jabez. He found a note that Dr. Gould had placed inside the cover for him.

"Therefore, an overseer must be above reproach, the husband of one wife...." (1 Timothy 3:2 ESV)

Oh, no . . .

Tom would anguish over "one wife" and The Prayer of Jabez until he....

Author Bio

PHIL KING was a military photographer, magazine photojournalist, songwriter, traveler, and historian.

His popular book, *Saint Augustine Carriage Tour*, combined a love of history with marvelous images. In his controversial new novel, *Rising Love: A Spiritual Journey*, Phil pours his talents into unlikely characters destined to share danger, love, spirituality, and awesome Grace.

This novel is the first book in his, *Way of Love* series. Phil lives and writes on St. Augustine Beach, Florida, where he was the memorable history writer at "Old City Life", its premier magazine.

He can be reached at ThisSky1348@gmail.com.. Find Phil and his books at www.WayofLove.us.

www.ingramcontent.com/pod-product-compliance
Lightning Source LLC
Chambersburg PA
CBHW020407210626
46816CB00006BB/2166